THE LADY
WITH THE
ALLIGATOR
PURSE

THE LADY
WITH THE
ALLIGATOR
PURSE

A Novel by

ERNEST FINNEY

CLARK CITY PRESS
LIVINGSTON, MONTANA

Library of Congress Cataloging-in-Publication Data

Finney, Ernest J.
  The lady with the alligator purse : a novel / by Ernest Finney.
    p.   cm.
  ISBN 0-944439-46-2 : $19.00
  I. Title.
PS3556.I499L34   1992
813'.54—DC20   92-32125
                                                              CIP

The chapters titled "Bertram's Slough" and "In the Avenues"
appeared in a slightly different form in *Threepenny Review*,
in the fall 1983 and fall 1989 issues.

"Lot No. 17" was included in Ernest Finney's *Birds Landing*,
University of Illinois Press, 1986.

"Old MacDonald" appeared in *New Letters* in the Summer 1990 issue
under the title of "Charming Billy."

Clark City Press
Post Office Box 1358
Livingston, Montana 59047

To my mother and father

CONTENTS

THE LADY
WITH THE
ALLIGATOR
PURSE

Kay, 1978
Ruby, Opal, Garnet

Billy found Ruby. Kay knew he'd been working on it for months. His voice sounded as calm as ever. "Kay, are you still there? Kay?"

"I'm here," she told him, adjusting the phone against her ear. At least, her body was; in her mind, remembering, she was getting ready to jump again, twenty years ago, the year after Ruby had disappeared. Poised on the edge of the tile roof, umbrella handle in her hand, cape, and a coil from an old bedspring fastened to the sole of each of her shoes with a roller skate strap around the instep. The springs made it hard to balance on the tile, two stories up, and her father's World War II helmet kept slipping to one side of her head. Billy had a grip on the back pocket of her jeans as she leaned out over the edge. She could see Ann down on the walk, looking worried, and hear the sound of her mother's Singer in the sewing room below.

It was a clear summer morning. They were out of school. What had she been thinking when she raised the umbrella and Billy yelled, "It's my turn next," and let go? That's what she was trying to remember. She stepped off the roof. The air whooshed upward as she passed the window where her mother was sewing. Grandmother was cutting out a pattern. There was plenty of time to wave.

She was taking hours to reach the cement walk below, bracing herself for the shock when the springs would hit the walk and bounce her back up. She'd soar, that was the plan. Soar. Soar high enough to take a big bite out of a cloud.

"Kay, do you know what this means? I found my mother. Say something."

"Okay, you found her, Billy. You talked to her on the phone. You and Ann go down there and see her, then. You went this far; you might as well go on with it."

"Will you come with us, Kay?"

How was it, she thought, that she'd turned into everybody's emergency rescue unit? If it wasn't Billy or the rest of the family, it was somebody from the Kansas Association. Just yesterday it was "Kay, Lilly's having one of her spells again; do you think Mental Health, or that doctor in Redwood City?" Before that, "Kay, where does a bad-conduct discharge leave me, exactly?" Everyone in California was from somewhere else; that's what her grandmother had always said, and though she herself by chance happened to be born in San Diego, her grandmother, her parents, most of her family and most of their friends were from Kansas. She knew more about that place, from listening to the stories and putting the pieces in order, than any of the others, and now that there wasn't anybody left back there, she was the only person who could keep it all straight. At least, she'd never met anyone else that could, that liked the stories so much: certainly not Ann or Billy. Stories: the whole thing with Ruby was like a legend or a fairy tale, Ruby some mysterious participant in her absence, which made her so much more interesting than Opal or Garnet who were present. Keeping the Kansas Association books was like keeping an outline of all the stories. So was helping to put together the Kansas Day Picnic. Or did she just like an excuse to be boss? That's what Ann always told her.

"Kay?"

"Wait a minute, I'm checking my calendar." She'd liked doing the Association accounts from the start. In high school she'd gotten the monthly Association newsletter out as well as the doing of the accounts; at sixteen she was a voting member of the executive board. In college she'd started investing the Association's money in mutual funds and built up enough profit to offer health insurance to members at reduced premiums. She had her own business now, but always had time for the phone calls. "Don't get married, Kay," they kidded her; "you won't have time for him and us." She always laughed.

"Okay, Billy. Saturday's fine with me."

"We'll take my car. I'll call you."

We're actually going to see Ruby, she realized with a start, putting down the phone. Billy'd done it. She wrote RUBY/L.A. in her appointment book. Then, under RUBY she wrote in OPAL and under Opal, GARNET. There wasn't a single day that went by, all the time they were growing up, that someone didn't mention Aunt Ruby. Not a day passed. Because she'd disappeared. She went to the store and never came back. The story had taken on all kinds of turns and elaborations that no one could prove or disprove. She ran off with someone. She was kidnapped or had amnesia, or she was dead. No one ever said dead in front of Ann and Billy, though. Everyone remembered a different reason why she had gone to the store that day. Billy always said for a loaf of Wonder Bread, but he was only six. Uncle Frank said to get him a pack of Chesterfields. Ann said a bunch of celery, which was possible; she was eight. But the way Kay remembered it, Aunt Ruby had gone for a box of powdered sugar. And most of the family agreed that it must have been powdered sugar: the Kansas Reunion Picnic was the next day, Sunday, and Ruby always made a layer cake. Uncle Frank went to the picnic the day after she'd disappeared, hoping she might turn up. He waited almost a week before he contacted the police, hoping she would come back on her own. She'd left several times before, but for a day only, and she was always home that night. For years afterward he'd blamed himself for not reporting her disappearance right away: it could have made a difference, six days, he always said, especially if she was sick.

After twenty years of speculation it didn't seem possible that they were really going to meet Ruby. It was like meeting Guinevere or Snow White. She dialed her office manager's extension, thinking how, when you're young, certain people resonate in your imagination. Grandmother. Ruby. How you try on the idea, I could be like that. At one point she'd told Billy not to keep on, once there was a chance of finding his mother. Why? It wasn't as if their lives were on hold and once they found her things would change. Why? Maybe she didn't want the real person to interfere with her own version of Ruby.

Ann didn't want to go to L.A. "What did she ever do for me? She ran out on us."

"You don't know that," Billy said. "Something might have happened. She could have had amnesia."

"You know something, Billy? You're stupider than you look if you believe that. She left us because she wanted to leave us, that's why. Amnesia my ass." Ann was about to say something else—her mouth was open—when a customer came in. Her whole face changed into a big smile. It must be a good customer, Kay thought. It was: he was the personnel manager of a big plant in Sunnyvale and did all the ordering of flowers for employee retirements and funerals. She watched Ann take down the order. Strange, the way Billy and Ann complemented each other: there was no sister/brother resemblance, but you needed one to understand the other. As if Billy were the transparent part of an X-ray and Ann the bone and gristle. Billy had been a towhead and still was fair, pink-cheeked, like he was slightly flushed from some inner exertion. No one would call him handsome, but he was stalwart, athletic-looking, slimmer than he should have been, the way he ate. Assured, if you didn't know him.

"She should go with us," he whispered. "It's her mother too."

"It's up to her. We can't force her." That would be a laugh, forcing Ann to do anything she didn't want to, Kay thought. How could Billy be so different? He was quality-control technician at a food processing plant. There were always calls in the middle of the night: "Better come down, Bill, this batch of asparagus doesn't test out right." More times than not it was just that the foreman didn't want to take responsibility, but Billy went every time without complaint. He had been married twice: both times the women left him. He'd called after the second breakup and asked her to phone his wife and find out what was wrong. "You've been married barely a year, Billy; she'll come back," she'd told him, but she did phone Jennifer. "Before you say anything, Kay, I'm not going back. I know he's your cousin, and I agree he's a nice guy. But this is it." Billy's first wife, his high school sweetheart Norma, who'd waited for him during his two years in the Army and married him in college, had said almost the same thing: "He's a good guy but he's boring; I might as well live alone." She told Jennifer the same thing she'd told Norma: change him. "Change, he'll do anything I ask him. But what does *he* want?" Kay didn't know. "You're his cousin," Jennifer had said before hanging up, "but living with him is like having a pet dog. I feel like a hostage to somebody who's trying to kill me with kindness."

"Now where were we?" Ann said after the customer closed the door. It was the commanding tone she used when they were going over her accounts at tax time and she wanted Kay to cheat. One of the women fixing arrangements in the workroom came out and waved Ann back. In a second they could hear her yelling, "For Christ sake, just follow the diagram, can't you do that? Look, this is April Fantasy: carnations here, Dutch iris there. I don't care if it does look better, carnations."

She came back out shaking her head and grinned at Kay. She didn't look thirty-two; she looked like the nineteen-year-old in her wedding pictures. She met her husband at the reunion: a Californian, but both his parents had been from Kansas. He lived for fishing; "I'm your second interest," Ann used to kid him. Carl supplied the whole family with fish every time he could get away from the gas station and garage his father owned. They'd been married eight years and had two kids, who were waiting with Ann on the beach the day he went clamming. While they watched, he disappeared under a wave, and his body was never recovered.

"When do we go?" she asked.

Kay wasn't surprised. She was like that, up and down. "Maybe you two should go alone," she said.

"That's a laugh," Ann said. Kay felt her face getting hot, but then Ann stuck out her tongue at her and she had to grin: Ann'd been so funny when they were girls. She'd kept them giggling through all those long holiday dinners, mimicking aunts and uncles at the other end of the table. "Believe I'll have some of those parsnips, Celia," she'd lisp through her nose, imitating Aunt Verna, and they'd snort into their napkins, eyes wet from laughter.

"What about Dad?" Billy asked Kay.

"I think it's better not to get him involved until after we go down and see." She saw Ann was giving her her look.

"We couldn't keep you away if we tried, could we, Kay?"

"Ann, is that necessary?" Billy said.

"I'll make reservations for Saturday," Ann said. "If we can get in anywhere, with all the tourists running around down there." Then she said, "What would you do without us, Kay?" as Billy held the door open.

Kay knew she would say something like that. "What would you do without me, Ann?"

"I paid you back." When Carl died, there had been insurance money, but not enough to buy the flower shop.

"You know I'm not talking about the goddamn money."

"Come on, Kay," Billy said, pulling her by the arm out of the shop.

"All these years and I still let Ann get to me. I know that's what she wants. I know it," Kay said, still angry at herself.

Billy was maneuvering through the heavy traffic. "That's the way she is; what can you do? She hasn't changed an inch since Mother left."

"Billy, don't start that; I don't want to hear it."

"It's true. I remember. I was old enough."

"Stop it, Billy. We spent the whole time we were kids talking about Ruby; that's enough."

Billy let Kay out at her mother's; she went there every Monday for dinner. They were both able now to remain fairly calm through the three hours. The table was set; the food was already cooked and in the oven to keep warm. Her mother, Garnet, was Ruby's older sister: was Ruby that old? she thought, startled. Opal was the baby. Garnet, Ruby, Opal. "What did Billy find out?" her mother asked as she put dinner on the table.

"He talked to her on the phone. She's down in Los Angeles."

"What did they say?"

"Mother, I wasn't there."

"How did he ever find her?"

"I have a friend, someone I went to school with, who was able to trace her social security number. Billy did the rest, checked about two hundred phone numbers."

"She's got the same name?"

"I don't know. We're going down Saturday." Kay said that before she could ask.

"Ann too?"

"All three or us."

"It's been years, hasn't it. What a family. We should never have left Kansas. I mean that. Your father would never have run off with Opal. I know that for a fact. Not back home. And they have the gall to come to the reunion."

Kay had been nineteen at the time her father divorced her mother and married her younger sister Opal. Just like that. Opal was a good fifteen years his junior. "Dad, she's more my age than yours," Kay had commented at the time. "It doesn't make a damn bit of difference," he'd answered. And it didn't: they were still together after fourteen years.

She was almost out the door when her mother said, "Say hello to Ruby for me. I still think about her a lot. We had some times back home. Ruby was the smartest of all three of us, always got her own way. She should never have let herself get involved with Frank. I don't like to say that now, especially the way things have turned out for all of us, but it's the truth." Kay had to ask why.

"You'd have to have been there to understand. Frank's family had a store. We rented twenty acres. Frank and Ruby got together for all the wrong reasons. Then again, I think sometimes it was California; coming out here after the war was like getting dropped down a well. Only the meanest got out, stepping on everyone else. Then, other times, I think it was just human nature."

Billy picked Kay up last, but Ann got out and sat in the back. "I won't have to watch him drive," she said when Kay protested. Billy sat through the switch and the comment patiently, unperturbed. They were on the freeway and everyone was sitting back for the long drive when he suddenly took the off ramp for Belmont. They knew where he was going but Ann said, "Damn it, Billy, what are you doing?"

"I just want to say good-bye."

"We're just going overnight."

"Ann, it'll take ten minutes."

"I know how long it'll take, but I didn't plan on stopping."

"You never see him anymore."

"What do you mean: I came over on his birthday."

"Not last year. Because Kay and I were the only ones there last year."

"The year before, then. Besides, it's none of your business when I go over there."

"Both of you calm down. We're supposed to be adults," Kay said. She hadn't lived on this side of El Camino; her house had been nine blocks over. Still close enough for her to walk Ann and Billy to grammar school. Her mother and father had been lucky; they could borrow from Grandmother, so they'd ended up in the tile-roofed house with the big lot on a tree-lined street. Uncle Frank landed where his G.I. loan put him, in one of the first tracts, butted up against an old neighborhood. She could remember when the whole place started to change, just about the time Ruby disappeared. Her grandmother would stop the blue Chrysler to watch as bulldozers took chunks out of the sides of hills. "Don't they know they can't put that back," Grandmother'd said. Whole hilltops went down, sliced off like you'd cut a potato in two, and were carried down to the bay in dump trucks. Houses went up on the terraced hillsides, shopping centers on the fill in the bay. They drove around on the weekends just trying to keep up with the changes. And to look over duplexes that came on the market. Once, driving back home in time for Sunday dinner, her grandmother had passed their turnoff and gone farther south on 101, Mountain View, Sunnyvale and Santa Clara, where there were miles of open fields: strawberries, artichokes, onions. Truck gardens, Grandmother called them. Orchards. She slowed down the car so they could smell the red onions being dug up. "I might have been a little hasty," she said, "buying in the city. I didn't see that the city and county of San Francisco is going to fill up and that will be the end of it. Down here is where everyone will come."

Frank looked the same, always. The house was clean, as always. She had envied Ann, not having to do housework when they were girls: Uncle Frank vacuumed, hummed along with the sound of the motor; Billy dusted; Ann did the dishes and cooked. Frank had fallen off a scaffold a year and a half ago, his third fall, and that plus his diabetes had put him on disability ever since. He looked tired.

She and Ann took turns kissing Frank. He smelled of the bourbon he sipped all day long, and Chesterfields. After they sat down and Frank asked how they were and offered them something to eat and drink, he turned to her. "Did you find out, Kay?"

"Not yet, Uncle Frank."

"I don't want them to take all the fruit this year. That old pear tree, half of it hangs on the other side of the fence now, and those new people take it all."

"I phoned someone; he's supposed to be researching it. I'll get on him Monday."

"Another thing, Kay, the state wants me to go to another doctor. I've been collecting disability all this time and never had any trouble and now . . ."

"Dad," Ann said, "we're going down to L.A. to see Mom." Frank shook his head.

"I didn't tell him we're going," Billy said. "Just that I talked to her."

"You don't have anything to say, Dad?"

"What can I say?"

"That's your answer? She ruined your life," Ann said. "She ruined Billy's and mine too."

"She didn't ruin my life," Billy said.

"Why can't you stay married, then?"

"That has nothing to do with it."

"We better get going," Kay said, "or we'll hit the traffic."

After the good-byes to everyone from the doorway, Frank took her arm and whispered, "Don't forget about the tree, Kay."

She kept her eyes closed until they reached the freeway. She didn't like to see the old neighborhoods where they grew up. All the vacant lots had buildings on them now; the trees looked like they were all dying. Could the leaves be turning this early, in August? Billy was yelling at Ann. "You didn't have to tell him where we were going."

"You wanted to say good-bye, didn't you? How could we do that and not tell him where we were going? You've always protected him. Like he was the baby and you were the father. It doesn't do him any good. He's not old, but he acts like he's a hundred, shuffling around."

"You want me to take you home, Ann?" Billy turned his head around to yell at her. Kay grabbed the wheel until he jerked back. Ann mouthed something but didn't make a sound.

They checked into the motel first. Ann and Kay had to share a bed. After a few minutes, Billy came in, clapping his hands. "Well, we made it this far without killing each other." He was smiling, pleased with what he'd said. "Well, what next: shall we have dinner, or what?"

"What does *or what* mean?" Ann said. "Are we going to see her tonight?"

"I'll have to phone her and make the arrangements."

"Can't we just go over to where she lives?"

"I don't know where she lives; all I got was an unlisted telephone number."

"Let's phone, then."

"You phone her; I'll give you the number."

"Why are you doing this, Billy? I just want to get it over with. How can you go out and eat something not knowing, when we're this close. Kay, tell him to phone."

"We could at least get the meeting set up for tomorrow or tonight, whichever is better," Kay said. "Arrange a convenient time for everyone. She may have to work or something."

"When I talked to her last, she said any time."

"We should give her some warning, Billy; phone her now, and we can see."

Billy picked up the phone, taking a card out of his wallet. He dialed, and they could all hear the phone ringing. No one answered. "Let's go eat," he said. "I'll try again after we come back."

They went to the motel restaurant and Ann ordered the first bottle of wine and Kay the second. When Billy confessed he'd finally found his true love, they all laughed. And Billy wasn't offended when Ann asked, "What about your other true loves?"

When they went back and phoned again, there was still no answer. "Come on, Billy, where is she?" Ann asked. "Do you think she went out for more Wonder Bread?" No one laughed at that.

"Try again," Kay said. There was no answer.

"Well," Ann said, "I'm going to bed. If I could wait twenty years to see her, I can wait another day."

When Kay came out of the bathroom, the lights were out. She lay down cautiously, not wanting to go over her half of the bed. She could hear Ann breathing; it reminded her of old times, when they'd shared her new double bed for almost a year, after Ruby left, when Frank was drinking heavy. She thought Ann was asleep until she said, "Do you want to play Twenty Questions?" They both giggled. It was what they used to play when they were girls. Billy, in the next room, would crawl to the open door to listen. "Mineral," Ann said.

"Your filling."

"You got it in the first question. I always started out with that, didn't I?"

"That or your barrette; it never failed."

"What happened to that guy you were going with all that time? You stopped bringing him to the picnic a couple of years ago."

"What category is that supposed to be: animal, vegetable or mineral? He wasn't what I was looking for. Why don't you get married again?"

"It's too much trouble. I have the kids; that's enough. I went out a couple of times. But I don't like having to be nice when I don't feel like it. Being myself all the time is a lot better."

"What are you going to say to her tomorrow?"

"I don't know; whatever I have to say to please Billy. I brought along a stack of the kids' school pictures just in case of any conversation lags. What's there to say: Hi Mom, did you get the cigarettes? She didn't come looking for me; we can agree on that. I don't like not knowing anymore. If we're both really alike, things like that. I'm going to sleep; I need to stop thinking about her." But she went on, after a minute: "I thought that was the worst thing that could ever happen to me, when I was a little kid. But the worst was when Carl . . ." She stopped. Went on. "My mother was one thing, but not Carl. How could that happen? He took half of me with him."

She stopped speaking. Kay could hear her breathing. It was so dark in the room. Ann had never said anything like that before. Especially about Carl. He was just gone. As if he had never been there in the first place. After the funeral his photos disappeared off the walls. His mounted fish. She gave his clothes away. Sold his tools, along with the old pickup he used to take fishing. Ruby they had discussed endlessly. Carl, never.

"All for a couple of fucking clams," Ann said and turned over, facing away from Kay.

No one wanted to eat breakfast. They checked out and loaded their luggage into the trunk of the car. They all sat still a minute before Billy started it up, looking at nothing in particular, waiting. It seemed to take hours before he gave the key a sudden twist and the car was moving. Billy watched the street signs, missing one turnoff and going back. "You know the way," Ann commented.

"I marked it on a map when she gave me the directions this morning. I know where I'm going."

But when Billy stopped the car, Ann said, "This couldn't be right."

"She said one-twenty." The numbers were in brass on a five-story building that covered a whole block. It was a combination motel, restaurant and convention center. The building was modern: tinted blue glass, redwood, with immense ceramic sculptures spotted around the outside walls. Each was a different color: cobalt blue, red, yellow, orange. There were beds of marigolds and petunias around the parking lots, and lawns with perfectly shaped trees dividing the various parts of the complex.

"We better get out," Kay said.

"She works here. She could have let us visit her at home," Billy said.

They passed under a marquee that said WELCOME NOBLES and through a hammered-copper door that led into a lounge. There were customers with name tags on their lapels drinking already, at nine-twenty in the morning. They wandered out of the dark lounge into a dining area where black-vested waiters stood watching, ready to rush forward to take an order or pour more coffee.

Ann whispered to Billy, "Ask someone." He ignored her and Kay and walked over to a sliding-glass door, the two women following. They could see several swimming pools, a couple of tennis and racquetball courts. "They've got everything here," he said.

"Go ask one of the waiters where Ruby works," Kay said.

"This place is too big: how are they going to know?"

"Ask. We'll never find her ourselves."

When Billy came back he said, "Fifth floor, take the elevator." They stood facing front as the elevator went up.

"Remember, we have to leave by noon or we won't get home by dark," Ann said. "No fooling around; we say hello and talk a little and then let's go."

"It's been over twenty years," Billy said.

"How did she sound on the phone, Billy?" Ann asked.

"What do you mean?"

"Was she happy to hear from us?"

"She was surprised, and she invited us over."

"Annie, relax," Kay said. "This is just the first visit; there'll be more. Maybe she can get rates at this place, and you and the kids can come down for a vacation."

When the elevator stopped, they followed Billy out and down a corridor, through one door, down another corridor, and through another door into a large room. If it was an office, it didn't look like one. There was a table with nothing on it, a number of leather armchairs. The walls were panelled in dark wood and there was a fireplace. At least a dozen pots of ferns were scattered around the room. There were a few of the same kind of ceramic sculptures embedded in the walls outside, but much smaller. From the window they could look down past the pool into the parking lot and see their car. "This is where they told me to go," Billy said. "We were expected, they said."

When they heard the door open, none of them wanted to turn around and look. They kept their eyes on the parking lot. It seemed like a long time before a voice beside Ann said, "You turned out more like Opal than me."

If Ann looked like Opal, and there was a resemblance, Kay thought, Ruby looked like no one they had ever seen before. She was suntanned, dressed in a dark blue suit with a white silk shirt. She looked out at them over the tops of horn-rimmed reading glasses. She hadn't aged like either Garnet or Opal, who had got chunky and wore pantsuits they made themselves. There were short lines running down from her mouth, but her neck was still good, Kay thought, and her shoes must have cost a hundred and fifty dollars at least. She was the picture of calm, slowly taking her glasses off, her head still tilted to see them over the rims. It didn't seem like Ann or Billy were even breathing, much less able to talk. No one moved. There were no hugs, no kisses. Not a handshake.

"I'm Kay, Garnet's daughter," Kay said to break the silence. "I'll wait outside."

Ann grabbed her arm. "Stay."

"How's Lester, Kay?" Ruby said. "I always liked your father."

"He's fine, just fine."

"Why don't we all sit down here. Have you had breakfast? I'll order some."

"We're not hungry," Ann said.

"Coffee?"

"Why did you leave us?" Ann said.

"Come over and sit down."

"I want to stand, Mother; answer me that and we'll go so you can get back to work."

Ruby sat down and crossed her legs, her forearm and hand flat on the table. "I knew someday I'd have to hear that. I used to think of different answers and different endings. Me coming back: that was after a few years. Rich. To change your lives. Or driving by your house to get a glimpse of you playing in the front yard. Arranging for you to spend the summer down here. I was busy too, and sometimes, to be honest, I never thought of you for months, years even. I have an eighteen-year-old son: did I say that yet? I didn't; yes, Christopher. We're pretty proud of him. He's a freshman at U.S.C." She was quiet for a minute. She still seemed perfectly relaxed. "Louis—my husband—didn't have anything to do with my leaving. I met him after I left. We became business partners first. Along with three banks, we own this place."

She paused, looking at each of them. Ann was tapping her foot impatiently on the rug. "You just dumped us like garbage. Never mind anything else; you got tired of us, and good-bye." Ann's voice was getting louder with every word and she was pointing her finger at Ruby.

Billy took a step nearer. "What you did wasn't right, Mother. I told myself we would come down for a friendly visit, to get acquainted again. But you act like nothing ever happened, that you didn't leave us."

"What do you want me to say, Billy?" She raised her voice just a little for emphasis. "What is there to say? I'm your mother, I'm your mother; don't you think I know that? I can't say why, now. It was a different time; there were different reasons."

Ann started crying. "She's not our mother," she said. "Not her. No, no." She broke into loud sobs. Ruby sat looking toward the window, although she probably couldn't see out because of the angle, Kay thought. Ann put both her hands over her face as her sobs became louder, and Billy led her toward the door.

They listened to the door open and close. After a minute Ruby said, "I would have recognized you anywhere, Kay."

"You don't look like I remember," Kay said.

"Maybe because of the surroundings here. They were a little different back then," Ruby said. Both smiled.

"Sit down here." Ruby patted the chair next to her. Kay sat down. "And my Kansas family?"

"Mother's fine; Dad ran off with Opal."

Ruby chuckled. "That Opal. I was surprised when Billy called. Billy who? I almost said. Do I seem hard? It's been so long a time. You can say what you want about Los Angeles, but this is where everything begins. Where everyone in the whole country with any get up and go wants to come. I waited tables when I first came down here. I was a Kansas farm girl."

Ruby stood up, looking at her watch. Kay quickly got to her feet: how much time would she have given Ann and Billy, she wondered? "I'm afraid I have an appointment. I know you understand, Kay." She put out her hand and Kay shook it. "You must think I'm terribly selfish, but I'm not. I'm really not. I never knew what I wanted when I was younger, not the slightest notion. But I found out what I didn't want. You take care of yourself, Kay, and say hello to everyone for me."

Billy and Ann were waiting in the car, both sitting stiff, looking straight ahead. No one said anything until they got onto the freeway.

"What did she say?" Ann asked.

"Nothing."

"You stayed long enough."

"We should never have come," Billy said.

16

"At least we know now," Ann said. "For years I was hurt because she didn't take me with her. A week before she disappeared she made us matching outfits, red cotton sundresses with wildflowers: I still have mine, put away."

"I don't know how anyone could live down here, so much smog, and the traffic," Billy said.

"Next year near reunion time I'll send Ruby and her second family an invitation," Kay said. "To the Kansas Day Picnic." There was a short silence while Billy pulled out to pass a truck and double trailer. Then Ann began to snicker and Bill laughed out loud, all three of them did, once they were safely ahead.

At Tejon Pass, just before they started down the Grapevine, she shut her eyes for a little nap. She had stepped off the roof and was soaring, soaring higher with each bounce, looking down on all of them below. Or they were looking down on her, Ann's head bleeding from when she tried to catch her. Her legs must be growing from all this exercise, and that was why they were going numb.

"Remember when we decided to jump off the roof?" she asked, opening her eyes. "I've been thinking about that the last couple of days."

"It was me that got the spanking," Billy said, "when your grandmother drove you two to the hospital. Aunt Garnet had grabbed me and kept yelling, 'You could have got killed' and hitting me on the butt."

"I remember the emergency room," Ann said. "The doctor sewing my scalp where the helmet hit me. Your grandmother was holding me around the shoulders. They had already X-rayed your legs and you were lying up on the table and the nurse said, 'You won't do that again, young lady,' and you answered as plain as day, 'I wouldn't say that.'"

"I don't remember that part. What I think about is that feeling, when you're suspended, neither on the ground or in the sky. That instant. It wasn't the jumping off the roof. It was more. A lot more."

Ann, 1978

The Interview

She could measure now with her eye how much green wrapping paper she needed to tear off, but it hadn't been easy. She'd had to learn everything, from how to order down to arranging the flowers: just putting the right amount of fern in with the roses was an accomplishment when she was starting out. But handling the flowers was always the biggest headache. Billy had come in to help once, when she'd only been open a month. Started right in making up a wreath, one that was supposed to have bronze mums in the shape of a saw and hammer. It was for the funeral of a carpenter. She hadn't been able even to start. "Okay, Ann, how does that look?" he'd asked. It looked like real tools lying on a white pillow. She still couldn't do anything like that.

But people came in and bought her flowers anyhow, which in itself still amazed her. Not just when someone died, which was the only reason she ever remembered anyone buying flowers in her family. Kay's grandmother's funeral. But for anniversaries, birthdays, or just to put on a table. Did her mother ever cut the roses that grew over the fence from the neighbor's yard and put them in a vase?

She could have done better when they went to L.A. She had even surprised herself, breaking down. Crying her eyes out. Where was her self-control? She'd gone in okay, ready for anything. But that disappeared when her mother gave her that look, like she was a waitress coming to take an order. Erased. Her past evaporated, all she'd done since she was eight. Along with all her energy. Since that visit, she'd had a feeling—what, inertia?—that stopped her cold. The feeling, it's no use. Sometimes she couldn't get up in the morning. Just to yell out "Rose, RubyAnn, get up, you're going to miss the bus" was too much for her.

She couldn't understand what was happening. She'd be paralyzed, unable to move, stuck under the covers. It got worse and worse. Once after the kids left she had tried to get herself ready, washing her face, brushing her teeth. It always got her going. Suddenly she felt like she had stiffened, arm locked. The blue handle of the toothbrush sticking out of her mouth, the grip of her fist: she watched, fascinated, in the mirror. She was never going to move. How long had she stayed there: a minute, an hour? What had she thought about?

It was Kay phoning that finally got her moving, Kay asking, "Anything wrong, Ann? Your employees are waiting out in front of the flower shop."

"My clock must have stopped," she'd said. "I'm not that late." Letting this happen was bad enough, but for Kay to know would be worse. But she couldn't stop what was happening, either. She'd given a key to Margie the cashier so she could open up. That solved that part.

She hated to think that what was going on with her had a name. When she went in for her pap smear, she casually mentioned a little of what she was feeling to the doctor's nurse, who was filling out her insurance form. "You're too young for menopause," the nurse said.

It kept happening, once a week sometimes, at least a couple of times a month. She stayed in bed one morning without calling to the girls to get up, fully awake, telling herself call, call, the covers pulled up over her head. Rose got up on her own, fixed breakfast for herself and RubyAnn, and they went to school late, while she lay there the whole morning, dreaming. But this time she was going back, seeing herself in civics class, as a girl. Her mind wasn't blank. She knew it was her. She recognized the dress. She felt happy, relieved, almost, and she could move. She got up and showered, got dressed. She was in the kitchen when the kids came home from school.

She waited for the next time, anticipating, almost wanting the inertia to happen again. Immobile was the word she liked to use. But it was what she thought about when she was that way that interested her. It was like she was translating a book in a language she didn't know, looking up each word, going on, page by page, thinking this is familiar, and realizing the words were about herself.

Maybe she should see a doctor. Kay would know someone to recommend. That seemed worse than what was occurring. Why had this happened to her? But it was fascinating too. From the pillows she could sometimes will the episodes to start, as if she were starting a favorite TV program, by remembering the clothes she had on. Plaid wool. Black Watch plaid.

She was wearing her pleated tartan skirt, bought two months before at Penneys to start high school in. It almost floored her when, one after another, three different boys came up to where she was standing, talking to Kay at the noontime mixer, and asked her to dance. She'd never expected that to happen, probably, she later realized, because Kay had never mentioned it happening to her. She got good grades because Kay did. Took the same business-math courses for the same reason. She didn't dance with any of them, just smiled, kidded around a little, and left the gym with Kay. She wasn't ready. Kay's face was red. She was a junior and no one had ever asked her to dance.

That made her understand she could be different in high school. That she didn't have to be like her old self. She didn't have to be Kay. She realized she dressed like Kay, wore her hair the same, in a ponytail, even though it was too curly and stuck out like a bottlebrush. Walked the same, as if she were in a race to get to the next class first.

She didn't have to experiment; she knew how to be different. Hair and clothes were easy, but signing up to be a reporter on the school paper was hard. She almost took drama but lost her nerve at the last minute, dropped that for public speaking. Had to take geometry, but it was going to be her last math requirement. Instead of business English she took regular freshman English. Dropped out of the Business Club and signed up for the swim team.

It was like the start of a new life, the second semester of her freshman year. Like she had moved, got a new father, to a different house in a different block with a whole different family.

By the time she was a sophomore, Kay a senior, she hardly saw her at school. They'd always studied together, but because they were on different schedules now—she stayed after school for swimming, the paper, any activity rather than go home—they never got together. The next year Kay went to college, and she really felt free.

That was the time she called up now, when she couldn't get out of bed. It made her loosen, thaw. She'd be made of stone but then an eyelid would twitch open, she'd feel a big toe move. Then wiggle her nose, watching one or another of the episodes. But she had to be careful to stay inside that segment of time, not to go beyond it, to where she met Carl at the picnic at nineteen, or before she stood next to Kay at the noon dance at fourteen. That was the most important.

She was the feature editor for the paper her junior year. In journalism class they were all given the same assignment, and she'd waited too long to pick a name from the list of people to be interviewed: all the interesting ones were gone by the time she got to it. She had to hurry, too; some kids had already turned theirs in. Took the bus, ran from the stop to the building, not to get wet. She hadn't wanted to carry an umbrella.

The door was half open. His name was printed in gold letters on the opaque glass, Milo Gorman. She stuck just her head into the office. The rain was coming down in sheets outside against the windows. There was only a small desk lamp on. She could see the place was a mess. Stacks of papers were ready to slide off the tops of the filing cabinets. Books and magazines were heaped on the floor and couch. Dying plants lined the windowsill like dry arrangements. White bags, paper plates with half-eaten food, and paper cups were scattered all over.

There was a flush and the other door opened. He came out zipping his fly. She was surprised: on the phone he hadn't sounded so old. "What are you looking at?" he asked. The loose skin under his chin and around his throat kept moving after he stopped talking.

"I phoned you," she started out. "For my journalism class."

"I don't remember," he said, leaning his elbow on a file cabinet, facing her.

She couldn't think of anything to say.

"Well, come in, I promise I won't bite you." He smiled. His teeth were worn down and yellow. She stepped inside but left the door open. She thought of flipping back the top of her writing pad but couldn't get herself to loosen her grip on her pencil. He had picked up a letter and was holding it away, reading it, when he asked, "How old are you?"

"Sixteen." She knew she didn't look sixteen. More like twelve. She'd worn a skirt and blazer to seem older. He humphed and went on reading.

Milo Gorman. His name had been on a long list of people her teacher had selected from *Who's Who in California*. She had picked him because the address was only one bus transfer from her house.

"How old do you think I am?" he asked.

"Forty," she said. She knew his age; it had been in the book.

He showed his teeth again. "I'm as old as the century, but I appreciate your guess." She was able then to open her notebook and write down, As old as the century.

"Are you going to sit down?" he asked. "If you're not, I am." He sat down on the swivel chair behind the desk. She backed up to a wooden chair that wasn't full of papers and lowered herself down.

"Sixteen," he said. "Have they got into your pants yet?"

She knew she was turning red but couldn't stop it. She wanted to run for it.

"I'm sorry," he said. "I shouldn't have said that." He didn't look sorry, she thought. "I've never got out of the habit of trying to shock people. I once introduced the attorney general as the number two bunghole of the state. And guess who's number one, I said. It was at a fund-raiser. He got some big money that night, enough to get the nomination for the U.S. Senate. But he lost in November by seventy thousand votes."

Sitting, he was still immense. He must be at least six-four or five, she guessed. Bald, with wispy gray hair scattered over the back and sides of his round head. He looked like a walrus. "What do you know about me?" he asked. He had been leaning back at an angle away from her, but now he suddenly swung his chair around to face her.

"You are as old as the century," she said.

He laughed. "You know I got two years at Terminal Island?" She shook her head. "Fraud. Can you imagine that, in this state? I had California in my pocket. I ran the place. The voters elected the governor and we told him what to do." She was writing it all down in shorthand. "It wasn't just because of the money. Not always, anyway. State government is too complicated. The new legislators always need some guidance. We were always there."

The phone rang. He picked it up but didn't say a word. "Who do you think would answer," he finally said, "my staff of secretaries? It's me, Milo."

She pretended not to listen. His voice boomed. "Jimmy boy, would I shit an old turd like you? Believe me, there's nothing in it. I have no memory. They just needed copy. No one has to be concerned. I had a lot of time to think about the past, if you'll recall. I don't want to dwell on it anymore. That's right. I've got to go now; I'm busy. Do you have to know everything? I'm just busy." He hung up. "Business," he said. "Old friend. Now where was I? Did I tell you this one? At a certain person's inaugural ball, we were all at the banquet table when someone asked me what I thought of the new governor. I said, loud enough for every-one to hear, 'He may be a son of a bitch, but he's *our* son of a bitch.'"

The phone rang again. Milo picked it up and listened a minute, then started laughing. "Don't worry. Calm down. Do it this way. It's not the right time for the bill, tell him. It's not going to be good for the state. It's not going to be good for the folks in your district. Don't mention anything about money. And then add, Milo doesn't like it. He owes me. No. No. Don't send anything. I don't want half. No. No envelopes. No." Then he hung up.

She'd got up and wandered over to the window. She looked down the three stories to the street at the parked cars, the few people hurrying by in the rain. The office was old-fashioned, varnished wood going four feet up the walls, high ceiling, floor lamps. She picked up a half-filled cup of coffee with green mold sealing its surface and dumped it on one of the dying plants.

"Well, now, where were we?" Milo said. She moved back around to the chair. The phone rang again.

"I better get going," she said.

"You'll come back?" he said, not reaching for the phone.

"I will," she said.

"I have plenty more to tell. You kids think you know it all. I could tell you things about this state. Be sure and come back," he said as she moved toward the door. "I'm not done yet."

She could hear the TV and the three of them laughing as she went up the walk. She opened the door and put her books down, watching too just as Moe shut Curley's head in a floor grate. They all roared. "While you're up, see if there's anymore coffee," her father said, "and bring me a cup." She went into the kitchen and turned on the gas burner under the pot. While it heated she watched them from the doorway: Billy on the edge of the sofa, the heel of his right foot jiggling up and down in excitement as Curley dangled at the end of a rope; her father slapping his thigh the way he always did; Kay sprawled back, laughing. The other Stooges were trying to haul Curley out of a cellar. Kay: if she was here on Friday it meant there was trouble; Aunt Garnet was raising hell again.

Later that night, in bed, she told Kay about her interview.

"Sounds like a creep to me," Kay said.

24

"You should have heard the way he talked to those people on the phone."

"I hear enough of that at home," Kay said. "I've got my name on a list for the dorm, but it's taking forever. You don't know when you're well off."

She tried to remember her mother. She never knew if her mind was making something up or not. They looked alike, Kay had told her. Small, fine-boned, dark hair and hazel eyes. "I'm not so well off," she said.

"I'll trade you any day."

Who did Kay look like? Not Aunt Garnet, who was small-boned too, her mother's sister. Maybe like her father: he was tall and had long arms and legs. Maybe she *was* luckier.

Poor Kay. Ann tried not to think that, but she knew she was smiling at the corners of her mouth in the dark as well as if she were looking in a mirror. Kay never had a date until Jack came out for a summer job from Kansas. He tried her first. Nothing doing. She might not have had a mother but she was smarter than that. Not Kay. Jack, who they called Stringbean behind his back, got Kay. Straight A's through her freshman year in college. "I think I'm pregnant," she confided one night in bed.

She couldn't think of what to say. Kay got up on her elbow and shook her by the arm and repeated herself. "I heard," she said, irritated. For something else to say, she asked, "Jack?"

"Who else, for Christ sake?"

"Where?"

"In the porch swing."

"Wasn't it cramped?"

"I never noticed," Kay said.

It turned out she wasn't pregnant, though, just late.

"Well, look who's here," Milo said. "I thought you'd forgotten the way." She had to grin. He was sitting at his desk, tapping his cigarette on the edge of a full ashtray every couple seconds. He looked the same, peaked, her father would say. Never outside, probably, she thought. He must have been even stouter once, the way the skin hung from his throat and the roomy way his double-breasted suit sagged on his frame.

"How are you, Mr. Gorman?" she said, going right up to the desk and putting out her hand. She'd noticed it usually disconcerted men to shake hands with a woman, or a girl, for that matter. She could never understand why. Not him. He took her hand, stood up, and kissed it.

"I'll never wash it again," she said.

"I wouldn't go that far," he said, and they both laughed.

Before he could start, she headed him off. "I have some questions for you." He closed his mouth with a snap; his old teeth clicked. She opened her pad to her outline. "How did you decide to become a career lobbyist?"

"Sweet Jesus, I never decided anything in my life. I just went and did it, that's all. I joined the army; they sent me to California. I could type and spell. They made me a clerk. An officer I worked for had a friend—this was after I got out— who needed someone to handle his office. In those days, men did that. He was a lawyer and was elected to the assembly the next year. So I moved up to Sacramento. One thing led to another. I got to know my way around. And most important, I got to know people."

"And they got to know you."

"That's right; from there it went on and on." She kept scribbling to catch up, wanting to finish with one question before she asked the next.

"I once handed a fella a million dollars in a suitcase. All in hundreds. I was sweating rivers. That's when I represented the racing association. Nice group, know how to appreciate people. Named a horse after me, Milo's Luck. What a time that was."

"Do you think your schooling prepared you for your profession?" she interrupted.

"Where did you get these questions?" He shook his head. "I finished the eighth grade and maybe a couple of months of high school. I learned to type through a correspondence school course. That was plenty then. I had to work in the orchard, pruning those goddamn trees. Riding herd on the apple knockers so they'd be able to pick in the morning. That was up by Spokane. After that, getting up at five-thirty, running for a couple miles, eating swill in the army, I thought I was on a picnic."

"Were you ever married and if so did you have any children?"

"Somehow I missed both pleasures," he said. Then he laughed. "I've had a lot of, shall we say, girlfriends. But I never married any of them. When I was incarcerated—do you know what that means?"

She nodded. "Stony lonesome." She realized she'd said it the exact same way her father did.

"That's right. When I had time to think about it, down at Terminal Island, I decided I must have been having too much fun to get married. I enjoyed what I did. I don't know if I'm saying it clearly. Maybe I didn't have the necessary time. I have a sister, though, and nieces and nephews."

He came to his feet suddenly, making her start. "Come on," he said, "let's go have lunch. No more of those silly questions." He put an old, wide-brimmed hat on his head and took her arm. She'd eaten before she came, but she didn't have to go back to school because there was a Teachers' Institute at two-thirty.

She had to keep herself from staring at the other people in the restaurant. The women looked like they'd stepped out of a fashion magazine, hair pulled back from perfect faces, and they all seemed to smile as they ate. The men wore three-piece suits and their hair looked like it was cut daily. The menu was in French without prices. The waiters knew Milo. He got nods and hellos from the other diners as they came through the room. Several men stood up to shake his hand. When they were seated, he whispered, "Isn't fear a wonderful thing? Look at them, half belong in jail and the other half have never done a day's work in their lives."

He ordered, adding at the end, "Knock off the hot stuff; they don't feed my daughter anything like that at the convent." The waiter never gave her a glance. She had to smile again at Milo. She felt comfortable here in the semidarkness. It was quiet: the only sounds were the soft murmur of voices and the faint clink of silverware. She belonged here, she decided.

On the way back downtown, Milo asked, "Well, what did you think of that place?"

She imitated a junior high kid being unimpressed. "It was all right." She started laughing first. "I liked it. I could go back a thousand times and never get tired of it."

"I don't know about a thousand, but I can arrange for a few more times."

She didn't plan to say it but she couldn't stop. "Do you know where we go out to eat?" He shook his head. "Down the corner to Danny's for the fish fry on Friday night. It's the only place we go to."

"Don't worry," Milo said. "If you want to go to those classy places, you'll end up going. But don't let it fool you. You pay twice in a place like that, once for the food and once for whatever it cost you to get the money."

"I'll pay," she said.

She was three hours late already, but she went back up to his office. Milo was tired; he sat down heavily in the chair behind his desk. She bustled around, throwing old half-eaten lunches in the waste basket. He watched as she emptied the ashtrays and then took water from the cooler in a paper cup to water the plants. "I wondered if you had any domestic instincts," he said.

"I hate housework worse than anything," she said, filling the cup again. When the plants were watered she stood by the door, her hand on the knob. He was pretending to read the paper. "Thank you for the lunch," she said.

He shrugged. "I wanted to impress you," he said. "I decided some time ago I hated the food in that place. That was after years of eating there. I'd give my right arm right now for some white gravy for my mashed potatoes. Liver and onions like my mother used to make me and my sister. You can't buy that anywhere that I know of."

"I'll be back," she said, opening the door. He nodded, looking down at his paper.

She could smell the Lord Calvert before he yelled, "Where have you been?" Kay and Billy were pretending to be watching the TV. Her father was standing in the middle of the room. "He worries about you, that's all," Kay had told her once, when she was crying because he'd yelled at her. "It's your mother; he thinks you might turn out like her."

He took another step toward her. She noticed the laces of his right shoe were untied. The little metal tips were dangling on either side of his foot. There was a special name for them; she'd read it in the newspaper. "Answer me," he yelled.

"It's none of your business," she said as clearly and slowly as she could. There was a flash, and her head struck the door as she fell. Kay was yelling "Uncle Frank, Uncle Frank." She was lying on her side on the floor. She could taste blood. She felt with her tongue for the split on the inside of her lip. Don't cry, she told herself, don't cry. She waited a minute before she got to her knees. Her father had backed up by his chair. Kay was standing by his side. Billy was at the far end of the couch. She glanced around the room as if she were seeing it for the first time, then went down the hall to the bathroom.

She had forgotten to lock the bathroom door. As she dabbed her face with cold water, Kay appeared in the mirror. "I'll never make it as a beauty queen now," she said to Kay's reflection, but neither laughed. She tried to wiggle her front teeth between her forefinger and thumb. None were loose. Both her cut lip and under her left eye were beginning to swell.

"What on earth were you up to?" Kay said. "I know you better than this. Where were you? It's eight-thirty at night. You're supposed to be home at four."

"I forgot to look at a clock."

"What's going on? It's me, Kay. Where were you?"

"That's for me to know and you to find out."

Kay slammed the door shut behind her. Ann went back to examining herself in the mirror.

She went back on a Saturday. The swelling had disappeared, and she had plenty of time. She tried the door and went in. He was looking out the window, his back to her. "I didn't know if you'd be here on the weekend or not," she said.

He swung around. "If you want to know the truth, I have nowhere else to go. Here or my suite at the hotel. And here is just a little better." She didn't know what to answer to that. "I expected you back sooner." She noticed he had a new shirt on now, button-down collar. He'd got a haircut, and even the hair that stuck out of his nose and ears was gone. His old double-breasted suit looked like it had been cleaned and pressed.

"The truth is," she said, "I got into a little trouble by coming home late last time."

"We don't want that," he said, taking out a pill from a plastic bottle and popping it into his mouth. "Well, let's get going. We have a heavy schedule today." He held the door open for her and then led the way down the corridor with long strides.

Once they were on the freeway he began talking again. "You have a sister?" he asked.

"A brother. Two years younger than I am."

"I don't know if it would be the same for you. But my sister Estelle was eight years older. She taught me to read. Took me to school and made sure I wasn't trampled on. In fact, gave me the three dollars for the bus ticket to run off and join the army."

She listened, wondering if she should have mentioned Kay; Kay was like a sister. Her father remembered like this sometimes, about back home in Kansas. Cows got into a cornfield and bloated up. The only thing for it was to puncture their stomachs in just the right place with an ice pick. He could go on and on as if the last twenty years in California hadn't existed.

"Those were apples then," Milo said. "Not this cardboard pap you get now. Grimes Golden. McIntosh. You kids today just don't know. Have no idea." They turned into the parking lot of a low building nearly hidden from the street by landscaping. She followed him into the building. He stopped at the drinking fountain to take more pills. She kept her eyes averted from the doorways where old people on beds looked as if they were dead, and concentrated on counting how many nurses greeted him as they went down one hallway after another. She waited at the door when he turned into a room.

A woman lay in a bed with metal railings. When she saw him she raised her thin arms and grabbed him around the neck as he bent down to kiss her. Milo waved her in. The old woman's hair had been recently curled, and she smiled. Her mouth moved and she made sounds, then put out her hand. She took the old hand and gave it a squeeze, feeling the oatmeal she'd had for breakfast come up to the back of her throat.

"She says hello," Milo said. "I can understand, pretty well. She's had a stroke." His sister spoke again. Milo cocked his head. "You have to listen," he said. "Estelle says you're pretty." She nodded and moved a little closer, trying to follow the words. She noticed Estelle's flannel nightgown was new, with a blue ribbon laced through eyelet embroidery around the neck.

They talked back and forth, but she couldn't understand Estelle, no matter how hard she concentrated. When Milo stood up to go, she stepped back. After Milo kissed her good-bye, Estelle held out her hand and drew her near. She closed her eyes and bent to kiss Estelle's cheek. She started when Estelle kissed her on the lips.

"We all have to grow old," Milo said, back in the car. "There's no avoiding it. That I know of, anyway." He pulled over in front of his hotel entrance. They stood on the sidewalk under the green canopy as someone came up and drove the car around back to the garage. She was looking forward to lunch in the hotel restaurant. "Wait a minute," Milo said to her, turning from the entrance. "Let's take a walk." She kept up with him as he strode down the street. The store window displays were beautiful. She'd never been to this part of the city before.

She followed Milo into a store. She didn't realize it was a jewelry shop until Milo said, "I want to see some watches. Women's wristwatches." The saleslady turned to a series of drawers built into the wall behind her and pulled out black velvet trays covered with watches and lined them up on the counter. "We want a wind-up," Milo said to the woman. "With numbers a person can see in the dark." He took out a big gold pocket watch. "My father's," he said. "Practical."

The woman pulled out two more trays. "Go ahead, look them over," he said. These watches were not like the one she got for graduation from the eighth grade and lost. She couldn't help seeing one price tag. Twenty-one hundred dollars. It made her nervous. She tried a watch on. And then another. "Take your time," he said. "Get what you really want." She took a deep breath and looked closely at the watches for the first time. There was one with a narrow band like a bracelet, with a safety catch. Gold. It had no price. She put it on and held it up for Milo to see. "We'll take this one," he said. He signed something as she admired the watch. "We can't have you late," he said.

She made sure she got rid of the box before she got to her street. Just left it on the bus. This watch looked something like the one she'd lost. She pulled the sleeve of her sweater down over her wrist before she went into the house. They hadn't got back to normal yet. Her father didn't speak to her when she came in. She made sure he noticed the stack of library books she'd stopped for on the way home. Billy waved as she went through the living room and then went back to reading his magazine. When Kay came over that afternoon she noticed right off. At supper she didn't say anything, not even when they did the dishes. She waited until they were in her bedroom, the door closed. "You think you're smart, don't you," Kay said finally. "I know what's going on."

She went back at least once a week to see Milo, sometimes more. The office was getting cleaned regularly now by a janitorial service. The clutter was gone. He had a new dictaphone machine that he was using to write a book. It was going to be about his years in Sacramento. "Listen to this," he'd say when she'd come in, and he'd play back a section. It was always a funny part, and she'd laugh. He must have bought at least a dozen suits, because it always seemed like he was wearing a new one, but he'd kept his old hat. They'd go out for lunch to a different place each time, or they'd go to see Estelle. She brought her flowers once, from a neighbor's rose garden. A former lieutenant governor sat at their table at lunch one afternoon. "I'm glad to see you around again," he said to Milo.

"No no," Milo said, "I'm retired. I'm just enjoying myself."

The lieutenant governor gave her a long look. Milo had introduced her as his niece. "I bet you are," he said. She watched Milo's face turn red. He had never laid a hand on her, never, not even when they jaywalked across the street because he was too impatient to wait for the light or to walk a few feet to a crossing. It was she who'd take his arm.

The night before it was due, she turned in an interview with the city district attorney who'd come to the school to speak on Vocation Day. She didn't care if she got a C or not. She had decided not to use the notes she had on Milo. There was just too much. She didn't know how to condense them and didn't want to leave anything out. She carried her notepad each time she visited him, but didn't open it now.

One Saturday on the way to see Estelle he asked, "Did I ever tell you the one about the auction?" She shook her head. He couldn't remain silent; one of them had to be talking. "From five to about nine I'd arranged to have a buffet put out over at the hotel across the street from the capitol. Free drinks too, naturally. We all congregated there: lobbyists, politicians, and hanger-ons. Well, a certain senator needed money: not a lot, I think it was ten thousand, but he needed it fast. There was nothing I could do for him. It was too short a notice."

"Why did he need the money?" she asked, although she knew Milo didn't like to be interrupted.

"Who knows. Someone always needed money. For a campaign payoff. Blackmail. Anything. He was standing around feeling sorry for himself, when his wife came in. I don't want to see your ears turn red, or I'd describe her." She looked at him; he'd stopped talking dirty months before. She missed it. "My mother would have said she was no better than she should have been. He, I might add, was known as a person who would do anything for money. And she was just plain known. Anyway, someone suggested a kind of auction. And it wasn't me."

"No one said it was," she said.

"The good senator was all for it, you could see that easy. She didn't seem too happy at first. A year is a long time. And some of those people there were low down. Word was passed and we all headed for one of the conference rooms. I remember there wasn't air to breathe in, there were so many people there. Her husband helped her up on the table. She was smiling by then."

"Maybe she was happy to be getting away from him."

"Anyway, the bidding started. I did not participate. I was attached, then. Within ten minutes, someone who will be nameless handed the senator the ten thousand and walked out with his wife."

"That's all?"

"That's all."

"What happened? I don't mean what they did. But did she go back to the senator after the year was up?"

"I don't know. I lost track of her. She could have, but on the other hand, she could have stayed with the high bidder or found someone else."

School was almost over: she'd taken her finals and cleaned out her locker. She got out at ten and hurried home. She had told Milo she was going to have a surprise for him, to be in his office at noon. She fried the onions first and then the thin slices of liver. The biscuits turned out light and the white gravy from the breakfast ham drippings was thick. She put the meal in vacuum containers, then packed a picnic basket with the good plates, napkins, and silverware, then ran for the bus stop.

The food was still hot when she got to the office and fixed his plate. "Well," he said, "she can cook, too." They used the desktop as a table. "This is better than I can remember it," he said.

She got home before everyone else and washed up the dishes and put everything away. When her father came in the front door and called out, "Liver and onions tonight; I can smell them," she felt shooting pains in her stomach. There was no more; she'd just bought enough for their lunch. When Kay came over, the three of them were sitting in the front room with the TV on, but only Billy was watching. Her father was sipping his fourth or fifth drink, mumbling something to himself every once in a while. Kay sat down beside him and he glanced over at her and said, "No liver and onions for me, Kay."

She didn't remember who started the talk about going back to Kansas for the summer to work in Aunt Clarice's cafe as waitresses. "Come on," Kay said, "it'll be fun." They were seated next to each other on the plane two days later. The three or four times she'd been free to phone, she hadn't been able to reach Milo. She promised herself she'd write him.

They were almost celebrities at the Wagon Wheel. Aunt Clarice would come out of the kitchen to talk to the customers and she'd always add, "These girls are all the way from California. Born and raised there. Ruby and Garnet Stecker's girls."

"I'll be," someone would always say. Everyone smiled and spoke to them as they rushed from table to table with their orders.

As soon as they got off their shift, cousins would be waiting to show them Kansas. They rode horses: she never thought she'd ever be yelling giddyup and whoa horsy. Went to the Dairy King at night. To meal after meal with relatives; Kay gained ten pounds. They tried to milk a cow. Went out to the small farm where their mothers were raised. The new owner let them in the house to look around. She tried to imagine her mother Ruby in one of those low-ceilinged bedrooms with faded wallpaper, sharing with her sisters Opal and Garnet. Her father's ranch, which belonged to someone else too, now, had miles of corn. Cattle grazed on green grass under locust trees. The road that ran in front of the farmhouse was named Bennett Road after her father's family. So was the park in town. The house had a porch with white pillars on three sides, draped with wisteria. There was no one home, and they looked in the windows. "Looks like Uncle Frank's folks had some money," Kay said.

They saw Jack. He was home from Kansas State for the summer. They were at the Dairy King in Aunt Clarice's car when he strolled up to Kay's window. She watched Kay, who hadn't seen him coming. "Well look who's here," he said, putting his hand on her arm. Kay didn't answer; she started the car and backed out of the space, leaving him standing there. "I was lucky last time," she said, after a couple of blocks. "I can do better."

They got back on the morning A's through G's were to register. She got most of the classes she wanted and was elected editor of the paper. There didn't seem enough time for everything. She meant to see Milo but kept putting it off. She hadn't had time to write back in Kansas. She had started several letters but never finished them. She had taken care of the watch, though, making sure she took it off before doing the dishes or taking a shower. She wore it all the time.

Kay never said anything more about it, just eyed her wrist now and then. It was no one else's business what she did. When she had more time she'd go see Milo. Maybe take him out to dinner. She had made more money than she'd imagined, just from tips. He would be surprised when she picked up the check.

She couldn't get Kansas out of her mind. It came back to her at odd times, vacuuming the front room, standing on the bus going home from school. It was slow one morning at the Wagon Wheel, and they were filling the salt and pepper shakers. Kay asked, "Could you live here?" She gave it some thought, screwing on a salt-shaker top. "If I could have a little air-conditioning unit mounted on my head to keep me cool." She didn't like the humidity.

"Remember my grandmother?" Kay asked. "My father's mother? She used to say we should never have come to California. You know, with my folks, and your mother running off. Things would have been different here."

She tried to imagine how it would have been, growing up in this little town, her mother at home. "I don't know," she said. "It's too late now anyway."

It was Kay who phoned at school. "The scaffold your father was working on collapsed. He's in a hospital up in the city. I'll pick you up at home." Her father had tubes running into his nose and mouth, but his eyes were open. They watched from the window in the door of the intensive care unit. "It was his pelvis this time," Kay said. "The foreman phoned my mother." They sat for a while watching the nurses and doctors go in and out of the rooms. Kay got up to talk to the head nurse. When she came back she said, "We might as well go. He's not going to come around, with all the drugs they gave him, until tonight. We can pick up Billy at school on the way back."

Kay took a shortcut across town to get home. They passed Milo's office building. The afternoon wind was coming up, blowing loose newspapers along the sidewalk. From a half a block away she knew who it was. That long-legged lope of a walk. He was bent a little forward against the wind, one hand holding onto the brim of his old-fashioned hat. She couldn't see his face. The car drew even and then passed him, and she stopped looking.

"What a day," Kay said.

What a day: that's what Kay had said when Billy dropped her off, coming home from L.A. last month. "What a day." Then, "That's over. Now you can get on with your lives."

She made it sound so easy.

Kay, 1979
Bertram's Slough

Kay always went alone. Her mother wasn't interested, and Ann and Billy weren't really related to her grandmother. Her father had moved away after he'd married Opal and had never been one for visiting cemeteries anyhow; never went, as far as she knew, when he came up now on selling trips. Never mentioned it, anyway, and she never wanted to ask.

She was always there, though, on August 29th. Never before. Then after, she'd go two or three times more, up until November. Then she'd stop until the next birthday. AUGUSTA ROSS CORTNER. 1891–1964. NATIVE OF KANSAS. REST NOW. She put the flowers in the little built-in vase, brushed off the top of the simple headstone with a paper napkin she'd saved from lunchtime. Granite, probably. She didn't know who was responsible for the inscription. It didn't sound like her grandmother. She'd always wondered, but didn't know who to ask.

She had tried her mother a few years ago. "How should I know?" Garnet was always aggrieved when her mother-in-law's name came up, even after she'd been dead for twelve years. "No one bothered to mention the subject to me. You better ask your father."

She didn't at first, because he didn't like to talk about his mother. Always seemed to change the subject to something else. One time on the 29th of August, still thinking about having been out at the cemetery, she phoned him. She'd done that before, but never mentioned going out there. Opal always answered: "Kay, how nice to hear from you. I bet you want to speak to Lester. He's right here watching the game. Hold on." They'd start slow. How's things? Business. They never mentioned Garnet either, of course. The weather down in Long

Beach. How bad the Kansas City Royals were doing this year. When he was going to come up again.

"I was out at the cemetery." She tried to sound as casual as she could. "And I was wondering about whose idea it was to put that inscription on the headstone."

"I have no idea. None whatsoever. I wasn't the executor; her bank was. They handled all the details."

"The *native of Kansas* sounds like her," she said, "but not the *rest now*." He didn't make any comment.

She knew her father hadn't received anything from the estate. Her uncles and aunts had. She had, too, a full share, and a lot of her grandmother's personal things. Her bookcase of books, the Cortner family registered branding iron, her size-six wedding dress, album after album of photographs.

She made sure she never opened the trunk where the albums were. It would be too much. That would let out all the secrets. She knew better. But she kept the trunk in the spare bedroom, inside the closet. She liked to think about her grandmother—it could be a comfort, sometimes—and always looked forward to the drive out in late August, September, October.

She wasn't thinking about having been at the cemetery when she pulled into her garage; she wasn't thinking about anything at all, because she went in too far, bumping into a stack six feet high of cardboard boxes of her father's. He had stored a lot of his things with her when he and Opal went to Long Beach, promising to move them, but he hadn't so far. The two top boxes came down, spilling their contents onto the garage floor. The next time she phoned him she'd remind him to stop and get his stuff when he came up. But she ought to have been more careful herself; she didn't have to nudge them like that.

She righted the boxes and started picking up the stuff. She wasn't paying attention at first, just picking things up and dropping them back into the boxes, until she yanked a stiff leather belt with a big silver buckle out from under the car. Still on one knee, she reached for a cigar box with a blue rubber band around it, then the magazine. Just putting her fingers on the faded *LIFE* cover was enough. His face was upside down, but that grin, even reversed, made her take in her breath. She felt actual small prickles of pain, as if someone were throwing darts to her chest, her neck. She couldn't let go, just drop them into the box. She stood up and went into the kitchen, set the cigar box down on the table, and rubbed her thumb across the engraving on the belt buckle. WALLY CORTNER. FIRST PLACE, BULLDOGGING.

She had always kept her grandmother separate, never let her get near Uncle Wally, when she thought of him. But neither was complete without the other. She hadn't realized that before now. Not just because they were mother and son. It was something more than that.

If anyone came close to being like Grandmother of all her children, it was Wally. He resembled her: almost rectangular head, round-shouldered, long-waisted, legs that looked like they could cross under the belly of a horse. Slim, lanky. Both had big farmer's hands. Grandmother was half his size, of course. And Wally did what he liked, just like she did. At fifteen she'd married a cowboy who didn't own anything but his saddle, lived in a sod hut till, with two babies, they'd moved to a shack closer to town with an abandoned boxcar in the back pasture. She turned the boxcar into a rooming house when the harvesting crews came to town, went from there step by step until she had the money for the house and the ranch. But Uncle Wally was different; he didn't do anything by design and never by a single step. He just did whatever occurred to him until his good fortune ran out. She had seen the whole thing end when she was eleven years old.

It wasn't easy to think about Wally. To look at his picture. To remember how he died. But it was worse not thinking about it, once it started. She went into the front room, switched on a table lamp. Sat down on the sofa. Wrapped up in the afghan. Held the LIFE magazine in her lap, and told herself the story, to the very end.

I went because Grandmother said there was room in her Chrysler, and I sat in the back on Opal's lap. I didn't get sick, but they still made me suck on a lemon and eat two crackers when the road started to zigzag through the foothills. I was looking wan, they said. Grandmother never talked while she drove, but as I dozed I heard her say, "This state is too long for comfort, and it's too changeable. You've got an ocean, rivers, bays, mountains, deserts, all that in the way, and they still grow more corn and raise more cattle than back home." She added after a few minutes, "In Kansas you can go anywhere in the whole state and it's still the same place."

They left me in the room to rest, but I couldn't sleep. From the third floor of the old hotel I could see the main street run south five blocks and stop against the fairground stands. "It's a small town," someone had said as we drove in, "but it's got the biggest rodeo in this end of the state." I could see down side streets lined with trees; there were houses with yards three times as big as ours in Belmont. Aunt Leila came bursting in. She'd been crying again and her nose was red and running. Then Opal came in and slammed the door shut. As long as I could remember, this had been going on: that Wally, everyone said. I stayed in my chair by the window, looking out.

Uncle Wally worked as a roofer when he wasn't following the circuit. When he was in the neighborhood I'd take my cousins Ann and Billy to watch him work, shirt off, driving nails as fast as you could look. When he'd see us he'd grin and shy a shingle at us kids. If Grandmother was with us, he'd yodel: she'd laugh and the rest of us would put our hands over our ears. He'd take a break and come down and visit, swigging water out of a gallon jug with a gunny sack sewed around it.

Ever since Uncle Wally had come back from the southern circuit there'd been more than the usual trouble. Twice a police car had stopped in front of Grandmother's house. Once they had talked him along to the porch, where we were waiting. The other time we didn't hear, and they left him leaning up against the front door. They didn't lock him up because he was in the papers now and LIFE magazine had his photograph on the cover. I don't know how many times taxis brought him to Grandmother's. He'd always give her address when he was drinking.

"Those LIFE magazine pictures didn't change him one iota," I heard my grandmother say at Thanksgiving. "He's still got that mean streak in him. He hasn't outgrown that by a mile."

Opal, my aunt but only seven years older than me, asked, "What's a mean streak?"

A cousin answered, "It's when a man beats up on his wife and kids and when he fights another man he pulls a knife."

"That's enough of that talk," Grandmother said.

But the cousin added, "He'd never have got away with the things he does here, back home."

Grandmother, my father's mother, came out to California after Wally, the youngest, ran off and joined the Navy during the war. There was no one left to work the ranch, so she came out too. She lived close enough to us that there was only one transfer on the bus. She owned property, duplexes, seven of them, and she was kept busy getting the rent and keeping them up. I learned that listening at the table after dinner.

On Fridays after school my mother would walk me to the bus stop, me marching along in my Girl Scout uniform, wait until the bus came, drop the money in the box, put my transfer in my hand, and aim me toward a seat. Grandmother waited at the other end, taking my hand without a word, then walking me up the boulevard, cars whizzing by, people rushing past us, fire engines and police cars, red lights blazing, sirens so loud it hurt my ears. But Grandmother didn't seem to notice; she kept going, leading me by the hand, as if she were in a tunnel.

It was quiet inside her old house because of the thick walls and heavy drapes. After washing up the dinner plates we'd put on our nightgowns and she'd get the shoe boxes of photos from the closet. It had taken hours, but we had divided them up into the Kansas pictures and the California pictures. We had almost all the Kansas pictures in albums. She called them snaps. She wrote the names for each picture, had to recognize everyone before it could be fitted under the four pointed corner holders. "See here, that's your mother leading the horse, when she was your age. They'd show up over to our place at least once a month to get your grandfather. They didn't know beans about cattle. One would go down sick and here'd they come. Your other grandfather was mostly a farmer. See back here, that's Opal and here's Ruby, you can just see her arms. Here come those Stecker jewels, I used to say when they'd come riding into the yard." It was a job. She couldn't always remember everyone's name, and those pictures were put aside. The California boxes grew with each visit. Everyone sent Grandmother photos, of themselves, their kids, grandchildren, family portraits, someone getting married or in a service uniform or graduating.

Uncle Wally was in a lot of the pictures, rodeoing, arm around his first wife that he met in a bar in San Diego. Then Aunt Leila with one child, two, three, four children, Grandmother would count. "There's no room for them out in this state. No work. What are they all going to do? I had six, but they were born into a job. The more you had then, the richer you were. Now you're poorer."

There was a snap of Wally and Leila and the kids in front of one of Grandmother's duplexes. Grandmother would rent to family, but there was an understanding that they were to be treated like everyone else; they were to pay by the first. Uncle Wally, no matter how much money he made, always owed Grandmother. Always. And she kept track and charged interest. He owed her three years' rent when he won seven thousand at Salinas and moved out and bought a house in a subdivision.

Everyone in the family waited. She didn't do anything. That next Thanksgiving they sat at the same table side by side and passed food back and forth and not a word. Liens, garnishments, lawsuits: an uncle whispered those words to my parents, but nothing happened. Grandmother even made bail once, when Wally got into a row down at a bar. "Favorite or no favorite," I heard, "when he was drunk he said, 'She can whistle for her money.'" Somebody told her. But she was silent, tight-lipped.

She took in Aunt Leila after he threw her out one night. I was over at Grandmother's that weekend. After we got Leila and the kids settled, I held the garage doors open and she drove out the Chrysler, then waited for me to get in. She didn't knock when we got to Wally's house; she walked right in. He was standing by the kitchen door, his shirt front flat and still, as if he weren't breathing. Grandmother held her big blue purse against her chest with both arms.

"You never in your whole life took time out to use your head," she said. "Not one minute. You're lucky your father's not alive."

"This is my business," he said, slurring the last word so it sounded like the buzz of a horsefly.

"Look at you. Some day you're going to have to grow up. Act like a man." Wally turned his face toward Grandmother and glared. "I don't know what is going to become of you," she said. "We should have never left. Back home none of this would have happened." She wasn't speaking to him when she said that. She took my hand. "Get yourself some sleep. I'll send Leila back in the morning."

I was used to seeing Aunt Leila crying. So I stayed in my chair by the window, watching for cars with out-of-state license plates, while Aunt Leila and Opal splashed water and whispered in the bathroom. It was just me, Opal, Grandmother and Aunt Leila staying at the hotel, because there wasn't enough room in a cousin's sister-in-law's house for everyone. Three carfuls of family had made the trip to watch Uncle Wally. He'd come up a few days before, towing his horse trailer with Toby inside. "That horse can do everything but talk," Wally would say, "and he's worth his weight in gold as far as prize money's concerned." But once at the stable I saw Wally kick Toby in the stomach when he tried to bite him.

Aunt Leila and Opal left again, and I waited long enough, then went downstairs. There was a restaurant dining room with a waitress in a starched yellow uniform setting tables. My grandmother would have been pleased at the way she lined the silverware up just right with everything else on the table. I got the silverware in the right order, but nothing was ever straight. "Young lady," my grandmother would say, teasing me, "you're nine years old and you can't do better than that?" I didn't mind; I had skipped a grade and was in the fifth. I had plans of catching up with Opal.

I eased by the desk where the hotel clerk was reading the paper and then slipped into the next open door. I'd been in bars before, but this was by far the best. It was so dark you couldn't see anything when you went in. The jukebox light came first, then the one over the bar. The glasses were stacked up high in front of the mirrors; they reflected the light like chandeliers. The cigarette smoke was thick and moved in hazy layers around the room. Eight people were lined up in front of the bar. Their voices were just loud enough to hear but not to understand.

The bartender saw me; I'd got too close. He tried to stare me down, drive me back out the door. I pretended I was looking for someone. I knew he wouldn't yell or stop what he was doing and come out from behind the bar as long as I didn't do anything to disturb the customers.

He stopped glaring at me and I moved back into the shadows. There were two women at the bar near the front door. Every time it opened they turned toward the spear of sunshine with big smiles, their chins up. The men were wearing high boots, jeans, blue work shirts, Stetsons. All of them were drinking draft beers and shots of whiskey, the women too.

When Wally came in there were big hellos and he hugged the two women and shook the bartender's hand. He stood between the two women, an arm around each one's shoulder. I waited until he spotted me. Then he gave out a whoopee you could hear for a block, picked me up on his shoulder and carried me over to the bar and sat me on top.

The two women made much of me and the bartender poured me a glass of

7-Up. This had all happened before when I was sent to get Uncle Wally or told to go along with Aunt Leila. He knew the same as me that it was all a game and sooner or later he'd have to come home. This time I'd come on my own. He did all the things he usually did, introduced me to the people in the bar: "This is my niece Kay, the smartest kid in the family, my oldest brother's girl." Someone said they had a daughter my age. One of the women combed out my hair and redid my braids. A man down the bar gave me a quarter and another one gave me two nails bent into a puzzle, which I figured out right away. The bartender handed me five swizzle sticks and a handful of olives to eat.

Uncle Wally danced with me, my feet dangling above the floor, until he got out of breath. He got me to name all the states and state capitals and won ten dollars from the bartender and five from the man who gave me the puzzle. I sang "Streets of Laredo," both women cried, and I got more money and the bartender gave me an alligator purse someone had left at the bar. I was going to sing another, everyone was making requests, when I noticed Grandmother watching me from the hotel lobby door.

She eyed us steadily from the doorway. I knew there was no use trying anything, crying or running to her. She stopped looking at us then and gazed around the bar as if she were interested in buying the place, then turned on her heel and went out. Wally pretended not to notice and took a gulp of his drink. I waited until she had time to get up the stairs and then followed, my cheeks burning. When I got to the room she was sitting in the straight-backed chair at the desk, writing a letter. She never mentioned it, ever.

Forty-Niner Days ran the whole three-day weekend. Rodeo, parade, carnival, street dance. It was exciting enough before Wally was out there, but when he came into the arena the first time on Toby, even Grandmother half raised in her seat. He wore his red shirt, and his long legs spurred Toby on, faster and faster.

The calf wanted to cooperate, kept running after the rope was around his neck, then jerked up his four feet straight up into the air like fence posts. Wally was right there, had him tied in record time. He got a good hand from the crowd, and he took off his hat and nodded his head in Grandmother's direction. I'd seen it all before, but I felt like it was the first time.

He won two events that first day, and when I walked by the open door to the bar, going to dinner, I could see him already inside. A fat man was slapping the bar top with his hand, yelling, "This man"—he whacked Wally on the back—"his money is no good, do you hear? No good. I'm paying for whatever he can eat, drink, or lay."

The second day he won one event, and that night he got a new '53 Chevrolet, donated by a local dealership to the cowboy who had the best time in the Brahma bull–riding event. He gave everyone a ride, filling the car with family and friends, driving around town honking the horn, blinking the lights, the police saluting us, Wally waving back with his glass in his hand. "Isn't this something," he said over and over.

Even Leila was happy, following Wally out from the sidewalk to be the first couple to start the street dance. Before that, they'd made him say a few words at the grandstand by the hotel. He didn't speak at first, looking down at the microphone as if he didn't know what it was for. Finally he chuckled. "I can't think of anything to say."

The mayor coaxed him. "Just say hello."

"Hello," Wally said, and everyone yelled and whistled.

The third day he won three events. He was driven around the arena in a Cadillac convertible, sitting up on the back, his big boots resting on the white upholstery. A pretty girl escorted him to where he was presented the prize money. He kissed the check first, then the girl. Everyone stood up and roared. He waved his hat and hugged and kissed the girl again.

That night we had reservations for dinner at the hotel dining room, all of us, the whole group that came up together. Even Grandmother spent a lot of time in the bathroom getting ready. We kept watching the doorway while we ate, but Wally never showed up. I didn't hear anyone say anything about it. We stayed in the dining room for the good-byes: a lot of the family were going back right after dinner, to be ready to go to work on Monday. Opal had to go, and Leila got a ride back too; her kids were staying with a neighbor and she had to get home to get them off to school in the morning. Grandmother let me stay, school or no school, without me asking. We'd go back in the morning, she said. We were both in bed reading our magazines when we heard the knock. It was the police. We got dressed and followed them to the hospital.

Wally was lying on a table and they were cutting off his trousers. A nurse was following the inside seam up the right pants leg with a pair of shears. His eyes were closed but his chest moved with his breathing and there was no blood. Grandmother watched, but I sat down in a chair in the waiting room. I dozed off and on, coming awake when someone spoke or the doors opened. The police came in again and asked Grandmother if she wanted the car towed to a yard. The two women with Wally were not badly hurt and were released from the hospital before Grandmother and I went back to the hotel.

We stayed on after Leila came up and left. We went to the hospital at morning and evening visiting hours. Wally was completely paralyzed, couldn't talk or move. He lay staring back at the two of us standing at the foot of the bed. The only thing he could move was his eyelids, which he'd blink occasionally. Grandmother talked to him like nothing was wrong. It felt like rain; the moon had a ring around it with two stars inside, but no weather was predicted. The insurance would fix the car. She'd got a letter from her sister that the price of beef couldn't go any lower. That we'd have to go tomorrow, but we'd be back. And to do what the doctors said. She kissed him on the cheek, and I did too. His skin felt like a smooth stone.

I didn't go back with her the next time she went up, but the time after that I did. He had shrunk. They had moved him to the veteran's hospital and the old building had small rooms without windows. Wally lay with his head propped by a pillow. Grandmother stood at the foot of the bed. She talked about the family, who was where and who was doing what. As she talked she slowly moved her head from side to side. He was always going to be paralyzed. What made it worse were his eyes. The way he stared. I couldn't watch for long. Then he started to blink. When he stopped blinking, his blue eyes stayed covered, and I thought he was dead. But after a few minutes he opened them and started to blink again.

We stayed the weekend, then went back. They let me go up to Grandmother's any time I wanted now. We didn't go through the photo boxes anymore but sat together trying to work on squares for her afghan or to write letters. She would stop whatever we were doing, making peanut butter cookies, polishing the silverware, frozen right in the middle of what she was saying, then go on as if nothing had happened. Other times she'd say something that had nothing to do with what we were doing. There was a mole on the side of her neck: she'd always trimmed the hairs away but now it sprouted gray, long hairs that I couldn't stop looking at. Once she said, "It can't go on this way," and was silent again.

After the second year Leila moved, sold the house and went to live in the southern part of the state near her parents. Grandmother was the only one who went up now, staying a couple of days at the motel near the hospital, then coming home. She took his nurses hard candy at Christmas, invited the head nurse to breakfast at the motel coffee shop.

Grandmother asked me to go along too, in early June, just after the last of the sweet peas bloomed. I took a bunch up to put in the vase by Wally's bed. He didn't look like Wally anymore, not even close up. It was like visiting a stranger. I did everything Grandmother did, waving to him, kissing him hello. I had planned to sing, but I couldn't. I wanted to try to make his eyes laugh. I always thought he'd beat it, leap out of his bed when we walked in the doorway to surprise us. Dance a jig, yodel. Something. But all he did was blink. He blinked the same letters, over and over.

Grandmother stood at the foot of the bed. She was smiling but couldn't stop clasping and unclasping the catch on her purse. She always brought a big bottle of cold orange soda, his favorite. She opened it and poured some into a spoon and gently without spilling opened his mouth and trickled it down his throat. She went back to the foot of the bed, still holding the spoon, and read a nice letter from Leila and the kids. He lay staring, waiting for her to finish.

After that she asked me to leave and wait downstairs. I went, shutting the door like she'd asked. She came down a few minutes later and we went outside. She didn't say a word as she drove over to the motel. When we were inside the room she didn't take off her coat or hat. She sat down on the edge of the bed with her hands clasped in her lap. I was frightened; I had never seen her look like that before. I felt cold as ice inside my new spring jacket. We sat in our coats and hats side by side on the bed near the phone. About an hour passed before it rang. The nurse's voice came through, loud and tinny, "Very bad news . . . so unexpectedly," and we rushed back to the hospital.

I waited a month after the funeral before asking. It was Saturday night and we were sorting the photos. "Who was Bertram?" She turned toward me, looking over the top rims of her glasses as if the lenses were in the way. She didn't answer. Handed me a photo. "Tell me who is in this snap." They were lined up in front of the open barn, and there was a puddle that was frozen and it looked like it was sleeting. Grandfather was wearing his overalls and an overcoat, with a gunny sack like a shawl around his shoulders. Grandmother—I had to smile—had on her high boots: she was deathly afraid of snakes; and overalls, a heavy man's coat, one of Grandfather's old Sunday hats. There were other people: Ruby, Uncle Frank, a cousin James, my mother, my father. The last in line was Wally. He had on a slicker and a hat with earflaps.

"He was only a couple of years older than you are now," she said. She ran her finger down the photo. "Three years later your grandfather died. And a year later he joined the Navy. And I came out after." She took the picture and looked at it again, tilting it this way and that to the light. I waited; it took her a long time to begin.

"Bertram's was a quarter section about three miles from ours," she said, still looking at the picture. "The land was no good, alkali. There was nothing left there by the time we bought our place. But later the railroad built one of the longest trestles in that part of the country, across Bertram's slough. When the river ran high in the winter it flooded most of the Bertram place. Your grand-father had died and just Wally and me were left at home. There were the usual storms; the roads were closed; several times during the winter a train had been derailed, and they sent crews out. They boarded with us. It was fine with me; I didn't mind cooking and cleaning up; they paid. They set up a telegraph key in the parlor to get messages out. There was nothing to it; the operator showed us both how. We took turns at spelling him.

"I read later it was the worst winter ever. It lasted a long time. Just after the crew had repaired some track and went back to town, the trestle at Bertram's washed away under a string of cattle cars. We went out but there wasn't anything anyone could do. The engineer and the fireman had got out, but the two brake-men in the caboose were drowned. Most of the cattle were drowned too, but some of the cattle cars had floated, smashed as they were, and were stuck against the bank, and the cattle were bellering and thrashing inside them. We could see them down there in the water, wild-eyed and hurt. Big slicks of dark blood on the water like oil. Wally ran back for his rifle. I held him by the legs and he dangled down the bank so he could aim into the open car doors and he shot each one in the head.

"Now here's a picture—I bet you can't guess who they are. They're all grown and out here now." It was a birthday party, a big cake. Everyone was looking straight at the person who was taking the picture. I took my time. It wasn't hard to tell. People don't change much, no matter what happens. You can tell. You can see the same faces at fifty as you can at five. I went right around the table.

Later that night when we were in bed I tried to settle myself. Grandmother never moved once she got under the covers. I could end up anywhere: at the foot of the bed, tucked up next to her, or half hanging over the side. We were laying there, neither of us asleep, when she asked, "Where did you learn Morse code?"

"It was my first badge in Girl Scouts."

"I should have known you'd notice," she said, and she squeezed my hand.

I thought she'd fallen asleep, but she said after a while, "You remember when I said we should never have left home? Never come out here? I was wrong to say that. It doesn't matter. It's not California. I want you to know that."

I didn't know what she wanted me to answer. So I said, "You think we'll ever get all those California snaps into albums?"

"Most likely we won't," she said. "But then again, we're not going to stop trying."

She didn't own a camera and she didn't have photos around, just Rose's and RubyAnn's school pictures on the refrigerator, and when the girls gave her the new ones each year she tore up the old ones. She got up, stiff from sitting cross-legged, and took the LIFE magazine back into the garage and closed the flaps of the box on Wally's face, then stuffed the belt down inside another box. Her ankles were aching and she limped back into the kitchen and put some water on the stove for tea. Her mother never let her forget jumping off the roof.

Grandmother had come over to visit when she was still in bed, her legs in heavy casts. She'd brought her a white bag full of lemon drops. "When I was your age I got a notion to see what lightning felt like," Grandmother told her. Kay's mother and father told stories about lightning storms too: no one stood by a window or used the phone during a thunderstorm, or touched a faucet for a drink or got in a car. Her mother told once how lightning came in the house, into the room where she and Ruby and Opal were hiding in the closet, and melted the metal doorknob.

"I climbed up the two-by-four ladder that had been nailed to the side of the house, up to the gable where the lightning rod was fixed," Grandmother said. "I grabbed that rod with both hands. It was raining, too, and I was soaked through. The rod on the barn got struck. I held on tighter. Pretty soon, I thought, I'd be holding on to something that was hanging down from the sky, and I watched each stab of broken lightning like it was the one for me." She chose a lemon drop and looked it over before she put it in her mouth. "My father saw me up there and got me down. When I think about it now, I know I'm lucky not to have got killed up there, but what I wanted to do, ride that lightning down to the ground, that stayed with me like a kind of talisman. You know what a talisman is?"

She shook her head no.

"You'll find out. You're going to have scars under there"—Grandmother tapped the casts—"where your bones came through. That'll keep you wondering, when you're my age."

It had her wondering now, what Grandmother had said. She poured the boiling water over a tea bag. If she had a talisman, it wasn't from jumping off the roof. It was Grandmother, spooning that last orange drink to Wally, like he wanted, that was her talisman.

Billy, 1980
Old MacDonald

He was going to go slow and do everything right this time. No one in his family had any luck with love. Even if it was only the chance of the draw, someone ought to win occasionally. No wonder Kay never picked a number and Ann wouldn't risk another try. His father.

Billy watched while Charlotte flopped down on the creek bank and put her face in the water, then he fished around in his pack for his watch. Four minutes to twelve. What timing. He spread out his poncho and laid out the picnic.

"You carried all that up here?" Charlotte said, her face still beet red from the climb and dripping wet.

"Uh huh," he said as he uncorked the wine bottle and handed her a glass. It was an elaborate spread, he thought, admiring the cake, which had come through the ten-mile hike almost unscathed. "My pack only weighed a little over twenty-seven pounds, not much for that sort of a hike."

"Does everyone go to this much trouble?"

"Some do," Billy said, offering her a sweet and sour chicken wing. "Sit down, let's eat."

"I can't believe it, Billy," she said, squeezing his arm. "You're all style." He glowed with pleasure as he filled their glasses.

By the time they'd finished eating, Charlotte's face had returned to its normal coloring. Billy took off his boots and socks and lay back on the fine meadow grass. She sat cross-legged, reading the label on the wine bottle. How did she stay so skinny, he wondered. She'd finished off all the chicken and salad plus two pieces of cake. That was what he'd noticed first about her: at coffee break her first day at the lab she'd gone back to the counter for a second doughnut and then a third. She'd caught him watching and winked. The next day she'd sat down beside him at break with two maple bars and a bran muffin. "Nervous energy," she'd said in her twangy drawl. "Coal for the old locomotive, my mother used to say."

He tickled her knee with his toes. "What about our sauce?" he asked, mostly just to hear her voice.

"What about it?"

"Do you think we have a chance? Think they'll buy it?"

"You've worked there for nine years. How many people have brought in recipes?"

"Hundreds, I don't know."

"How many did NatureFresh buy?"

"None that I know of."

"Does that tell you something?"

"Yeah, that they weren't as good as ours." His voice was louder than he meant it to be. "If you don't believe it's going to be a success, why do you spend so much time on it?"

"Guess," she said, putting down the bottle, then throwing herself on him, giggling wildly as she kissed his face and neck.

"Come on," Billy said, holding her away. "We're going to have our barbecue sauce in every store in the country."

"I know we are," she said, unbuttoning his shirt.

Next day at the plant they were all business. When the batch samples came in from the floor, it was hectic. Charlotte worked quickly as Billy poured, separated, and checked weight and viscosity. It was the only time during the day that they had to hurry, and she set the pace. If everything checked out okay they could slow down and go back to their regular work. He surreptitiously pinched Charlotte on the rear as she bent over a microscope. She pretended not to notice. She was head chemist and in charge of the entire quality-control section. He was a technician. No one on the staff guessed there was anything between them. She waited until no one was looking to clamp the hem of his lab coat in a vise.

He stepped into the flower shop Tuesday afternoon and winced: he could hear them both in the back. He'd wanted to see Ann, but both at once was too much. The bell brought a clerk out. Maybe they wouldn't know it was him. "I'd like a bunch of violets," he said in a low voice.

The clerk called over her shoulder, "Ann, are there any violets left in the refrigerator?"

"Wait a minute," Ann said. His sister came out carrying a small bouquet wrapped in green paper. She started laughing when she saw him and yelled back through the doorway, "Look who's here!"

Kay came out. "My favorite cousin," she said. "And buying flowers." She started in. She really thought she was funny. "You promised, Billy, and you still have eleven months to go," she went on, resting her big ass against the counter. Ann laughed too. They always did, no matter how many times they repeated it all. He'd only agreed to wait to make them stop. Always bringing up his two divorces. He didn't like to be reminded all the time. He'd marry Charlotte tomorrow if she was willing. The hell with them.

Then Ann had to say her piece. "Billy boy, love is not for everyone. Love, and especially marriage . . ."

"Goddamn it," he interrupted, "let me get this over with." He lowered his voice again. "Why I stopped is to invite you to dinner Saturday at seven." Both women gave each other a look. He went on. "You two have been chosen to be the first to try my new experimental barbecue sauce." They smiled; it was the old Billy they heard now. "I'm cooking enough ribs to test the final three variations of my sauce, which is sure to bring me fame and fortune. Also, my partner Charlotte will be there."

"The chemist from work?" Ann asked.

Billy nodded. "I'll be expecting you at seven sharp, with big appetites." He started backing out.

"The flowers!" Ann thrust them into his hands.

He reached for his wallet. "How much?"

"Oh, come on, Billy. On the house."

He put a five on the counter and hurried out. As he moved his car into the traffic he started going over the whole business again. Right from the beginning, like always. He was two years younger than his sister and four years younger than Kay. He was always the baby. They were always there waiting for him to ask for help. And he did, he always did. Norma. Dumped him for a bartender she'd known for a week. He couldn't believe it. When everything else failed he asked Kay to go see her. Tell her I love her. I'll take her back, anything. I don't care. Was he crying that time?

Kay knew everything. She was a C.P.A. before she could drink legally. "Maybe it's better this way," she said.

"Please, Kay, I'm asking you. Please talk to her; she'll listen to you."

"Did she ever do anything like this before?"

"I don't know; I don't want to know."

Kay phoned him back the next day. "No go, Billy. She's not coming back. And if you want my opinion, it's no loss."

He married Jennifer eight months later. Slipped off to Reno one Saturday night after she got off work. She wanted out in less than three months. He talked her into something he wished he'd talked Norma into: going to a marriage counselor. Listening in the office, Billy couldn't believe it was him she was describing. He bores me sometimes. He's so particular. Everything has to be planned down to the letter. When I say "Let's go see this movie," we can't just get up and go, not him. He has to read at least three favorable reviews first. Has to be there fifteen minutes before it starts. Sometimes he even phones the candy counter to see if they have Good N Plenties before he'll go. It's like living with an old woman.

The counselor convinced her to give it a two-month trial. He took him aside. "Be innovative," he said. "Be impulsive."

He tried. He waited for Jennifer to open the front door of the apartment after work, then sprang out of the closet with nothing on but a gift-wrap bow stuck on his belly button. She shrieked and leaped back. He hadn't known she was going to bring her mother home. Although she hadn't mentioned it to the marriage counselor, she'd always told him he was too fussy about personal cleanliness. He stopped changing his clothes daily, forced himself to wear his shorts and T-shirts two days in a row, although he couldn't bring himself to do that with his socks. She complained about ironing him a clean shirt every day. He sent them out to a laundry. He kept it up for three weeks. She never noticed the difference.

Charlotte came early to help, but he had everything nearly ready. While he was cutting a clove of garlic into tiny slivers, she started running hot water in the sink to wash up the pots he'd dirtied getting dinner going. "This is a switch," he said; he was always after her about the mess she left in the lab for him to clean up.

"You're lucky I'm doing this. I swore once I left home I'd never touch dishwater again. My mother made me do the dishes because it was women's work," she said. "My brothers got to watch cartoons while I was in the kitchen."

He measured out a small pile of peppercorns on a scale. "Why is it," he asked, "that everyone always remembers the bad things?"

"It's probably easier," Charlotte said, hurrying to the living room at the sound of the doorbell.

Glancing through the kitchen doorway at Ann and Kay on the couch, he realized how close to opposites they seemed: Ann slight, dark, gesturing with quick movements as if she were stubbing out cigarette butts; Kay big-boned, fair, deliberate. They were facing Charlotte on the recliner. He'd stayed in the kitchen to finish up, but he could catch most of the conversation. Ann was talking about her daughter Rose. "She's just turned thirteen and it's an acne crisis every day. She's miserable. I can't say anything to her. You'd think it was my fault she's got pimples."

"I don't know if I could put up with kids. I'm glad I'm single," Kay said.

"Do you have children, Charlotte?" Ann asked.

"I had one. She was born with Down's Syndrome." Billy stopped stirring the sauce. She'd never mentioned that to him before. "I was absolutely in shock. I'll admit it now; I couldn't touch her for a week. It was my husband who insisted we bring her home. I didn't want her." She paused, then added, "She died when she was seven months old. I was so wrong: I should never have rejected her. No matter what. Now I have my mother." He watched her through the doorway. She was leaning forward, caught up in what she was saying. "She's been going through a bad time. She regressed to about a nine-year-old when my father died; can't live alone, of course. There's three of us kids and we take four-month turns. Mine starts this fall."

"You're divorced now?" Kay asked.

Charlotte nodded. "He's remarried and has two children."

When women got together it was so revealing, he thought, turning off the oven. It wasn't like men, maneuvering to establish a pecking order. With women it was facts laid out, face up. He had never heard Ann even hint before about seeing Carl die. Or Kay say that after the second break-in on her block she'd started to sleep with a knife under her pillow. He hated to interrupt, but the ribs were getting cold. "Well," he announced, coming into the living room, "I hope you all have big appetites, because there's going to be a lot of eating done here tonight. You'll notice by each plate there is a card and pencil. After each sample, I want you to put a check under excellent, fair, or poor, for flavor, texture, adherence, etcetera. This is an important moment, and we ask you to be objective." As he held Charlotte's chair for her, she patted his hand. He saw Kay and Ann smile approval at each other as they sat down.

Ann and Kay had left, and they were cleaning up. "What did you think of them?" Billy asked.

"Well, they didn't physically assault me." Charlotte laughed. "No, I liked them. Did you really promise not to get married for three years?"

"I did, but you have only eleven months to wait."

"Is that a proposal?"

"Maybe."

"You know my mother's coming. I promised my brothers. I have an obligation. She's going to stay with me four months each year, no matter what."

"That's fine with me," Billy said.

They decided to take their vacations together, two weeks hiking and camping in the Sierras. "I can't believe I've agreed to do this," she told him at coffee. "I could never stand to sleep out in the backyard with my brothers, not the whole night. I always ran back in the house after they fell asleep. It was too scary. Not everyone could have talked me into this, Billy."

A week later he brought her the first list of camping gear she'd need for the hike. "Why do I need all this stuff?" she said. "Three pairs of shoe laces? An Ace bandage?"

"In case."

"In case what?"

"Just get the things on the list."

"All right." She looked at the list again. "I will, but answer me this. Why the mothballs? Humor me."

Exasperated, Billy said, "For the bears."

Charlotte started to laugh. "Oh Billy," was all she could say. She was laughing so hard she held her sides and tears came streaming down her face.

"What's so funny?" Billy said, getting hot.

"Mothballs," she got out, and started hiccoughing. He patted her on the back. "I'll get them," she moaned. "Mothballs!" She started laughing all over again.

The second morning out she saw an osprey catch a fish out of the lake where they were camped. "Did you see that!" she yelled, grabbing Billy by the arm. He'd never enjoyed himself more. Her seeing everything for the first time made it new for him too. And she never failed to laugh when he put out the mothballs. "I thought it was some crazy California environmental group's idea to rid bears of their moths," she explained the first time he did it.

"It keeps them away, Charlotte. You don't see any around, do you?"

When it got dark they lay on their backs watching the stars, talking about old movies, high school, anything that came to mind. "My brothers made a friend of theirs take me to the junior prom. I had a pink eyelet dress. We sat by the punch bowl the whole time because he couldn't dance. They meant well, I know that, but I made up my mind then that I'd never let anyone step in like that, make decisions for me, again. But later, when I met my husband, I did. He was the one who insisted on the divorce. We'll never be compatible, he said. I gave in. But looks like I got lucky after all," she said, running her finger along his jawline.

He rolled over, facing her. "Are we going to be lucky together?" he asked.

"We can't miss," she said, squeezing his hand.

When Joanna, Charlotte's mother, arrived, Billy found it hard on all of them. There were too many scenes. At her sons' homes she'd been allowed to sit and watch TV all day. Charlotte insisted she go for therapy at the mental-health clinic. Joanna seemed to get more obstinate each day. "I'm not going," she'd say, stiff-legged, shoulders rigid.

"Mother, you're going." Billy would avert his eyes.

"You can't make me."

"Get your coat."

Some of the time Joanna was docile; she'd take his hand when they went for a walk and skip along beside him. When Charlotte had evening meetings he'd take her out for ice cream, and she'd slurp her soda and act coy when he helped her on with her coat. She startled him once during intermission at a Disney double feature by asking, "Have you ever smelled a putrid body? Have you ever noticed how a dead thing bloats?" He knew the story from Charlotte. Her parents had taken a Caribbean cruise. Her father took sick in port. The ship left them; they were to catch up later. He suddenly died. The body was iced and she accompanied it north by train. A bridge was out and they were held up eight days on a siding.

He tried to make it easier for Charlotte. When Joanna knew he was coming she was always, for a short time, on her best behavior. "You have more patience than I have," Charlotte told him. "You're my rock, Billy. I've never known anyone like you. You're so good." He was touched; he didn't know what to say. His former wives had never said anything like that about him, ever.

The barbecue sauce was almost perfect. Charlotte was ready to submit it to the company, but Billy kept holding back. "Just take it easy. It has to be just right," he told her, tasting a spoonful from the latest batch they'd put together in Charlotte's kitchen.

"What more can we do with it?" Charlotte asked.

"I want to try a little less cayenne pepper."

"Billy, you did that a month ago."

"I want to try it again, just to be sure."

"You're fussing over nothing," she yelled. "You just don't want to find out what they'll say."

"Remember, we agreed I was going to decide," Billy said, putting down the spoon. "And I'm not ready."

"I don't like people who vacillate, Billy."

He went to the door without looking back or answering, opened it, and walked out. That was on Saturday. He hadn't spent a Sunday alone in months. He changed the mantles on his Coleman lantern, oiled all his boots, took his car to the car wash, steam cleaned the engine. The day went on forever.

Monday wasn't much better. A couple of weeks before the argument he had volunteered to pick up Joanna at the clinic each afternoon. He felt he had to keep on, but he dreaded that now. She had started acting up with him, too. Last week she'd taken his keys out of the ignition when they were stopped at a red light. "Now Joanna, you know better than that. Please give me back my keys."

"Make me," she'd yelled back.

Friday, when he'd opened the door for her at the clinic, she'd yelled from the sidewalk, "I know your dirty game. You're trying to get rid of me. I know what you two do when I'm not there." He hadn't told Charlotte. This trip is the last, he promised himself, working through the going-home traffic Monday night. Joanna was belching beside him on the front seat. She'd been doing it since she got into the car. When she got out, he saw she'd peed on the seat. She smiled sweetly as he closed the door. He wanted to yell something, but he couldn't think what.

He stayed away. Enough was enough. He stopped in to see Ann at the flower shop. "You know why I don't have any luck with women?" he said. He didn't give her a chance to answer. "Because the ones I end up with always think that one of us has to lead. And because I'm the way I am, they take over."

"What happened?" Ann asked.

"Charlotte and I aren't speaking. I changed with another technician and I'm on a different shift now."

"Well, look at the good side," Ann said. "At least this didn't happen after you married her."

When he picked up the phone one evening and it was Charlotte, he was so excited he dropped the receiver. "What's wrong, Billy?" he heard her say as he fumbled for it.

"Nothing, nothing."

"I just phoned to say I should have kept my big mouth shut about the sauce."

"You're right, Charlotte, you should have."

She laughed. "Billy, did you think I was going to let you get away?"

"You had me worried."

"Let me finish the other things I was going to say. One, I shouldn't have let you do so much with my mother. Two, she's a pain in the ass. But she's my mother. She always treated us kids good. I owe her. But on the other hand, I think she's putting most of this stuff on. And three, I'll be glad when she's gone. Four, the weather is so nice this week, let's have a picnic up where we went before."

"It's cold up there now," Billy said. "I bet there's still snowdrifts."

"Good, then I can throw snowballs at you. Of course, I'll have to take her too, my mother. Do you have any comment on that?"

"No, I don't care."

"I'll bring the food this time. I've get everything planned. If you want to bring anything, pick up a bottle of wine. I love you, Billy."

"You have every reason in the world to, Charlotte," he said, pleased that he could think of something clever in reply.

It was a perfect day for a picnic. It was warm in the sun; birds sang in the trees; buds swelled on the branches of the alders by the creek. Joanna ran ahead like a little girl, splashing in the puddles from the last rain. She insisted on going higher when they reached the meadow where they'd had the first picnic. Finally, Billy said, "Enough," and spread the tablecloth on a flat rock as Charlotte began to unload his pack.

"Billy, cut my sandwich," Joanna demanded, thrusting it in his hands. "You know I can't eat them this way." He cut it in two. He was going to stay calm. He watched her eat, big snapping bites. Joanna didn't look anything like Charlotte. In photos from before the cruise she'd looked well dressed, a weekly beauty-shop customer, a member of the Oconee County Historical Society and the Republican Women's Central Committee. Now she was down from a hundred thirty to ninety pounds, with cropped hair, no makeup, shrunken in the rumpled cotton jumpsuit of ten years ago she'd insisted on wearing. "Give me a piece of that pie."

"Please give me a piece of pie," Charlotte said.

Joanna glared at her, working herself up with little grunts until Billy handed her a piece. She gobbled it up and then skipped off, dropping her paper plate on the ground. "Pick that plate up," Billy yelled after her, but she kept going.

Charlotte reached over and patted his hand. "I hate repeating that she'll be gone in three days, but she will." He fiddled with the top button of her blouse. "I don't know if I'll have enough strength to take her back next time, either. I'm not saying that for you, Billy. Are you listening?" It had suddenly got chilly, and he was looking for the sun, which had gone behind a bank of dark clouds. "Ever since she's been here things have gone wrong," Charlotte was saying. He'd forgotten how beautiful she was, how transparent the skin seemed at her temples, so you could see blue veins underneath, how her eyebrows advanced unplucked toward the bridge of her nose. The wind started to blow, and he grabbed the paper plates before they took off. There were little crow's-feet at the corners of her eyes. The two weeks after the argument had been almost as bad as his two divorces. She poked him in the ribs. "Have you been listening at all? What did I just say?" Charlotte said. He kissed her.

When the first big snowflakes came sailing down like miniature kites he jumped up yelling, "Grab the stuff; I'll get Joanna." He'd just seen her a couple of minutes ago out of the corner of his eye, but it took a long time to find her. When she spotted him, she tried to hide. "Goddamn it, come on, it's going to snow. We have to go," he yelled. She ran behind some bushes. By the time he caught her the ground was covered white. Going back, he lost the path a couple of times. It didn't help that Joanna kept trying to break away. He got a good grip on her arm and began yelling, "Charlotte, Charlotte." The snow was coming down thick and fast. Finally he heard her yell back, and he saw her, holding his pack and looking anxious.

They hugged each other until Joanna whimpered, "I'm cold, I'm cold." Charlotte buttoned her mother's raincoat and turned up her collar for her, Billy grabbed his pack, and they started off down the trail. They were about an hour and a half from the car, Billy thought. Maybe two hours, with Joanna. They lost the trail. He realized it when they found themselves at the edge of a ravine. He tried to retrace their steps, but the snow had already covered them. He didn't know what to do.

They ended up huddled on a fallen log in a gully out of the wind. The snow kept coming down, faster, piling up on the plastic tablecloth they held over their heads and shoulders. Joanna was subdued now, hunched in her raincoat like a furtive animal. He and Charlotte were in ski jackets, but it was getting colder. "How long do you think it will last?" Charlotte asked him.

"No telling." He looked at his watch. "It started about two hours ago, and there's more than a foot already. It can't go on this way."

The wind died down, finally, but the snow kept on, gathering so fast that he had to constantly brush it off their plastic cover before it got too heavy. "This is the first time I've seen so much snow," Charlotte said. He was trying to think of another alternative. This was going to end badly; he knew that. Tonight it was going to get really cold. He kept trying to think of other solutions, but he always came back to the original. There was nothing he could do to stop what was going to happen.

It was after five, and it had turned dark. The snow was almost three feet deep around them. No one had spoken for a long time. He told himself, I have to do it now; I have to do it now. He felt through his pack for the plastic salad bowl. He ducked out from under the tablecloth, found a level place, and scooped out a trench in the snow with the bowl. Snowflakes piled up on his jacket in just the few minutes it took to make the trench. He floundered to a small stand of manzanita and broke off some limbs: it seemed to take a long time, wrenching with stiff hands in the dark cold. He got the branches over to the side of the trench. Then he got the down mummy bag he always carried in his pack and spread it out in the bottom of the trench. Brushing the snow out of his face, he laid the limbs across the trench.

He went back to the women and pulled Charlotte up by the arm, and then yanked the plastic tablecloth from over Joanna's head. He led Charlotte back to the trench and pushed her into the sleeping bag. He spread the tablecloth over the limbs and scooped snow over it with the salad bowl to weigh it down. Then he stuck his feet into the opening.

"What about my mother?" Charlotte yelled.

"There's only room for two in the bag," he yelled back.

"What's going to happen to her?"

Angry, Billy yelled down into the hold, "She's going to die. That's what. Anyone outside is going to freeze to death." He tried to force his legs into the sleeping bag.

She slid over, blocking him. "If she can't come in, I'm not staying."

"There's no room," he yelled as loud as he could. She didn't budge.

"Charlotte," he yelled. She didn't speak. There wasn't time for this. "Charlotte!"

He wanted to turn his face up to the sky above the falling snow and howl what about me? What about me? Instead he got up and waded back through the snow to where Joanna crouched. With numb hands he brushed her off as well as he could and guided her back to the trench. Charlotte's eyes and lips were clenched shut. Her shoulders were shaking. He made sure they were both zipped in good, and closed the opening. He stuck a branch upright by the head of the trench, warmed his hands under his arms until his fingers would move again, and tied his blue handkerchief to the branch. What about me? What about me? He heard himself saying it out loud. He stepped back. Screw you, he said. I'm not going to die.

He crawled up out of the gully. The wind wasn't bad now, but the snow was as thick as ever. He wandered around, trying to find a boulder or log. He felt calm; there was nothing to worry about, he decided. He stumbled into an old stump, cut high, about three feet across and well up out of the snow. He pulled himself up on top of it and kicked off the snow. He remembered the picture in the book as if he'd seen it only an hour ago. Kay used to read to him, before he learned how. She'd sit there and read by the hour, turning the book around to show him the pictures. Snowshoe Thompson, delivering the mail over the Sierras. When it got so it was impossible to go on, he'd take off his skis, climb up on a boulder, and jump up and down and bang his arms against his sides, yelling at the top of his lungs and singing until the storm passed.

He started out slow, a little self-conscious. Old MacDonald had a farm, he sang into the darkness. This wasn't so bad, he decided, once he got moving. With a moo moo here and a moo moo there; here a moo, there a moo, everywhere a moo moo. I can do this all night, he told himself. Or forever, if it meant telling Charlotte what he thought of her. What about me, goddamn it, what about me, he kept thinking between songs.

He was still singing the next day when they came, didn't hear the sound of the snowmobile, in fact, over the sound of his own voice. But his feet weren't working very well; he'd had to quit jumping up and down some time before dawn. "Good thing for you we went out cruising," the snowmobile driver said as Billy guided them to the blue handkerchief marking the place he'd left Charlotte and Joanna.

He guessed it was Charlotte out in the corridor before she came into his room from the way the shadow paused just outside the door. Thinking what to say? He was too, when she stepped through.

"I'm sorry about your toes," she said.

"There isn't any pain. And I only lost two. So far."

She came closer, even with the foot of the bed, but she didn't speak.

"How's your mother?"

"She's fine; my brother came for her. She didn't want to stay anymore." She took another two steps closer. There was a patch of red on each cheek, and her voice was high. "What in the hell do you think you were up to out there? You asked me to let my mother die. Choose her or you. How could you do that, Billy?"

He couldn't believe his ears. He'd saved her life. And her mother's. And here she was, giving him this. Was it too much to want to live too? He was so overcome with indignation he couldn't answer.

She was leaning over him now with her hand on his arm. "Get away," he finally got out, jerking his arm back. "I saved your life. You left me out there to die," he yelled. She backed away. "To freeze up like a popsicle. You made your choice. Go on. I'm alive."

She strode out the door and he could hear her footsteps hurrying away.

Ann and Kay had been stopping by ICU every evening. Tonight Ann had a bunch of early daffodils. "How much longer?" she asked as she arranged them.

"Another couple of days. Unless they decide to take more toes off." He tried to smile, but his eyes kept watering as if he were going to cry. He was remembering the little blue veins.

"Charlotte phoned me this afternoon," Kay said.

"She wasn't for you, Billy," Ann said. "You can do better."

"She got her transfer to South Carolina," Kay said. "The moving van's coming this Friday."

"Good, let her go back," Ann said. "You almost died because of her, the bitch."

"Shut up, Ann," Kay said. Billy saw Ann's mouth clamp shut. It'd been a long time since he'd heard Kay talk to her like that. "Charlotte mentioned that her phone wouldn't be disconnected until tomorrow afternoon."

Ann finally spoke, something about the shop, a delivery that went wrong. Kay didn't add anything more, stood looking out the window toward the airport. Chances, he kept thinking. How many was he going to get? The guy with the snowmobile coming by like that. He was alive, that was one thing. That was a start. Charlotte was alive. So was her mother. He closed his eyes.

They were leaving. He felt them take turns pecking his cheek. The good-byes.

He lay back, eyes still closed, and let pictures drift across his mind. Not the cold, this time, the Old MacDonald had a farm. Last night he had seen himself as a popsicle, bare legs and feet clamped together for the stick. Now he imagined himself lying on the bed with his bandaged foot. With his hand raised, reaching for the phone.

Kay, 1981
Sailing to Tasmania

She finished with one client and another sat down in the chair by her desk. Sneaked a look at Ann, in the deacon's bench by the door, and heard herself say, much louder than she meant to, "I'm not going to accept those receipts, Ann."

Ann patted the shoe box on her knees. "There's no reason why these can't be figured in too."

Kay knew everyone was listening, but she couldn't stop. "You might as well throw them away. I know they're no good."

Ann stood up. "All right, if that's the way you want it." She emptied the shoe box onto the floor and stalked out. Kay watched the pink and yellow receipts flutter to the parquet, then turned again to the startled gray-haired woman. "How many dependents was that?" April 15th was always the same.

It was past eleven, all the help had punched out, and Kay was just finishing with the last client when Ann came in again. She must have made a late stop at the flower shop, because she had her work clothes on. She went straight to the janitor's closet and got out the push broom. Kay ignored her, exchanging good nights with the client at the door. Then she stretched and yawned, watching Ann sweep around the copy machine. "You don't have to do the whole office," she told her.

"That's what I get," Ann said, "for trying to pull one on the I.R.S." She picked up the pile of receipts with the dustpan and returned it and the broom to the closet. "Did you see the look on that woman's face, the one who was sitting at your desk, when I dumped the box?" Kay had told herself this was it: Ann could take her account somewhere else; she'd had it with her and her snits; but she remembered the surprised face and had to laugh. "I came back to invite you over. I went straight home and made an apple-walnut cake just to get back on your good side."

"Come sign your name on these forms, first." Ann was fitting her signature into the space when the street door opened. Kay wished she had locked it; she was ready for home. Someone tall, sandy-haired, suntanned poked his head into the office and gave them a tentative grin. "I hope I'm not too late," he said, "Gordon Brown recommended you to me. My name is Gene Flynn. I just want some advice."

Ann was the first to speak. "How did you get that tan in April?"

"I just got back from eleven months on the Great Barrier Reef."

"Come on in," Kay said. She bundled up Ann's forms. "Ann, sign the rest, here and here." She added her own signature and put everything into a large envelope. "Mail this now; I won't be able to stop tonight."

"I'll wait for you," Ann said.

Kay didn't argue. She sat back, ready to listen. "Go ahead, Mr. Flynn. Ann's my cousin; her lips are sealed. Start with Gordon Brown; I haven't seen him for years, not since he sold his warehouse. He was one of my first accounts."

"He's fine, Gordon's fine. He was at a dinner party the other night when I happened to mention that I needed to see a good accountant and get my affairs straightened out. He said you were the best C.P.A. he'd ever run across. I put it off and put it off, but then I started worrying a little, all those stories about the I.R.S., and so I've finally looked you up." He paused and smiled self-consciously again at Kay. "About two weeks ago I was carrying some money. And somehow I left my attaché case on the plane. When I went back for it, they insisted on opening the case to make sure it was mine. I had a lot of cash in it. It got into the papers; you know how they like those kinds of stories."

"What do you do?" Kay asked.

"That's just it; it's hard to explain." He fidgeted in the chair.

"When was the last time you paid taxes?"

"Practically never: a couple of times, I think, while I was in the service."

Ann made a sound that was half cough, half laugh. She was still wearing her black vinyl shop apron that had BOSS printed across the top: where the vinyl had cracked, she'd patched it with gray duct tape. Her washed-out broken-zippered sweatshirt had green stains on the shoulders from carrying bunches of flowers. She needed to have her hair cut, too. She was perched on the front edge of the chair looking quizzically from Gene Flynn's face to hers and back to his again like a cat listening to a conversation between two humans. Why did that make her think of when they were kids, hot mornings in August before the wind came up, Ann in a white T-shirt and Levis, hands flat in her back pockets, jumping; Billy turning the rope, one end tied to the garage door handle, all of them chanting *Sally called the doctor, Sally called the nurse, Sally called the lady with the alligator purse* while she waited, arms half raised over her head, for the exact instant to run in, watching Ann jump straight-legged up and down, up and down, barely lifting her feet off the driveway so it seemed the cotton rope couldn't pass beneath her tennis shoes: *IN came the lady with the alligator purse!*

She came back to the present. "But you've had income from whatever you do, Mr. Flynn?"

He exhaled and reached into his shirt pocket and took out a folded check. Kay had to look twice before it registered. "This cashier's check, it's made out to you for eight hundred forty thousand dollars. And you want to pay taxes on this, Mr. Flynn?"

"I'll pay my fair share, but I want to keep all I can."

"This is out of my league," Kay said, shaking her head. "You need a tax lawyer."

"Wait now, listen, I want you to handle it. I think you can. It'll take a while, but let me tell you about everything."

At ten minutes to twelve, Kay remembered Ann. She interrupted Mr. Flynn to yell, "Ann, go mail that now, or it won't have the postmark on it." Ann jumped up and rushed out the door. Kay turned back to Mr. Flynn. "Excuse me. Go on, please."

"That's about it."

"I don't know what to say, I really don't. All I can think to do is ask for an extension, get some time, and then try to set a course."

"That's a good nautical term," he said, touching her arm.

"Here, take your check. I'll think of something," she said.

Over at Ann's, Kay couldn't stop herself; she had three pieces of cake. She knew better. The weight didn't come off like it used to, with a few missed meals and her once-a-week exercise class. She gained it all in the rear. Last month she and Ann had been trying on dresses down at the mall. "My God, it looks like a big balloon is under my dress with me," she'd said, looking over her shoulder into the mirror. "More like a couple of basketballs," Ann had said.

"You think that check was good?" Ann asked, cutting herself another slice.

"It was a cashier's check."

"How about the story? Hurricanes, sinking ships, rescuing people?"

"I don't know," Kay said, carefully picking up cake crumbs from her plate with the flat of her index finger and putting them in her mouth.

"And Tasmania: I thought that was next to Rumania somewhere, not an island. He loans thirty thousand to a friend, which he got from an insurance company for saving a ship. Ten years later, after striking it rich mining in New Zealand, the friend gives our boy almost a million back. I'm surprised he didn't have a chest of jewels somewhere in the story."

"It sounds crazy," Kay said. "But that doesn't mean it's not true. I like this. I like playing around with all the possibilities. I could incorporate him; that would open up all kinds of options. I could average . . . It's going to be interesting."

Ann got up and put the encyclopedia back on the bookshelf. Kay yawned, covering her mouth with both hands. "I'm going to sleep till noon tomorrow, now that the rush is over."

"If I had your money, I'd take a month off," Ann said.

"I'd go nuts with nothing to do."

Ann walked her to the car. It was after two. "I almost forgot," she said, stopping, "everyone at the shop's saved up a whole stack of mysteries for you, must be a couple of dozen. I'll go back and get them."

"Like they saved up those receipts? No, no, that's all right; I'll get them next time," Kay said, sliding into the car. As kids they'd both been readers: Ann had read nine books in one day, once, to edge her out by two, the last day of the library summer reading contest. She'd been so mad at losing that she'd yelled at Ann, "You didn't read that many, I know you didn't, and I'm going to tell everyone." Ann had yelled back, "I did too," and burst into tears. She'd hugged Ann until she stopped crying; then later they'd taken the prize, a five-thousand-piece puzzle of a cable car, and burned it in the fireplace. Kay slid back out of the car and gave Ann a hug.

"What's wrong with you?" Ann said.

"Nothing, go back in. Go on, you'll get mugged out here, waving good-bye to me."

She stretched and pulled the covers up to her chin. She knew it was after ten. She really could take a month off and go somewhere. The business could take care of itself; her office manager could handle things. She hadn't gone on a real vacation since that trip back to Kansas years ago. She remembered how green it had been, green in the summertime at a second cousin's farm, and wondered what it would have been like if her parents had stayed back there, had never left: would she be doing the farm accounts while her sunburned husband did the chores? Out here you always had the feeling you were missing something, that you were right on the edge of some chance that might change your entire life. From the stories she'd always heard, Kansas was always the same: you knew what to expect there.

She rolled over to the edge of the bed and put one foot out on the rug. Kansas. No one had ever gone back there to live, retired there with their California money. They stayed here in the sunshine. But they kept telling their Kansas stories. They could remember every detail from fifty years back, even the dogs' names: Dandy, Soupbone, Sport. There must be thirty or forty of them among her clients: just last week an old man had come in with his middle-aged daughter and told her, "I knew your grandmother. She was one of the big girls in school. She taught me my letters."

She put her other foot on the floor. No vacation yet; she had to clear her desk first. She jumped up and stretched her arms out in front of her, ready to do her exercises. As she was dressing, the phone rang. When she said hello the voice on the other end said, "What? Me worry?"

"You must have the wrong number."

"Is this Kay?"

"That's right."

"It's me, Gene Flynn. I came in last night about my taxes, and you thought you might be able to help me."

"Well, all I can say is I'm working on it. I'm going to need your business records."

"But I don't have a business."

"Your boat. Didn't you charter, carry cargo? You mentioned that last night."

"But that was only in an emergency, when someone needed help."

"That's good enough; it's a business."

"Oh, I see."

"You still have the boat?"

"It's in a yard up on the Sacramento. They're going to do repairs. I let it go too long this time; sea worms got into the planking. I'm going up today, in fact, just to get things started. That's what I phoned about. Would you like to go with me? Just go up and come right back?"

She said yes.

She was surprised when he walked her to an old, battered pickup truck and opened the door. "Watch out for that broken spring," he said, helping her up. "I folded this blanket over it, but it might come through."

The truck wouldn't go past forty-five. They had to yell to talk over the noise of the engine. "Not much of a getaway car for a guy in trouble with the I.R.S.," he said, laughing. "The owner of the yard lets me use it when I have my boat in dry dock. I've known him for years. I had one of those deals where the Navy helps pay for your college and then you serve four years. When I got out I knew what I wanted to do, and I talked Jesse into taking me on. And then finally I knew enough to build my boat. I've been sailing ever since. Been around the world twice. I anchored in a lagoon I found off Madagascar for a year, once."

The words came out of Kay's mouth before she could stop them. "You know, C.P.A.s don't just add up figures. We can help with all sorts of business decisions too." She could have bit her tongue. That was something she used to say when she first started out, to entice prospective clients. Nothing was going right. She wasn't picking up on what he was saying; she was laughing thirty seconds too late at his funny lines, and then too loud. When he'd phoned and used the Alfred E. Neuman opening, she should have caught on: she'd read *Mad* as a kid.

Gene geared down for a stop sign. She yelled, "How did you manage . . ." and realized that she didn't have to shout; the truck had come to a halt. "How did you manage day-to-day expenses?" she asked in a normal tone of voice.

"It's kind of complicated. Money doesn't really mean anything to me. I'm sure you've heard that before. But in my case, it's true. I can get along without it. Wind doesn't cost anything. I rarely use my engine. Food—well, I eat a lot of fish. When something comes along and I need the money, I barter. I'll take some passengers to an island or out to fish if they'll fill my tank with diesel or trade me a sail. So my day-to-day expenses are really nil." Kay listened, startled, when he parked the truck, to realize they were there.

The boat yard was just what she'd imagined: up on pilings, a big wooden ramp going down to the water, workmen in knit caps and sweaters hammering away. Gene introduced her to the owner, his arm around the older man's shoulders. "Kay, Mr. Jesse Bullard. Jesse is the boss here. It took me a lot of talking before he'd allow me to work for nothing to learn how to build my own boat." Mr. Bullard said very little: dour, she thought. He'd stepped out of Gene's grasp, and he gave her a nod and went back to work.

"This is it," Gene said, patting the bow of a boat. It looked too small to be sailing around in the middle of an ocean, propped up with boards which ran from the sides of the boat to the floor like insect legs. "It looks like a spider," Kay said, walking around it. "A daddy longlegs."

"It does," Gene said, getting a ladder.

The boat looked even smaller from inside the cabin. She sat on a stool sipping white wine while he explained how they had built the boat. As he talked, she watched a workman on the boat alongside them: with measured taps of his mallet on the chisel he cut away a section of rotten planking as if he were cutting a window in the hull to expose the wooden ribs underneath. Someone else was planing long curls of wood off a plank. That wood-shaving smell always reminded her of the Kansas Day Picnic: kids searching for coins in a big pile of shavings and sawdust, mostly Roosevelt dimes, but sometimes quarters. She'd been too old the last year they'd had the coin hunt, and so was Ann, but Ann was in there with Billy anyhow, both of them scrambling on hands and knees with the rest of the over-sevens and under-tens. She'd been turning hamburgers on the grill instead, the job her grandmother always had until she stopped coming, the year Uncle Wally died. The grill was next to the beer keg. A group of men stood in a half circle by the keg, drinking beer out of paper cups: her mother's cousin Gilbert, who was a surveyor; her father; Uncle Frank with that half-tanked smile; two brothers from Wichita who worked at Swifts and got the ground chuck and hot dogs at cost; a couple of others. They were griping about the city. "You know how the Peninsula's shaped: just like the pizzle on a bull," Gilbert was saying. A couple of them snickered, and she started to listen: she hadn't heard that word before. "Well, you know what end gets all the pleasure;

the rest of us do all the work. Just listen to that goddamn airport: anymore, you can't hear yourself think. The tourists don't bring any money down here to us; it all goes to San Francisco."

"As long as there's enough work for everyone, I can put up with those jets," Uncle Frank said. He had more work than he could handle. He had his contractor's license now and was able to bid on bigger jobs, storage tanks, hangars; at times he had twenty or so painters working for him.

"You live in Belmont. You wouldn't say that if you lived in Lomita Park; it's worse than an earthquake."

"I'd say it wherever I lived." Uncle Frank straightened up. No one wanted to argue with him, not only because he might punch you in the nose, which was a possibility, but because he never forgot, sober or drunk, and would continue the argument every time he saw you. He had changed since Aunt Ruby left. She could remember him good-humored and laughing: he had more back-home stories than her father. Jokes. You could barely get him to talk now, unless he was drinking, and then he talked too much, butting into conversations, not staying on the subject.

Gilbert changed direction. "We've got all their drinking water. Without us, they'd be a small name on the map."

"Well, Gil," her father said, "if they try to come south and take anymore ground, it'll be Colma first, all those miles of cemeteries. Just headstones and dead people."

Everyone laughed but Uncle Frank. "You can always go back home and shovel shit like you did before if you don't like it here," he said.

Gilbert got his back up then. "Who do you think you're talking to?" He set his full cup down on the table.

Her mother came over then. "Let's play horseshoes; come on, Frank. You were just plain lucky last year." She hooked her arm through his.

"You must be daydreaming," Gene said. "Your eyes aren't focused. More wine?"

"Just thinking," she said.

During the day they worked on the inside of the boat. They steel-wooled the whole cabin before putting on the marine varnish. He was even more meticulous than she was: no drips, paintbrush hairs or holidays anywhere on the teak panelling. She wore an old pair of overalls Gene had found at the boat yard and a faded baseball cap when she painted, and at night, when they got back to the motel, one of his T-shirts.

She had surprised herself, staying. She hadn't expected it at all, but when he'd asked, she had nodded. The third night, wrapped in a towel, just out of the shower, she sat down next to where he lay looking through a chandler's catalogue and ran her fingertips over the long welt of a scar on his upper arm where a Portuguese man-of-war had wrapped around it. "Outside of this, you're flawless," she told him.

He'd wanted them to stay longer up at the boat yard, but she knew she couldn't delay getting started on his file. The office had its Saturday smell of floor wax and furniture polish. She straightened the cushion on the deacon's bench, watered the ferns, and settled down with Gene's folder. She had thought out a plan, but it was going to take some doing. She was on the phone when Ann came into the office. She didn't want to talk in front of her, but she couldn't end the conversation. "I promise he'll pay what he owes, Bob. I just need more time to work out the details. There's no need to impound his boat or his funds. I know he should have made some moves before this. But that doesn't mean he wasn't going to do the right thing. Have I ever asked a favor before?"

She wondered if Ann could hear when the director answered, "For you, Kay, this once." She had never phoned his home before.

"Would you have done that for me?" Ann asked as Kay hung up the phone.

"You don't need that kind of help."

"What if I did?"

"Ann, for goodness sake, I'm busy."

"I brought you those books. I stopped over a couple of times last week, but they said you were gone. And when I phoned you at home, there was no answer."

"I took a little vacation." She started writing notes on a pad.

"Oh," Ann said. There was a long silence. Kay kept on writing. "I was telling Billy about your pirate or whatever he is, that guy that came in here."

"How about my mother; did you tell her? Or my father? I don't have to remind you . . ."

"You know something, Kay," Ann said, getting up and taking a pile of paperbacks out of a shopping bag and slamming them down on the desk. "You're too touchy. You always were."

Gene came by that evening to pick her up for dinner. She was concentrating on his folder and didn't hear him come in. He crept behind her chair and put his hands over her eyes. "Keep your eyes closed," he said.

"What?" she said, startled.

"Keep your eyes closed. I have a surprise." She heard him move the papers off her blotter. "Okay, open them," he said.

There were at least a dozen pearls spread out in front of her. "I never knew they came in so many colors," she said, amazed.

"These are culls; I won them in a bridge game two or three years ago. Take one, any one you want."

"Really?"

"Go ahead."

She picked one that was almost coral pink. It looked like electricity was running through it. He gathered up the rest and put them back into a black velvet pouch, then squeezed her shoulder. "Come on, let's go."

Instead of the pickup he was driving a sleek, silver gray foreign car. "This is a lot more comfortable, isn't it?" he said. "I have it on approval. It's custom made, sells at the bargain price of fifty-one thousand dollars." He never stopped surprising her. The night before he'd driven up to one of the best restaurants in the city in the pickup; tonight he took her down the coast to an old woman's kitchen where they sat family style at a long table with twenty other people. There was oilcloth on the table, but all of the women were elegantly dressed; one, with diamonds that had to be real, said hello to Gene. "I went to school with her brother," he told Kay. She knew he meant Stanford. They had a kind of fish stew that the old woman ladled out into thick bowls. They drank red wine out of juice glasses and tore hunks of sourdough bread from big loaves, covered them with slathers of butter and dipped them into their stew. She cracked a piece of crab with her teeth and it exploded juice all over her new silk blouse, but she didn't care. She'd never laughed so hard before in her life.

Ann came in, wandered around the office, looked out the window, checked the plants. She didn't say anything, but Kay knew what she wanted: for her to tell her what was going on, to introduce Gene to everyone, for them to go out some-where, Gene and her and Billy and Ann. She dreaded that. She'd mentioned the family, told Gene about her father marrying her mother's younger sister Opal. He'd been interested, amused. He said he'd have to go to the Kansas Day Picnic. She dreaded that even more. All those fat women in pastel pantsuits, men in Western outfits, boots, cowboy hats, big leather belts with silver buckles. Why did they have to do that? She remembered the yellowed snapshots: four or five of them lined up in front of a car or a barn in wintertime, lace-up boots, bib overalls, flannel shirts, coats, any kind of coat to keep the cold out, shapeless old felt hats or caps with earflaps, women dressed the same as men. In the pho-tos from the first picnics out here, the men wore sharkskin suits and fedoras, the women, rayon dresses. Now they tried to look like they had a palomino tied up outside. They had never looked like movie cowboys in Kansas.

Billy and Ann picked them up at her office. There were introductions; everyone shook hands, laughing self-consciously, trying to make conversation. "I hear you're a sailor," Billy said.

"Something like that," Gene answered.

"I work for NatureFresh Foods," Billy said. "Quality control. You wouldn't believe what went on in the lab today." He was off on a long anecdote about finding the tail of a mouse in a jar of gherkins. Nothing could stop Billy, Kay thought. He had that totally untouched and innocent look about him. The only other people she'd ever noticed who had that look were simpletons.

Somehow they finally got into Billy's car. "Tonight," he announced, "I have reservations at a place which will provide a new eating experience for all of you." He started to snicker. Then he laughed out loud.

Ann poked him. "Come on, Billy, where?"

"The last drive-in in California," he said. He took them way out to what used to be the interstate, still lined with old motels, tiny tile-roofed strings of stucco cottages rented by the month now instead of by the night. From a couple of blocks away they could see the broken neon sign over the drive-in flashing DRI N in pink. "I found this place by accident," he said.

Kay was relieved there weren't still carhops so they'd have to eat in the car. Billy led them into the octagon-shaped building. The walls were purple tile, chipped and faded, up to the windows. Booths ringed the outer walls and a counter circled the kitchen in the center. Kay could remember an uncle taking the three of them out to a place like this when they were kids—they'd all come home with good report cards. They had eaten in the back seat of his old Chevrolet and Billy, who must have been in first grade then, had spilled his Coke all over her.

Billy ushered them into a booth. He was enjoying himself. When the waitress brought a menu he said they didn't need one. "Four specials," he told her. Was Gene noticing the grease-stained ceiling, the cigarette burns on the floor? When the food came, he rolled his eyes: jumbo-sized hamburgers, french fries covered with brown gravy, and mugs of hot coffee. Kay tried to grin. "Takes you back, doesn't it," Billy said happily.

The hamburgers were good, but no one but Billy ate the french fries. It was difficult to talk because of the noise from the jukebox and because of the other customers, who were yelling back and forth to each other. A lot of the men at the counter were wearing Western shirts and boots. There were a couple of cops and a sailor in uniform too. The booths were occupied mostly by families. Two babies in high chairs near them had thrown a lot of their food all over the floor. No one wanted dessert except Billy, who ordered a hot-fudge sundae. He ate it slowly with apparent relish. It was as bad as when they were kids: you were supposed to eat slowly, chew your food, but Billy made a career out of it. He'd sit there and sit there, taking quarter forkfuls while everyone watched, unable to leave the table until he finished. Ice cream was the worst. Even Ann looked uncomfortable now.

"That was quite an experience, Bill," Gene said on the way to the car. The only empty parking place had been about a block from the drive-in. Somehow, when they got into the car, Kay ended up in front with Billy, and Gene and Ann were in the back. Billy rolled his window halfway down and started the car. He was just releasing the emergency brake when a hand thrust a pistol through the window. "Okay, folks," a voice said. "I need your cash."

None of them could speak or take their eyes off the gun. "You're the boss," Billy finally answered. As if he had all the time in the world, he reached back for his wallet. At the same time he pressed the button so the window went up against the mugger's arm, and popped the clutch. The car bounced forward and the gun went off with a flash of yellow flame and a deafening roar, shattering the windshield. Ann grabbed for the robber's arm and Kay yanked at the pistol in his hand. The pistol dropped into Billy's lap. The robber was gone. They sat there a few seconds before Ann said distinctly, "Well, on the debit side, he broke your windshield, but on the credit side, you've got his gun." Kay caught Billy's eye and they both started to laugh the same instant.

An account of the incident made the ten o'clock news. People Kay hadn't heard from in years phoned her about it. Her mother phoned the next afternoon. "You kids," she said, laughing. "Always were fearless. That time I got mad at you and wanted to give you a swat. All three of you climbed that acacia tree that used to be in front of the house. You scared me half to death, you were so high, two or three stories. You made me promise I wouldn't paddle you before you came down. Of course I gave you all a good whack anyway. That's not to mention the time you jumped off the roof with the umbrella."

Billy and Ann were in the office when Gene stopped by to pick her up. "I see we made the papers," he said, putting his arm around her waist. "Funny, same kind of thing happened to me in a port one time; a native tried to rob me, came at me with a machete. I took care of it. Still have the knife up on my boat. You remember it, Kay, in the locker with the life jackets."

She hesitated, then agreed. She'd emptied that locker, painting; there hadn't been a machete. There was a short silence until Billy said, "Well, come on, Ann, if you want a ride. I've got to be off; tonight's a game night. Company baseball team," he said to Gene.

She waved them off from the doorway. Gene nuzzled her neck. "Alone at last," he said. "We've got to celebrate. I knew you'd get that extension from the I.R.S. In fact, I made a bet with Gordon Brown right after I met you that first night that if anyone could do it, you could. He owes us a case of Moet."

They spent a whole week on the delta in a cabin cruiser Jesse had loaned Gene because his boat wasn't ready yet, stopping at night just far enough offshore to escape the mosquitoes. He showed her where to dig freshwater clams and how to fish with a drop line. Each night they swam, letting the current take them to the shore, where they'd rest on the warm sand of the bank until the mosquitoes came, then swim back to the boat. Gliding through the water, she felt like someone else, like someone in a travel poster, suntanned, with flowers in her hair.

She'd let her hair grow longer, bought expensive new makeup, which she put on, squinting into the tiny mirror in the cabin, while Gene waited with their drinks on the deck.

"This is nothing," he told her, "nothing. Wait until I show you what sailing means. No dirty smell of diesel, just the wind slamming against the sails. The bow knifing through the waves. Think about sailing around the world, take a couple of years." They were stretched out on deck chairs, and he sat up, excited. "I have friends everywhere; we can stop in every port. There're so many things I'd like to show you."

She wrote a postcard to mail when they went in for supplies: Ann, are you going to believe I caught a sturgeon yesterday? Baited my own hook? This is the life for me. Don't forget your quarterly payment. We're going to try scuba diving tomorrow. Love, Kay.

They got the usual Kansas Day write-up in the newspaper. "Wouldn't miss it for the world," Gene said when she showed him the article. She thought she could survive introducing him to some more of the family, even to her mother. Even to her father and Opal, if they came.

There was always a lot to do at the park. Their area was already reserved, but someone had to be there early to show the beer distributor where to set up the kegs; someone had to put out the horseshoe sets and baseball equipment and volleyball nets. Kay had a lot of the gear in her garage. Each year she and Billy dug it all out and hauled it out to the picnic. They got there at seven: at nine people started showing up. By ten, Kay felt there was something wrong. Gene had said he'd be there to help at eight-thirty.

"Don't worry, he'll come," Billy said. "He's probably feeling shy, all these people going to look him over."

At twelve Billy and Ann made her sit down and have a sandwich. "Eat something," Ann said. "You're going to need it: with as much beer as we've got this time, this'll go on all night." At one-thirty she phoned the hotel Gene sometimes stayed at. He hadn't registered. She tried the boat yard. There was no answer. She hadn't seen him since yesterday at lunch, when she'd shown him the Kansas Day article.

He had to be somewhere. She drove to her office. No one had left a message with her answering service, nothing in the mailbox. She took a shortcut to the freeway and headed north to the boat yard. There was nowhere else to look. She knew something was wrong. So many things could have happened, an accident: they wouldn't even know to notify her. It was after four when she pulled up and parked in front of the locked gate. Gene's boat wasn't there.

She rattled the cyclone fence, but no one came. There was barbed wire on the fence around the yard, but not on top of the gate. She took off her shoes and started climbing. Two of her toes were bleeding by the time she dropped into the yard. She checked everywhere. No boat. It had to be inside the shop, then. She tried the door to the office, and to her surprise it was unlocked. It was dark in the shop, but she could see that it was empty. She turned back to go out and saw Jesse watching her.

"The frump," he said, the word echoing in the empty building. "And I'm the chump," he added. He was sitting on a saw horse, a half-pint bottle of whiskey in his hand. He motioned her to sit down beside him and handed her the bottle. "Go on, take a drink; it won't hurt you anymore than what I've got to say." She took a tentative sip and then a whole mouthful.

"Years ago when he first came up here, you should have known him then; he was different. Just a big kid. Right out of the Navy, best apprentice I ever had. I offered him half if he'd be my partner and stay. No. He was for the deep water on his boat. He'd come back, and we'd haul her up to make some repairs. But each time I'd see changes. Before, he could charm monkeys out of the trees. Now he's not even polite. And he'll cheat and lie when he doesn't even have to. The first time I noticed, eight or nine years back, he'd ordered butane lanterns for his cabin. I handed him the bill when it came, and he crumpled it up. 'Let them collect it in New Zealand; that's where I'm headed,' he said, and he laughed. And I didn't say anything that time. Maybe with the sail and all, I did about twenty thousand dollars worth of work on his boat this time. I was going to charge him sixteen, even though he has plenty of money; he's always had a lot of money. He broke in here last night and launched his boat and now he's gone.

"You want to know the rest?" he asked Kay.

"Go on," she said.

"I heard him talking to Gordon Brown, another no-good bastard in my book. That's where the frump came in. They were using you too. I guessed that, but I didn't say anything there, either. You know another thing? It finally dawned on me: they use that boat to run dope. That's what he must have been doing. That's where the money came from. A bunch of dope fiends. I remember Brown saying, 'Where else can you make a thousand percent profit?' It all just came to me." He paused and said, "So there you are." He almost drained the bottle, then handed it to Kay. "Take a snort." She tipped it up until nothing else would come out.

She took her time driving back. She made herself drive carefully. Slowly braking to a complete stop at a stop sign she thought: nothing worse than this can ever happen to me. Kay, Kay, C.P.A. The frump. I.R.S. A ruined frump. She'd told herself she wasn't going to cry, but about halfway there she started sobbing and had to pull over until she could stop shaking.

She slowed for the turnoff to her house, but then she went on. When she got to the park, it was dark. She sat in her car with the window down a little. She could hear the music from the bluegrass group they'd hired for the dance. She couldn't get herself to move. She didn't know how long she'd been there when Ann and Billy found her. They had been checking the parking lot for her every half hour or so. Ann made her get out of the car. Billy locked his arm through hers; he never said a thing the whole time Kay told them what happened. She couldn't tell it all, not their plans, not sailing to Tasmania. But enough.

When Kay was through, Ann wet the end of her handkerchief with her tongue and wiped the mascara off her cheeks. Then she took her other arm. "Come on, Kay," she said, pulling them both along. "It's Kansas Day, we've been doing this since we were kids."

"No, no," she said, stopping. "I've had enough." They didn't argue. They let her go and she got into her car. She watched them in the light from the headlights as she backed away, and then she turned the car and they were gone. Ahead of her, across the lot, the exit sign seemed miles away, beyond hundreds of empty cars. Home would be worse. They were still standing there when she turned the car around and went back.

Kay, 1982
Lot No. 17

"Three hundred and one cent," Kay called out. She could see Jim Warren trying to keep a straight face when he caught her eye in the crowd. One of the regulars laughed out loud. She knew no one was going to bid against her; there were enough containers for everyone. The lots, big plywood boxes, van-sized, were stacked like toy blocks. Their sides were splashed with blue and white and red rectangles of paint covering years of stenciled numbers.

"Sold." Jim banged his gavel. "Sold to Kay Cortner for three hundred dollars and one cent."

Ann followed her, docile, as she paid the cashier and arranged to have the container delivered. Their prizes, Ann called them. Kay was never sure if she was being sarcastic or not. She didn't know what Ann expected: they'd been doing this long enough that she must enjoy it a little, at least, or she wouldn't be here. She'd walked out of the aerobics class they'd stopped at one night. The women were doing some routine that involved prancing backwards, then kicking their legs up over their heads. Kay, watching them, hadn't seen Ann leave. She found her sitting in the car, steaming. "This is the last time," she said after Kay pulled up in front of her house. "Don't bother thinking anything else up. Don't include me. You've been doing it since we were kids. I had to be a Brownie because you were. I was a Girl Scout for the same reason. Job's Daughters."

Kay had heard this before, so she waited her out. In fact, it was kind of nice: in the last few years, Ann hadn't even bothered bringing up the past. The flower shop didn't take much of her time now. The girls were getting older. Ann needed outside interests. She was getting too moody. Sometimes she reminded Kay of Mrs. MacFarland, who used to live next door. Once when she and Ann were jumping rope, one end tied to the garage door handle, Mrs. MacFarland had come out and surprised them by asking for a turn. During red-hot peppers she tucked up her legs and came down on her knees, but she insisted on another turn. She fell again, and Ann ran for the house yelling "Aunt Garnet, Aunt Garnet!" Mrs. MacFarland didn't seem to notice the blood running down her legs and soaking into her socks. She stood smiling, unconcerned, as her mother tried to stop the bleeding. They ended up taking her to the emergency room. Sometimes Kay thought Ann was starting to act like that. Not crazy, but indifferent to what was happening to her. It worried her. Ann had always been so sure of everything: now she barely talked. She'd seen Mrs. MacFarland once more after that, through a split board in the fence between their yards. She was standing in her underpants and socks, cutting her long red hair with edging clippers, singing Buttermilk Sky.

So she began again when Ann stopped for breath. "Tomorrow the customs people are auctioning off all the things they confiscated in the last year."

Ann gave her a look.

"Think about it. You like a bargain; you'll have to admit that. These are things people tried to smuggle in without paying duty."

Ann got out of the car. Before she shut the door she asked, "What time?"

"Nine."

"Stop on your way. If there's nothing doing, I'll see."

The last time they'd wound up with thirty-some boxes of office records from a defunct foundry. The time before that, a trunk from Greyhound that had, under stacks of chef's aprons and hats, a mounted stuffed cobra dodging what she thought had to be a mongoose, though it looked like a roof rat. The time before that, a carpenter's tool chest, which they had divided. The old tools were beautiful: worn cherry-wood handles on the braces and saws, brass fittings on the levels and rules. They'd never made much on any of their buys except the trunk: it had been brass and they got $150 for it. "You wait, this is going to be a good one," she said, reaching over to touch Ann's arm. "I know it."

"It couldn't get worse," Ann said.

The container was delivered to the old garage a block behind Ann's flower shop. She'd used it for several years to park her delivery trucks; that was before she could afford the addition. Now they used the garage to look through their treasures. There was a Cash and Carry sign nailed to one of the rafters, which always made Kay wonder what kind of business it had been. Ann had the doors pegged back, their tools laid out, the old kitchen chair they used to stand on near the container, when Kay walked in. She was excited, taking off her jacket; she could feel her heart racing. I must be getting old, she thought, if sifting through someone else's junk gets me going.

"Rose's counselor called," Ann said, working her pry bar under the edge of the container lid.

"What did he have to say?"

"Nothing, same old thing. She's not going to graduate. She's going to be expelled with one more tardy. And she's failing P.E. now."

Kay pulled a bent nail all the way out and dropped it into a coffee can.

"Grab it," Ann yelled suddenly, sliding the loose top section over Kay's head. "You're too damn slow " She tipped the lid down to Kay. Nails stuck out around the sides like teeth.

"I pull my nails all the way out," Kay said, "so no one will get stuck."

Ann got down from the chair and dragged the lid out of the way, propping it against the wall. Then she grabbed the side of the panel Kay had been loosening and walked it around, forcing the nails to pull themselves out. Kay stood up to look at the contents of the container. It was like looking through the glass wall of the ant farm they'd had when they were kids. In front was a large steamer trunk with old shipping line stickers—Cunard, Adriatico—on its sides. Suitcases. Cardboard boxes. What looked like a desk.

"What do you think?" Ann asked.

Kay pulled out a small suitcase and released the snaps. The clothes inside were neatly folded. She held a fur-collared coat up to the light. "Old," she said. "Twenties style, maybe. Look at this." Ann moved closer. "It's a fox head. See the ears and eyes?"

"I'm glad I didn't live then," Ann said. "Think of having that around your neck. You might as well be in the circus." She gingerly put it over her shoulders, away from her face. "Wouldn't it mortify the girls if I wore this?"

Ann went back to prying off the side, and Kay started pulling boxes out and stacking them on the floor. She didn't open anything else. It was their practice to go through the things together. The goods weren't much, so far. Nothing outstanding. They would probably lose money on this one too. But it didn't matter.

Her stomach growled. She hadn't eaten anything yet today. That was something. She was up to 141 pounds. She couldn't seem to stop the pointer on her scale from moving further and further up the numbers. She glanced at Ann's legs, slim in shorts; she never gained, never. Same size dress she'd worn in high school. "Enough," she said aloud as Ann dragged away the last plywood side. "Let's call it quits. It's getting dark."

"It's going to be another dud, huh?" Ann said, looking over the contents, her hands on her hips.

"Think of the exercise you're getting."

"I get enough of it during the day. Remember? I work for a living."

They both started laughing. At one time Kay would have got hot and come back with something; then Ann would have said something else. They would have been mad at each other for months. Ann locked up, as Kay stood by, musing. "How about tomorrow?" she asked. In the fading light she couldn't see Ann's face. "Do you have anything on?" That used to bring a chuckle occasionally. Not anymore. Did they say that when they were girls? She couldn't remember. She'd got straight A's. Ann went to the proms.

"Let's start earlier tomorrow. How about three; can you get away?" Kay nodded, taking out her keys and moving toward her car. She had nothing better to do.

Kay thought all day about going to the garage. There wasn't that much to do now, just the regular accounts, and April was six months away. She had exactly a dozen employees; that was enough. She didn't really have to come in at all in the slack season. Who was she kidding: she could walk out of the place this minute and never have to worry. Seven years ago she'd bought 300 acres of artichoke fields on a whim. Then the real estate boom hit, and she sold. She had too much money; it bothered her sometimes. She'd phone in every couple of weeks and tell her manager she wasn't coming in that day, then hop back in bed and spend the whole morning reading the papers, drinking coffee and eating toast and raspberry jam. No wonder she was getting so fat. She'd done that just last Wednesday. Too soon to do it again. Then Ann had phoned at eleven to say she was on her way to a flower farm over at the coast; did she want to come? "What, and miss the Business and Professional Women's luncheon at the Ben Franklin Hotel with guest speaker? Pick me up," she'd told Ann. They spent the early afternoon loading buckets of flowers into the back of the delivery van, the water sloshing up her arms, the gladiolus and carnations smelling like cheap perfume.

She didn't stop to change her clothes, went straight to the garage at three. The door was open and Ann was hard at it, pulling apart the mound of contents and spreading them out on the floor. Kay went right to work, prying open the big steamer trunk lock with the wrecking bar. Women's clothes. She didn't recognize the labels. She started taking them off the old wooden hangers and dumping them on the floor. The rehabilitation center would take them. The others were too picky. They wanted new stuff, they wanted to make a profit.

Ann was on her knees going through four boxes of books and grumbling crap, crap when Kay looked up from the clothes and saw the two women watching them. The younger one's hair looked like it was done daily, it was so perfect. Her clothes were too young for her but she carried it off. Probably a few years older than she was, maybe forty, Kay guessed.

"Hello there," the older woman said, taking a tentative step toward Kay. The skin was pouchy under her eyes: mother and daughter, Kay thought. "I hope we're not interrupting." Ann was watching them, still on her knees, holding a book by its spine and shaking it. They did that now; they'd both read in the newspaper that a letter worth thousands from Henry Ford to someone had been found in a book, Kay read everything, all the old letters, then checked on the stamps before she threw them away.

Kay didn't say anything. There was an awkward silence. The younger woman came forward, stood with her back to the light from the doorway. The older woman went on, "My daughter here, Laura, thinks we're making fools of ourselves. Well, I told her, it won't be the first time. We found out where the container was delivered. So we came over."

"Mother, get to the point," the daughter said. The woman ignored her.

"My father was a surgeon, had an office in the city, on Portola, for years."

Her daughter moved next to her. "Mother."

"Oh what is it, Laura, don't you see I'm talking?"

"I see, Mother, I see." She put her hand on her mother's arm. "We just stopped by," she said to Ann, "because we wanted to meet the people who bought our family's things." This brought Ann to her feet. "All this belonged to my father's sister Elinor. My aunt. My mother's sister-in-law. She never married." A faint smile developed as she talked; she seemed perfectly at ease, as if she were talking to old friends, Kay thought. "We didn't get the notice until the day before yesterday that she'd had these things stored. Then, as you know, we were too late. We were just passing and stopped on an impulse."

Kay had gone back to work, pulling more clothes out of the trunk and throwing them on the pile. The mother gave a shriek that made them all turn. She was pulling the coat out from underneath the pile. "El's fox," she yelled, and she slung it around her neck, poking the head at Laura, yapping and barking. Ann laughed.

"Oh Mother," Laura said. Kay kept sorting the clothes.

"Can I have this?" the woman asked Ann.

"Sure, go ahead."

Kay didn't say anything, but she knew she could have sold that coat to a period clothes store. "Just call me Sally," the mother said to Ann, and she started helping her drag a box clear from the container. Laura looked on, smoking, one arm across her waist, hand grasping the elbow of the other.

"You're not sisters?" Sally asked Ann.

"No, cousins, first cousins. Our mothers were sisters."

"I didn't see any close resemblance," Sally said.

No one said anything for a while. Kay noticed Sally was developing a pile of things she was going to take. She felt her heart beat faster. But she wasn't going to say anything. They had no right.

"Here's something you'd like," Laura said to her mother, handing her a silver framed picture she'd taken out of a box. "It must be Elinor when she was young."

"Quitting time," Kay said, shaking out an empty suitcase and putting it on the floor. She walked over to Sally's stack, and, trying to keep her voice steady, said, "We usually try to recover our money by selling these things." She tapped the silver frame with the toe of her shoe.

"Oh," Sally said.

"We'll pay you," Laura said.

Before Kay could open her mouth, Ann said, "Let her have the stuff." Sally immediately began putting the things into a yellowed pillow case.

Kay went over to the doorway and turned off the first set of lights, waited a second, then turned off the next, then the last, except for the one outside over the door. She didn't look to see if Sally had got all the stuff or not or was even outside before she started closing the doors. She snapped the lock and marched over to Ann's car and got in.

Ann talked to Laura and Sally for a minute, then came over and got behind the wheel. She started the car and backed out into the street. "I'm not going to start anything," she said. "I promised myself," she added.

Kay waited.

"That was nothing but rudeness. There was no point in acting like that."

"I thought you weren't going to say anything," Kay said. "I don't like people who do what they did. Come up and presume like that: 'Can I have this?' Put us in a position where we can't refuse. It irritated me." Ann wouldn't answer, and drove Kay all the way home without speaking again.

The first thing she did at the office the next morning, without even sitting down at her desk, was to phone the auction house. "You gave them my name," she started out, recognizing Jim's voice. "This is Kay. After I bought that last lot on the sixth." They'd got to know each other since she'd started going to the auctions two or three years ago. He had appraised with a straight face a textured print that she'd thought might be an impressionist oil. She had advised him several times on annuities. He started phoning her when they had something she might be interested in.

"Without thinking, Kay. I'm sorry. When I thought about it afterwards, I realized what I'd done and almost phoned, but I didn't. They came by the other night and said they were relatives of the former owner of that lot you bought. Talked me into it."

"This makes it very awkward, Jim. I imagine there's a policy."

"You know there is, Kay. Do you want to speak to the owner?"

"No. What good would it do me?" She hung up.

When Ann got to the garage, Kay was going through a box of old papers, mostly doctors' bills, just a few letters. She read one aloud. "My darling William, I was saddened by the *total* lack of response from you regarding my request for some monetary support. You forget quickly, you dirty son of a bitch. I gave you the best years of my life and asked nothing in return. I've lived on your promises since 1927, but no more. Your family doesn't have to know. You have until Tuesday. Yours, Elinor."

"Looks like Aunt El had a close friend," Ann said.

"Looks that way," Kay said, throwing the letter into the trash box.

It took both of them to pull the old desk out of the container. A vacuum cleaner cord and a twist of frayed drapes were tangled around its legs. It was like the one her grandmother had, Kay thought, walnut, with a drop leaf. It was small enough to fit easily in the back seat of her car. She remembered the hiding place behind the top drawer, space enough for her grandmother to put all her deeds there. She got the notebook and wrote in her section: one desk, net worth one hundred fifty dollars. She always put too much, but it was better that way. Ann did the same. At the end they'd tally up the value of what they'd taken. It usually came out pretty much the same; if it didn't, they'd subtract the difference from the other's share of the cost of the bid.

Finally they had everything out of the container and spread out on the garage floor. Elinor had liked to sew. There were bolts of expensive Scotch plaids, silks, a cast iron treadle Singer, canisters of buttons, boxes of thread. There was a whole wooden barrel of china. "We're going to make our money back," Kay said.

"We better. This is too much like work," Ann said, listing the things she was taking: the buttons, the thread, all the bolts of cloth, a sewing basket with colored beads and Chinese coins dangling from the outside.

It was dark when they closed the garage. Kay was half way home before she remembered the desk. She drove back, parking across the street when she saw the car. They were so brazen they'd left their car running, its lights blazing into the garage. Kay watched from the doorway. They were even more methodical than she and Ann had been, Laura examining each piece of clothing, turning out the pockets, feeling along the seams, shaking them out with a snap over the floor, Sally dumping out a box of kitchen utensils, looking over each one before putting it back in the box. It was Laura who noticed Kay and stopped what she was doing and called over, "Mother." She didn't hear at first. "Mother." When she did, she jumped up as if she had been shocked.

Kay raised her voice over the car motor. "I forgot the desk," she said, pointing to where it stood. She wasn't angry. The situation seemed humorous, if anything.

"We have a right," the mother started out.

Kay cut her off. "Did I mention that I've called the police?"

Laura hurried over to the car and got in. The mother walked slower, reluctant to leave. As she passed, Kay smelled her hair spray. She knew the woman was going to say something, some parting shot. But she didn't. She got in without saying a word. Laura started to back the car down the narrow driveway without turning her head or looking in the mirror. Kay reached into her purse and took out her notebook as the car passed her. Making a show of it, she leaned forward to see the license plate and scribbled down the number, walking the car all the way to the street.

She phoned Ann when she got home and told her about it.

"What were they looking for, you think?"

"Beats me, but they sure were looking. I don't think they'll come back. I don't want to call the cops and go through that. They could say anything: we let them in; it was their stuff."

"How did they get in?"

"They broke the lock somehow. I put it back on the hasp. It looks like it's all right from a distance. Tomorrow I'll get another one and put it on."

When she hung up she remembered the desk. She carried it into the kitchen from the garage. She checked the secret compartment first, then took each drawer out, feeling in the back with her hand and, still not satisfied, getting a flashlight and taking another look. There wasn't anything. What were they looking for, she wondered, putting the desk back in the garage next to her father's boxes. When he came through on selling trips he used to make a stab at going through some of the cardboard boxes. "One of these days I'll get these out of here," he'd say. "As soon as I get organized." By then he'd been married to Opal six years.

Kay remembered watching once from the doorway while she cooked their dinner. He was sorting things out of a box with HOME written on the side, pulling out a stiff pair of leather chaps, a silver trophy. When she called him in to dinner, he was wearing the top part of his old Navy uniform, three red stripes and a white propeller on the sleeve, and what he and Uncle Frank called a crow but was really an eagle. He and Uncle Frank used to talk about the Navy: "we had almost six years in; two more hitches and we could have retired." Her mother always put in, "You'll notice neither of them ever stayed in one day longer than they had to." The uniform top still fit him except at the cuffs; his arms must have got longer. At the time of the divorce, his only comment was that twenty years was long enough with one person. Kay had always wondered how her father had decided on that amount of time, twenty years. He'd kept the Navy top on after dinner too, while they watched the news. That was the last time he ever looked over his things or asked about them.

Kay went over to Ann's for dinner Friday night. Rose wasn't talking. Ann rolled her eyes when she caught Kay's attention. Rose didn't answer when Kay asked "How's school?" but RubyAnn piped up, "She's got three D's, that's how school is."

Later Kay helped RubyAnn with her fifth-grade math homework. "I don't remember any of this," she kept saying as RubyAnn explained it to her. Rose had got up in the middle of dinner, her plate still heaped with food, and hadn't come back. Ann was muttering to herself, stitching the hem on a skirt she'd made for RubyAnn out of the plaid material they'd got in the container. Kay kept hearing something as she worked with RubyAnn but she couldn't place it until finally she identified hiccoughing between sobs. It was Rose crying in her room.

"I never acted like that, never," Ann said.

Kay didn't say anything.

She'd just got to her office and was watering the plants when someone asked from the doorway, "May I come in?" She realized she'd never seen Jim Warren in a sweater: he usually wore suits and ties and his shoes always looked new. He looked out of place away from his microphone.

"This is an errand of mercy," he said, coming into the room and sitting down. "Your mercy and my errant behavior." She couldn't resist smiling at him. He made the worst puns. They usually sailed over the buyers' heads. She sat down too, scooting her fat legs under her desk in a rush. He took out a notebook. "The two women in question are antique dealers; at least, the older one is." He opened to a page of notes and read, "Sarah Herrington. She and her husband own, I think, three shops. One here, one in Carmel, and one up north. They gross about one and a half million a year. That's a rough estimate: I got that from a friend in the trade. Her accomplice is Janet Simpson; she's worked as a buyer for them for years. I had our attorney phone Mr. Herrington. He tried to laugh it off as some kind of game, the women impersonating relatives and so forth."

Kay wasn't surprised. "But what were they after? We've been through that stuff. Old clothes?"

"I checked my records. They bought a container from the same storage bankruptcy last month. This is conjecture, of course, but there must have been something in that first container—a letter, a photo, something—that described something in your box. They must have belonged to the same person. That's all I can guess. Then again, maybe they were just chasing rainbows. They didn't find what they were looking for, as far as I could determine from the conversation."

After Jim left she sat doodling on a piece of paper, going over in her mind the contents of the container. She'd looked: nothing could be hidden in that junk, nothing. Those women were good actors, she thought. How could they pretend that well? She was sure she couldn't. She had believed them.

She dialed Ann at the flower shop. "Busy?"

"No, slow today."

Kay told her what Jim had said.

"All I can guess is we must have missed something somewhere. Or whatever gave them the idea was wrong. Most likely the latter," Ann said.

"This afternoon I'm going back over to the garage and try a few other places I've thought of. I'll let you know if I find anything."

She looked inside the pedestal of the table. Hollow and empty. She unscrewed the bottom of the lamp, undid the handle on an ornate hand mirror. Felt the seams of all the coats again. Had there been something in the fox? But the women had come back after Sally had taken that. At the end Kay just stood staring at the heaps of clothes on the floor as if they would give her some clue. She was going to come back tomorrow. It was only a matter of working out the possibilities.

On an impulse she stopped at Ann's. Even before she rang she could hear them yelling.

"Get in your goddamn room."

"I don't have to."

"You will if you know what's good for you."

Kay pushed the door button and heard the inside chimes. The shouting stopped. RubyAnn opened the door. Ann was standing in the middle of the room, Rose over by the hallway. Rose's chest heaved as if she had been running.

Neither looked at her when Kay came into the room: they stared at each other, frozen. They looked so much alike. It was like seeing Ann twenty years before and twenty years after.

"You're so good," Rose said, gesturing with her right arm. "Why don't you tell Aunt Kay what you found. Why not?" she said, shouting now. Then she turned and ran down the hallway. A door slammed.

Kay stepped back and found the door knob, trying to think of something to say. Ann went over to the couch and picked up the sewing basket, then pushed it into Kay's hands. Kay wanted to drop it and walk out, but she couldn't move. The worn brass Chinese coins clinked against each other when she opened the lid.

She shook the basket. The buttons moved around and downward. The pearl on the end of a hat pin came up. She reached in and took it out. There were six or seven rings on the shaft of the pin. A piece of crumbling wine cork was stuck on the point, keeping them on. One of the rings had a big green stone; the others were diamonds in old-fashioned settings.

Ann had sat down on the couch, one hand in a fist buried in the cushion next to her. Kay still couldn't think of anything to say. She dropped the rings back into the basket and set it on the table.

"I wasn't going to tell you," Ann said, looking straight ahead. She paused and added, "Even before I knew what they were worth. Then I had them appraised. The diamond rings are worth about thirty-five to fifty thousand. The emerald anywhere from seventy-five to a hundred thousand," she said as if by rote. "I was going to keep it all."

Kay only wanted to get out of there. She could feel the sweat run down her back. "Take the rings," Ann said. "I don't want them here in the house. Take them." She said it louder this time, and Kay bent over and picked up the basket. She backed to the door and got it open without fully turning. There was nothing she could say.

She got to the sidewalk, then around to the driver side of her car. She wanted to get away. She fished out her keys and unlocked the door and got in. She had to put down the basket to insert the key in the ignition. She was ready to give it a twist when she looked across at the house. The door. Ann inside. She sat there, feeling the little beat of her pulse at her wrist. She got back out of the car.

Ann opened the door. Her eyes were red and her face seemed swollen. At first Kay thought she must have fallen down, but she was crying. Kay couldn't remember the last time she'd seen Ann cry. Then she remembered. L.A. Ruby. She opened her mouth and heard herself saying, "Jim said he has a whole warehouse full of crates stored since 1911. Can you imagine what's inside?" She kept going. "We get first choice. He promised. I'll pick you up tomorrow at nine." Ann tried to nod. Kay reached toward her and patted her shoulder. "I'll see you," she said, turning and hurrying away from the open door.

Ann, 1982
The Great Gorman

She brushed the stems and trimmings off the worktables and then got the push broom because there was so much litter on the floor. Both cans were filled, and she had to empty them in the dumper before she could pick up with the dustpan. She kept moving around the workroom, putting things right. Saturday afternoon everyone wanted to get home; she'd let them go early.

She went out front and made sure everything was in the cooler for Sunday. That left the jungle of plants. She'd already emptied the cash register and was giving the glass-topped counter another swipe when the phone rang. She was about to say, "Go ahead and eat, Rose; I have to finish up," when a booming voice said, "This request is important; don't hang up."

"It's after five," she got in. "We stop delivering at two on Saturdays."

"Anything else?" the voice asked.

"We probably don't have the flowers you want. Or the ones we do have are too old to sell."

"How did you know I want flowers?"

"Well, I hazarded a wild guess because this happens to be a flower shop."

He wheezed, trying not to laugh. "Promise you won't say no until I finish."

"Okay," she said. "But hurry, I'm wearing rubber boots and my socks are damp." He talked and talked.

She phoned home but the line was busy. "That damned Rose," she said aloud, breaking her promise to herself not to criticize, not even to think critically of the girls. She loaded the cut flowers into the delivery van. Didn't half fill the back; it was Saturday and she didn't have that much on hand. He'd said over the phone, bring everything. So she started loading the potted plants. She'd always kept too large an inventory of these things. She had every fern ever discovered. But it made the place look like a flower shop, when everything was put away in the cooler. If they didn't have the azaleas and the rest, it would look like a butcher shop, or at least it would to her; she could imagine sides of beef hanging in the refrigerator units.

She drove slow, looking out for the address. It wasn't where she expected it to be, where the banquets were usually held. There wasn't a hall around here that she knew of, anyway. She had to look at her county map. She kept going farther out, away from El Camino and up into the hills. Neighborhoods changed into estates. Los Gatos. Up where the rich people live, Kay used to say.

She finally saw the number on a big gate, and spoke into the call box. The gate opened, and she drove for another half mile before she came to the circular drive. She was looking for a delivery entrance but was waved to the front steps of the house. It was unpainted redwood, half hidden by the big overhanging trees.

It went fast. She didn't have to unload; three waiters came out to help. She just stood aside. The grounds weren't much. No lawns or clipped hedges. Just the big oaks, losing their leaves everywhere. She got her clipboard from the front seat and wrote in the total. She hadn't taken the full retail markup because the plants were so rangy from being around for so long, for years, some of them. She'd felt a kind of relief at getting rid of them. What would Kay say: "You discount only if there's no other option. You paid the full wholesale price and your overhead is horrendous." She managed to feel irritated. To get to herself, second-guessing a good sale. She must be nuts.

She shut the van door with a slam and followed the last waiter through the front entrance into a room where several people were already putting the flowers in vases. Paused, ready to ask who was in charge. Wandered to the double doorway at the far end of the foyer. The next room was the size of a basketball court, with already-set tables arranged on the hardwood floor, and a long head table set higher than the rest. There were candles on the tables, and a fountain in the middle of the room, lit by red lights. There was a podium up by the head table and someone was testing a microphone.

"Excuse me, ma'am; you brought the flowers?" She readied a smile and turned around and handed him the clipboard. Waiters were setting the flowers out on the tables. The red carnations looked exceptionally nice against the white linen tablecloths. They'd arranged the potted plants around the walls and the fountain.

He was going over the bill, looking up at her occasionally as if she'd confess she'd overcharged. This always happened with these people. The more money they had, the cheaper they were. She'd been given bad checks by people who drove to the shop in Jaguars. She had told that to Kay, who'd given her one of her doubtful looks.

He was looking at her funny, too. He was one of those people you couldn't tell about. Big, suntanned, gray hair combed smooth with a perfect part, a dinner jacket that fit him. Her father's age, maybe older. Condescending look replacing the silver spoon he'd been born with. "I took some off," she said. "The potted flowers and plants have been around a while." It was better to be first. He was still looking at her like Kay did, looking over her clothes. She'd taken the apron off. Her maroon sweatshirt was clean that morning, black flannel pants tucked into her rubber boots. She'd brushed her hair as she'd driven up, but she'd forgot to put on the lipstick she kept on the dashboard.

"I can see why your feet are wet," he said, looking down. Now he sounded like the same person she'd talked to on the phone. That surprised her.

"That was an exaggeration. I get some water down them because the flowers are always dripping, but it's mostly because my feet sweat so much."

"Would you step over this way, please?" She followed him. Right down the hall, wondering why she had to explain everything to everybody, and if he were the butler. He stopped and knocked on a door and opened it. There was a woman in an ivory-colored slip standing in front of a three-way mirror looking at her raised throat, her left hand holding down the skin. It was a bedroom, but there was an opening in the ceiling the size of a Ping-Pong table. You could see the treetops and the first stars.

"Elizabeth, we need some shoes."

"Grace will help you," she said as another woman came into the room holding a dress. They followed Grace out into another room where the four walls were covered with framed photographs. He sat her on a soft chair, got down on one knee, and pulled off a boot. She watched him, bemused. Then he pulled off the other and started peeling down her sock.

"Now wait a minute," she said. "I sell flowers and that's all I sell." She'd meant it to be funny, but not that funny. He started laughing until tears came to his eyes, slapping his leg and blowing his nose with a big honk into a white handkerchief.

The maid came in with a stack of shoe boxes higher than her head. He started trying shoes on Ann's bare feet, and she played along. She'd once shown a woman how to load her dishwasher before she was paid. The shoes were the right size.

"Do you like these?" he asked at a pair of black satin sandals.

"They're fine," she said. The room must be close to the front of the house, she thought, because she could hear more cars and voices.

"I want you to do something for me," he said.

"First things first," she said. "Pay me for the flowers."

"I forgot," he said, standing up. From his inside coat pocket he took out a stack of new bills like the bank gave you when you asked for a lot of money, still kept together by the paper band. He slipped some out and handed the hundreds over.

"Too much." She gave him one back. Wrote PAID in big letters on the receipt and handed the pink one to him.

"Now," he said, "I want you to stay."

"You don't even know me."

"That's beside the point," he said. "I promise you'll have a good time. It's true; if you're willing, money can buy that."

She was going to ask what makes you think I'm looking for a good time? But she wanted to stay, too, though her instinct was to pick up her boots and damp socks, kick off these sandals, and go. She didn't want to sound coy, ask "What do I have to do?" People were walking by the open door, going into the dining room. Guests in evening clothes. "All right," she said. "I'll stay."

"You'll be my guest, sit with me up front. Don't fret; there's an extra place; my wife couldn't make it. You're going to enjoy yourself; remember that. Now what do you have under the sweatshirt?"

She didn't remember, stretched out the neck to see. "Tank top."

The maid was standing at the doorway. "Grace," he said, "can you find something my friend can wear? Makeup, and some jewelry too? Take off your sweatshirt."

She didn't hesitate, pulled it up over her head. There was a certain satisfaction in doing exactly as you were told, she decided. Grace came back and led her into a bathroom with enough cosmetics for a drugstore spread out on the counter. She started doing her face.

He was gone when she looked again. She put on more blush than she usually did. She'd been yelling at Rose lately for doing the same thing. She had to phone. Her hair wouldn't stay down, no matter how hard she brushed. It was impossible. Still, she liked what she saw in the mirror. She never took the time to do this. Wearing the blouse outside like that made her slacks look like they were part of some stylish outfit. Was that wishful thinking?

She was going to ask the maid what the occasion was, but the woman barely spoke English. She was from Jakarta. Grace fitted a necklace of blue beads around her neck and a single gold bracelet around her left wrist, then sat her down and applied more lipstick. She allowed everything, smiling, nodding her head in encouragement. Grace tried to get her hair to stay down too, but she couldn't either. Catching her eye in the mirror, Grace made a face, and they both shook their heads.

Grace took her by the arm and led her back to the big room, which was filling up; it looked like hundreds of people. A few were already up at the head table. Grace stayed by her side, as if she expected her to collapse or run. Was she crazy?

He came back, looked her over, and started laughing. Then she started too. "What am I doing?" she said to him. "I'm a mother. I have a house, two children."

"And a business," he said.

"My van," she said. "It's in the way."

"No, it's been taken care of. Don't worry about things." He was looking her over again. A woman passed; she recognized her from the bedroom. "Elizabeth, may I borrow this?" He didn't wait for an answer, took the gardenias from the woman's shoulder and put them in her hair. She didn't feel them there but they must have weighed her hair down, because he said, "Very good. Now come with me." He took her by the hand and led her up to the head table, stopping by a tray to pick up a glass of wine for her. "Drink this," he said, and she took a sip. People made way for them. He was nodding, smiling at everyone. Pulled out a chair for her to sit down on.

She was blushing. "I can't," she said.

"Yes you can," he said. She sat down and he left her there. She told herself, no one's looking at you; no one cares. But she had to sneak a glimpse around. People were filling up the tables. She hadn't done anything like this, unplanned, impulsive, for a long time. Ever. She'd never done this. Never. That wasn't true; she did act without thinking sometimes. When she took the rings, didn't tell Kay. She still felt bad when she thought of that. The girls knew, too. Why did she have to learn everything the hard way? Everything by her mistakes?

"When's he coming back?" she asked Elizabeth across the three empty chairs.

"It better be pretty soon; he's the master of ceremonies," Elizabeth said. Then she leaned over toward her to ask, "Have you known him long?"

"For two hours," she said. "Is he your husband?"

Elizabeth laughed. "No, no, my husband Troy is over there," and she pointed at the man standing by the podium adjusting a microphone. She said something else but it was drowned out by a bleat from the sound system, then an announcement: "Ladies and gentlemen, welcome, welcome. Thank you . . ."

"Enjoying yourself?" the master of ceremonies asked, coming up behind her. "It's about to start now."

"What is this? I still don't know what's going on."

"It's a ball, a gala, a fund-raiser. A roast, too. Those swell folks out there have paid, what, Elizabeth?"—she shrugged her shoulders—"fifty-five hundred each to hear me and others make a fool of one of the richest of them."

"The wealthiest man in California," Elizabeth put in. "Over there at the first table."

He looked like anyone else, she thought. "Is this your house?" she asked the master of ceremonies.

"No, no, it's hers," and he patted Elizabeth's hand.

"So you're giving this?" she asked Elizabeth.

"Remember, it's a worthy cause, but it's basically extortion," Elizabeth said. "If they don't come to mine, I won't go to theirs. And it's a tax write-off. Also I want to see if Milo here can still wow them like he's done the last five years."

She heard the name *Milo*. Said it to herself again. It couldn't be, she decided. He was too young-looking. Milo Gorman would be an old, old man now. If he were alive. Elizabeth's husband was building up to the introduction: "And now, ladies and gentlemen, I give you the one, the only, Milo the Great Gorman, and thank heaven for that."

When the applause died down he began, "You can always gauge how important you are by who introduces you. Folks, that man used to be my caddie."

The food was delicious. Veal, she thought. It didn't bother her, sitting up here now; the lights were so strong she could barely see past them. The champagne helped. And so did Liz, who had slid into the chair next to her and kept whispering funny comments. Right now she was saying, "See that man over there at the third table, with the mustache and the very long nose? They call him Two Dicks." Both of them were giggling like kids. It was like being in the eighth grade, talking dirty.

She kept imagining things. That when the MC spoke, he was sounding more and more like the man she'd interviewed when she was in high school. But there was no resemblance, except in the way he laughed. Sarcastic. She leaned over to Liz. "Who is he? Is he *the* Milo Gorman?" Liz nodded. "The lobbyist?"

"Among other things. He's a consultant now; that's what he wants to be called. You bring him in and he handles everything. He can raise money for anything. He can made the dead rise up and write a check. Someone said that before me. He knows everyone in California. Tonight is a million-dollar event. We've never been so ambitious before."

Was she dreaming? Was this one of the times at night she thought she wasn't asleep but was, having those dreams of the past where everything was changed? She was playing hopscotch and she had to make a three-square jump, knowing if she made it her mother would come home. She leaped high, cleared the squares, but came down on her mother's back. Or Carl did come back home; they found him, finally; he knocked on the front door, but his face was like a fish's now. She was awake. She was awake. It was Milo, it had to be, but she had to know. "How come he looks so much younger than before?"

"You *did* know him. I was speculating on that. Milo is basically shy: he wouldn't invite someone he wasn't sure of."

"I didn't realize it was him."

"The new Milo Gorman, thanks to the best doctors money could buy. My husband had the same problem, time catching up with him, and he's a generation younger than Milo. He says he always knew Milo as pretty dilapidated; older than he was, anyhow. Troy's had some work done too, but he didn't come out as well."

She could hear her sixteen-year-old self repeat, *as old as the century.* "He's different now."

"From what I can gather, the change isn't only physical. But I didn't know him then. What stories, though. My husband was his protégé, after he got out of law school."

"You don't look that old," she said, and then knew it was the wrong thing.

But Liz cracked up, putting her hands over her perfect face. "I'm Troy's third wife."

Milo came back and sat in his place, wiping his face with his napkin. "This is hard work," he said.

She had to ask. "Do you know who I am?" The audience was hooting at the speaker standing behind the podium, and she repeated, "Do you remember me, Ann Bennett?"

"The flower girl."

"No, from before."

"You mean the liver and onions girl."

Tears started rolling down her cheeks. She was so surprised she didn't wipe them away. She leaned over and kissed him on the mouth. He turned red on top of his tan, but managed a wisecrack. "What if my wife finds out? But it's not likely; she's home with bronchitis. Do it again."

"I saw that," Liz said.

"You remembered me, didn't you. From the first."

"It's my business, remembering. You haven't changed that much."

All she could think of was how she hadn't written him from Kansas. Never went back, afterward. He had treated her so well. Bought her a watch. Took her out to those restaurants. Listened to her. "You look so different," she said.

"I look exactly the same as I did back then. Real human hair"—he lifted a strand—"except now unfortunately it's not mine." He stopped speaking; everyone was clapping, and he did too as the next roaster got up to be introduced.

"That was a bad time for me," he said. "I was feeling sorry for myself. The dumbest of all emotions. You helped me. I would never have pulled out of that slump."

"I read your book," she said.

"None of the big New York publishers would touch it. Too libelous. I had to tone it down before it ever saw the light of day. None of them even thought it was funny. I never dreamed the university press would go for it. But that book helped me put the business behind me. Then I could go on from there. I made a few false starts, nothing disastrous. I got married and divorced. And now I'm married again. I'm beginning to like the feeling. I still talk too much. What about you?"

She felt reluctant, telling about herself. "I'm Ann Bergstrom, now." Then she asked, "Did you know it was me when you phoned?"

"Not a clue, random choice, and you were the only one who answered." He took a drink of water. "It's the best kind of choice. But I should have put things together before. You're the one that brings flowers to my sister Estelle. With the little cards, from your friend Annie."

"My C.P.A. says I get to write them off. Those potted mums, the blooms start to go, and I can't sell them anyway. I just have my driver drop them off."

"Quit that," he said, "take my thanks. I appreciate it. Up until the year before last, I think she would have remembered you. Old age is not always better than the other option. But don't get me wrong. I'll put up with the cutting and pasting. I've had a quadruple bypass, half my stomach removed, all of my prostate. Let's see what else. My right hip joint replaced. Plus a hair transplant that failed, thus my rug. New teeth. Several face jobs to pick up some slack." He held out his hands to her. "I've even had my liver spots removed. You have to stay young and money-looking in this business."

"I never recognized you. I didn't believe Liz when she told me who you were."

"It's me; I've had a second chance. It's not just a matter of time. We all waste our first chance and then look back, knowing given another chance we'd end up doing the same things again. When I got my second chance, I decided to do the same things, but for a slightly different reason. And it works, sometimes."

"That's why you do this?" She made a gesture with her arm.

"Part of it. Like everyone, I have various motives. I was always good at making money. And always good at extravaganzas. There's a certain pleasure in knowing you're thwarting your own worst instincts."

"You're the same."

"How can you say that; do you know how much I've spent on cosmetic surgery? My doctor will be horrified. My first wife's idea. Probably just a little older than you are. I was smitten; I went along. And now my wonderful personality depends on these aids and accoutrements." He patted his hair. "It was about the time I met you that I decided I had to stop being the old Milo. And how's life treating you?" he asked.

She had to think that over. She was going to say, like always. Why not the truth? I have nothing. But that wasn't true. Better than expected? "I'm all right," she said. "I have my ups and downs, but I'm all right."

"You don't sound sure," he said.

"It's just that nothing ever turns out the way you expected."

"That's a real problem. But from my perspective, and that's from eighty-two years of age, no one's life does. Not mine, not yours, not anyone's. You have to learn that first, and it took me until I was in my sixties. Just imagine how far ahead you are."

He was going to say something else, but Liz's husband called over, "Milo, get up here; we can't let them get away with this." Milo tiptoed up behind the speaker at the microphone: "Excuse me, excuse me, sir, but I have a message from your spouse—who's locked in the trunk of your car . . ."

"He's a character," Liz said, leaning toward her. "He's one of the few people staging these affairs you can trust. I'm not saying he's easy to get along with, but he always comes through."

Milo came back. "This part won't last much longer. I don't know why everyone insists on roasts; the novelty's long gone."

The flowers were holding up well despite the heat and smoke. A large space had been opened up in the middle of the room for dancing. An orchestra was setting up; people were wandering around talking; some still sat at the tables. She hadn't seen Milo for a while.

She'd phoned Rose again, finally got through. Said she'd be late and not to wait up. Aunt Kay had called. Twice. That meant she'd have to listen, watch Kay circle, but never hear the question "Where were you, Ann?" She better go home. She'd been up since five-thirty.

She found Liz in the kitchen helping the catering people assemble a dessert buffet. She took the gardenias out of her hair and stuck them in Liz's, told her thank you. Took off the necklace and bracelet. "I feel like Cinderella," she said. Started helping unload trays of petits fours from a rack to be carried into the dining room. "If I could remember where I put my sweatshirt and boots, I'd give you your blouse back. I have to get going."

"I think Grace put them in my bedroom. Keep the blouse. It never fit me like it does you. I'm glad you came," Liz said. "I got to talk to someone. If you're not doing anything, I'll phone you next week . . ." Liz trailed off, watching her face.

"I'd like that," she answered, not sure what kind of look Liz was seeing, never sure herself what her face said or meant to other people. Should she practice in the mirror? She tried a smile. "Do," she said, with more emphasis. "I'd like that."

She ought to say good-bye to Milo. She'd found her sweatshirt and boots and put them back on. She felt completely at ease now, walking through the crowds of people, stopping to pick up a small green pastry. It was still hard to believe it was Milo. But it was. She hadn't been paying attention. As always. Didn't notice things. He hadn't changed that much. Not what he said or what he thought. The orchestra started playing all of a sudden, and she looked toward the sound. She didn't see him until he took her by the arm. "Come on, I know your card's filled, but I insist on the first dance."

"I haven't danced since my senior prom."

"The world's loss."

"I have my boots on now; I have to get home."

"Try not to leave any marks on the floor, or Liz will kill you."

They were the first out. "Have you been taking lessons?" she asked him.

"I was always light on my feet. And born to dance." People were moving around them now. Liz and her husband sailed by as if they were professionals, all smoothness and style. "She's holding up well," he said.

"She's beautiful."

"They had to put Jamie in a place, their son. That's what all this is for, research for kids like him. Autistic. It's hard for anyone, but especially for her. She can't accept the fact that he's never going to improve. Last year she had him here at the gala. Bought him a tux. It was a disaster. He set his hair on fire."

She didn't know what to say. Liz seemed so in control of everything. Milo was getting out of breath. He glided them over to a table with rows of filled glasses. Took one, but still kept his arm around her waist. "No more twirls and flourishes. The important thing about getting old," he said, "is you begin to understand time. Am I going to tire you out with this?"

"No, not at all." She was trying to remember everything he said.

"At first you mostly consider how you filled in your own life, used up your years. People who say they have no regrets haven't had any laughs, and the ones that say they wouldn't change anything haven't tried anything. The big problem about time is there's just too much of it. You can't use it up with any dignity. So you fall into these numb or mindless patterns. No wonder kids watch TV ten hours a day or whatever it is now. You have to be mighty lucky in the atomic age to be hit by events that force you to use time differently. Wars do it. Depressions. Stealing will do it. And so will trying to do good. Well, that's my latest theory. Now you tell me something. Anything. Tell me a nightmare or two. You listened to me. Now bend my ear."

"Nothing happens to me. I go to work and I go home. Get up in the morning and do it again."

"Then tell me the worst, the very worst thing you've done since the last time I saw you."

"I stole some rings." The words startled her; she hadn't even been thinking about that. "From a friend, from my cousin. She would have given them to me if I'd asked her."

"When was that?"

"Last year. The rings were worth a lot of money; they were half mine and half hers. But I found them first and kept them. And she found out."

She waited, but he didn't make any comment. They were dancing, barely moving along the outside of the room. By the time they passed the orchestra again he said, "I used to pull things like that on clients, friends, people who'd treated me well. Who were kind and generally good. I always thought it was my own greed, but later I decided I couldn't compete with their generosity of spirit. I had to do something to compensate, so I'd do something stupid. I absolved myself when I thought up that explanation, and I absolve you too."

"I wish it were that easy," she said.

She was getting tired; her eyes felt like they were going to close and she would never be able to get them open again. But Milo wouldn't let her go. When the music stopped, the musicians taking a break, he held onto her hand, took her over to the buffet. They drank and ate more, and it revived her. "Come on, let's dance." No one seemed to leave.

He told her about his wife, who he met in the hospital when he had his prostate out; she was having a mastectomy. About his two stepsons, who were grown, and the grandchildren. "I started late," he said, "but I started. That's what's important." Some Eastern university had asked him to speak about his experiences after his book came out, and now he went back there every year. "Our future national leaders. I give them an earful of California politics."

He listened while she told him what happened to Carl. Went back even further and included her mother. The flower shop. The girls. Her brother. Father. And Kay. He listened like she listened to him, she thought, while they danced. She couldn't stop talking. It was like trying to get the last bit out of the sugar bowl, chipping it away. "I still have the watch you gave me," she said. "It needs a new band. That's why I'm not wearing it now. I used to think I'd see you some day to thank you for all the times you took me out to lunch. Treated me the way I thought normal people treated each other." She heard her voice trail away. It was almost four in the morning. She felt so tired. She had to stop. "I have to go home," she said.

He was walking her to the van when he said, "I don't know if it'll work for you, but for me, I found out it helps if you do something to repay the good times. There's nothing you can do about the bad. But you can give some good back."

She was awake enough to ask, "What can I do?"

"Think of something. Something that will give others pleasure. Like what you did for Estelle."

Now that she was actually going to leave, she didn't want to. Someone was calling him from the front stairs: "Milo, telephone."

"It's my wife. I promised to phone and I didn't. We'll all get together. I promise."

She got home at almost six but didn't feel like going to bed. Stayed up and made batter for waffles, got out the old waffle iron. Called the girls. "It's Sunday. I have to sleep late," Rose said at first. RubyAnn got up, half-conscious, and ate waffle after waffle.

At eight o'clock the phone rang. She wasn't surprised to hear Kay's voice. "I've made waffles; come on over," she got in first.

"I'm on a strict diet. I phoned last night." A short silence. "I wanted to find out if you wanted to go to an antique show this morning."

"I can't," she said. "I'm going to roost today." But she couldn't sleep. She lay down on the couch, but it was no use. She was too excited, still going over what had happened. She finally went outside and mowed the lawn.

Milo phoned her at the shop on Tuesday. "Have you recovered from your Saturday night ordeal?" he asked.

For a minute she was confused about who it was. But there was no other voice like that. "Almost," she said. "I'm getting back to normal and only yawn occasionally."

"For all I know, that fandango may still be going on. I left that afternoon, and there was no slackening of the pace. I phoned because I just wanted you to know, and I hate to use the word *nice* but I can't think of a better one, how nice it was to see you again. I always felt you were lucky for me. Am I talking silly?"

"No, you're not."

"Well, I'd like us to get together as soon as we get back. I have to go to the East Coast for six weeks; Yale calls. I always mention the place when I get a chance. For a high school dropout, this is definitely a step up in the academic world. You have my card; I'll phone you or you phone me. But let's stay in touch."

She kept his card in her wallet next to her driver's license, where she could see it. She kept going over the time, elaborating, improving, until the ball was like something that happened before, a long time ago. Like the first time she'd met Milo when she was a girl. Some of the things he had told her then had turned out to be true. And maybe this time he was right; you should return your good fortune. But she didn't have time; she had the shop and the girls. Remembering made her look at a customer, a young boy, and smile while she was ringing up the box of tiger lilies he was buying for his mother. What was it Aunt Garnet always said: it only takes ten muscles to smile and eighteen hundred to frown, so if you don't want wrinkles on your face at my age, you better be cheerful. But she wasn't assembled—it was the wrong word—wasn't made up to be happy, to trust her luck. There was no use pretending. But she would try. When she saw Milo again, she'd have to be able to say she'd tried.

She didn't tell anyone about meeting him. It was no one's business. She hadn't when she was sixteen. Kay never knew. She wasn't that astute about people anyhow; it was numbers she was good at. She had the watch repaired, and thought briefly about giving it to Rose, but decided to wear it herself. A little too pretty for the work she did, but it did keep good time, and it was waterproof.

Liz, who used more flowers in a week than most people did in a lifetime, started ordering from her. She'd hand washed the blouse she'd borrowed and sent it back. They talked on the phone. She could be different with Liz. There wasn't that past between them. No attempt on her part to do . . . what? She couldn't explain what happened with Kay, or why she thought of their phone conversations as times to be pissed off. How's it going conversations. "How's it going? How are the girls? Did you get your quarterly payment in? There's a sale at Penneys on those dishes you were looking at." Kay would be perfectly pleasant, and all the time she'd be working herself up with wrath and indignation: "Business *would* be good if those thieving funeral directors would stop that *no flowers* shit in the obituaries. Why give contributions to some charity or some church where the staff uses the money to drive around in a limo? Or that bishop in L.A. who bought himself a helicopter so he wouldn't have to put up with the traffic. Flowers are a traditional sign of respect for someone. You know the most expensive, the biggest wreath I sold last week, you know who it was for? Dolly, a German shepherd. That tells you something about people and flowers." She'd be breathing hard, so irritated she'd have to sit down after she hung up to calm herself.

Liz called her on a Wednesday and invited her up to play tennis. She couldn't speak for a minute. "Are you kidding me?"

"How about bridge?" They both started laughing. "Listen, Ann, I have to come down Saturday and shop. Have lunch with me."

"That's my busiest day," she said, "and I don't eat lunch." As soon as she said it she realized that's what she would have said to Kay, the exact same thing. "Okay, one of these days, and I get to pick the place."

She made time to have lunch with Liz one Saturday afternoon. Liz cut her big old-fashioned hamburger in quarters when it came. "Bringing those flowers saved our lives; I want to thank you for that. That was my part, getting the flowers, and the place I ordered them from put the wrong date down, and I never checked."

"You don't have to thank me. It's my business. Milo paid me."

"Milo said you were a realist. A no-nonsense person. He thinks a lot of you. Said you saved him from the black dog, once."

"He has it backwards. He helped me. He's just saying that." She took a big bite of her hamburger and wished she hadn't; lettuce and tomatoes shot out one side all over her fingers. "Besides, if I'm a realist, it's because I have no choice. In a small business, it's dog-eat-dog. And I have no one to do it for me."

"How would you handle an autistic son? When no matter what you try, it doesn't work; it's always wrong." Liz's eyes were filling up, but they didn't run over.

"I know how I handled my husband's dying. I pretended he was never there. I tried to forget he ever existed. But I didn't understand until recently that that doesn't work so well."

"I can't do that with Jamie; he's alive. I can't give up on him when he's fourteen. It would be like giving up on myself."

"How's my favorite flower girl? Or excuse me, flower woman: you get ten years for gender slurs in this state. What I phoned about—we're having an outing on the Bay Monday. We want you to come, bring your girls. Meet my spouse. I've told her the whole sordid story, and she can hardly wait. It's Troy and Liz's boat; they'll be there too."

"Milo, I have to work for a living. The kids have to be in school. I can't get away from the shop . . ." But she wasn't indignant, not like when she talked to Kay and made that answer.

"We'll make it next time, then. I just wanted you to know I hadn't forgotten anything."

She didn't go that time or the next time either because RubyAnn caught scarlet fever. Then Milo was gone again on a national speaking tour. She'd still never met his wife, but she'd talked to her on the phone a couple of times. He wrote her a postcard from South Bend, Indiana. "I've been called all the *ists* now: sexist, fascist, communist, and now exhibitionist. The audiences are genuinely kind; they wait until intermission to leave. Milo and Spouse."

The day after she received the card, Liz phoned. "I've got some bad news,

Ann. Milo died of a heart attack early this morning. In his sleep, Roberta told me."

She closed the shop Wednesday and went to the memorial service. Thursday she phoned everyone again and told them not to come in; she was going to stay closed. She drove out to the rest home where Estelle was. Arranged the flowers she'd brought, not looking at the old slack face with the pale blue eyes like Milo's that didn't see anything. Sat next to the bed for a while, holding her hand. Talked at random for a few minutes about Milo, what a good person he was. Couldn't think of anything else to say. Felt uncomfortable, blurted out something dumb about the weather before standing up. And at the door she turned around to say, "It's impossible to buy wildflower seeds this time of year unless you order in bulk. It was good seeing you again. I have to go, Estelle."

Billy, 1983
In the Avenues

Billy saw Rupert and his collie Prince walking on the other side of the street, but he didn't have time to stop. He had to get to the hospital with the slippers before nine. His father had to have his own from home; he said the hospital's didn't fit right. Billy honked and waved but there was too much traffic and he didn't think they noticed.

"You could stay at my place," his father said when he put the slippers under the bed. He'd had gallbladder surgery. He seemed almost the size of a boy, lying there in the high hospital bed with a plastic identification strip loose around his wrist. His gray hair was neatly combed and parted. Billy wondered who had done that for him. "I've got plenty of food in the house. Kay took me to Safeway Thursday."

He knows he has me, Billy thought; he had to bite his lip to keep from laughing. Kay did the things he should be doing, he and his sister should be doing. Ann hadn't come to his birthday again this year. "I've got the time too, haven't I?" he said, smiling. New condominium, and no one waiting for him.

"You do," his father said. "You're all set."

He made a bed up on the couch. It didn't bother him coming back here like it did Ann and Kay. The house, the old neighborhood, all the changes: he could separate the past from the present. One didn't have to depend on the other. His two divorces: he'd taught himself to forget about them. What good had it ever done him, dwelling on that. Or his mother for that matter, walking out on them when he was six; then, almost twenty-five years later, a fifteen-minute visit in her office. It was too late. The time in between was used up. He had learned a good lesson from that.

It was too early to go to bed. Despite the breeze through the screen door, he could still smell his father's cigarettes. It was quiet out here in the avenues. Not much traffic, the streets were wide, no kids' voices. There was nothing on. He flipped back through the channels again to be sure. He decided to take a walk. He hadn't done that for years: he'd drive in, spend an hour or so, fix the lawn mower, put a few shingles that had blown off back on the roof, adjust the antenna, then take off. There was always a little chore waiting.

Sometimes Rupert would be there visiting his father, the two of them just sitting, Prince, Rupert's collie, stretched out on the rug. Once he'd stood at the screen door watching them, his father inhaling, then blowing out smoke, Rupert taking small sips from his glass, neither saying a word. After a few minutes he'd stepped back a pace and rattled the door handle. "Well look who's here," his father'd said. And Rupert added, "Long time no see."

All the vacant lots he remembered were filled with apartments, parked cars lined up and down the street. Most of the houses were dark except for the blue glow from the TV showing where the curtains met. There were grates on the windows now, and most entrances had wrought iron-work doors. Outside lamps lit up the front of each house. Alarm boxes.

He realized after a minute where he was: his feet had taken him in the same direction he used to go when he was a boy, down to Danny's with Ann or Kay to get his father. On Friday night they all went to Danny's for the fish fry. His parents—his mother was still home then, though they still went after she left—Ann, Kay, himself and their half-beagle terrier Henry. Sometimes Kay's mother and father or his other aunt, Opal, would come, or Rupert and his wife and Prince's grandfather Duke would sit with them. There was always a crowd from the neighborhood on Fridays, sitting around the tables, oval plates heaped with coleslaw and fried smelt. Billy's mouth watered thinking of it now, the comfortable sounds of people eating and drinking around them in the semidarkness, Henry and the other dogs waiting politely under the table.

He reached the intersection and stopped for a traffic light. This block of small stores still seemed healthy. No boarded windows. He knew Danny had died and the place had been sold two or three times. It must be hard to make a go of it, he thought, in a neighborhood bar with customers that nursed a drink for hours and talked with their friends. A few years before, when his father had found out he had diabetes, he'd stopped mentioning Danny's. That didn't mean he'd stopped drinking, though.

This was the corner where they'd waited as kids for their parents to catch up. He took a step closer to be sure, but the door, the family entrance, wasn't there. He felt with his hands; he could tell where it had been stuccoed over. He walked around to the front door. The old neon sign was still there: Danny's Restaurant and Bar.

He stopped just inside the door. There was no restaurant. The tables and kitchen were gone. In their place were pinball machines and video games. He looked down the bar. There were only a few people. He didn't see any of the old timers. He turned around and went back out.

As he walked back toward his father's house he remembered he hadn't seen any dogs. Not one. There were always dogs at Danny's place when he was a kid. His father had told him how it started: one night someone's Airedale had hopped up on a bar stool and, sitting on his haunches, his paws on the bar, had lapped up his owner's beer. The man was too busy arguing with his wife to notice. Danny had a sense of humor; he didn't mind as long as someone paid for the drink. It must have gone on for a long time, he thought, because the novelty, if there was any, had worn off before his time. He could always remember one or two dogs at the bar, their long pink tongues whipping between their big teeth as they lapped up their drinks, and no one gave them a second glance.

What had struck him as a boy, more than the dogs drinking, was what they could do. There had been a dog once, Moses, who could actually sing "I left my heart in San Francisco." He'd heard him dozens of times, and you could tell the words plain as day. Someone would sit down at the piano and he'd start in. People would buy him drinks after, though he remembered some of the customers got annoyed after four or five times. Moses' voice was kind of high pitched. There were dancing dogs; he remembered that every one of them barked while they danced. A schnauzer named Rainbow was probably the best; she did a fast jig. He'd taught his own dog Henry to roll over, fetch, count, and play dead, but a lot of other dogs knew those tricks too. One of Rupert's collies could take an eight-foot two-by-four through the front door in his mouth.

He went back the next night to see if anyone he knew would come in. There was nothing else to do around the house, and he was tired of just sitting. There was a dog at the bar. He took the stool next to him. Looking closer in the semi-darkness, he noticed it was a Doberman. The dog's eyes were red and his axe-shaped head seemed all bone. He was grinning as he lapped his Tom Collins. He'd never been up close to a Doberman before. There weren't dogs like that around when he was growing up. The dog's owner must be one of the customers over at the video games.

The bartender acted as if he was doing him a favor, setting him up with a beer, and then he tried to short him a buck with the change. The noise from all the machines was bad enough, but now they allowed customers to play box dice on the bar too. They were hitting so hard the vibration made his drink slop over. Another attraction he hadn't noticed last night was a punching bag with a meter: kids were taking turns to see who got the best score.

Rupert and Prince came in. Prince hopped right up on the stool next to his, and Rupert shook his hand. "Where is everyone?" he asked him. "Old Gus. Shorty. George Larson?"

"You can see for yourself," Rupert said. "They don't come here much any-more." He was going to say something else but stopped and looked down the bar. "Here comes the new owner now," he said. "Leonard."

He was sleek looking, in his fifties, Billy guessed. Suntanned in January. Ca-nary yellow trousers hiked up to the middle of his paunch. Gray chest hair showing in the V of his open shirt. A pinkie ring. He moved down the bar, grinning, making cracks. "How they hanging, Alice?" He stopped in front of a balding red-haired customer. "Red on the head," he said, patting his comb over.

"Well, if it isn't the friend of the working girls," he said when he got to Rupert, laughing.

Rupert cut him short. "Give me a draft, and Prince will just have a brandy; his stomach is off." Leonard took care of Rupert first, leaving a big head on his draft beer, all the time talking. "You still get it up, Rupert?" He winked at Billy. "I get a lot of offers: the ones I can't handle I'll refer to you. Ha ha." Rupert ignored him and stroked Prince's neck.

Billy could remember watching Danny do it a thousand times, wipe out the clean heavy glass ashtray from the stack on the back shelf, set it down in front of the dog. Leonard did the same thing, set it in front of Prince, who was watch-ing every move, then poured from a bottle into a shot glass and emptied it into the ashtray. Prince started to growl and then snapped at Leonard, who jumped back. Rupert took Prince's head and held on to his muzzle. "That dog's a mean one," Leonard said. "I know what I'd do if he was mine."

"But he's not yours, is he," Rupert answered. He held Prince's head until Leonard left. Then he turned to Billy. "Did you see that?"

"What?"

"That bastard is shorting drinks. I've seen him do it plenty of times before. That's why he upset Prince. He knows how much he's supposed to get. Watch him now." Billy turned as Leonard poured someone a drink. "See, he fills the jigger halfway, pretends he's still pouring from the bottle, and dumps the bourbon into the glass over the ice."

Billy shook his head. It was true.

"There is nothing in the whole world worse than a man that won't give you full measure," Rupert said. Prince downed his brandy and sat back on his haunches, licking his chops. "These kids in here don't know any better," Rupert said. "He's taking advantage. I'd call him on it but he can always say it was a mistake or I need new glasses." He tapped the side of his fist on the bar.

"Is that why there's no one around from before?"

"I don't know," Rupert said, blinking at him through his thick glasses. "A lot of people have died off, and this place has changed so much. It's not tranquil anymore. But I have no choice, if I don't want to drink alone. I can't walk any further than a couple blocks with my knee."

He had to laugh at how fast it had become a habit, less than a week. On the way home from work he'd stop off at the hospital, be patient, stay the whole hour, then race to his father's house, shower, grab a bite and hurry down to Danny's. Rupert would be waiting. They never had more than three or four drinks. Closing time always came as a surprise. Leonard would be at the light switch, flicking it off and on, calling "Down the hatch. They caught me twice already. I'm not going to lose my license. Drink up."

Kids would stop by their stools now and then and say what a well-mannered dog Prince was. They were right. The other animals sometimes got out of hand. Before, with Danny, two drinks was the limit for a dog. He'd never seen a dog lose control; the other owners wouldn't have stood for it. But no one said anything now when they started howling or barking or trying to get at each other after a few drinks. "Didn't use to be this way," Rupert would say, shaking his head.

Billy always agreed, but he knew it could never matter to him the way it did to Rupert. It was just another change to him. But maybe he'd had more of that than Rupert. After he'd left the neighborhood at eighteen, he had moved seven times, twice out of state, not counting his two years in the army. Coming back, it was as if he was just another spectator. The only thing that made it different was his father.

A girl was heading their way. Billy was amused, the way Rupert would straighten up on his stool when one of the young women would come over and kiss and pet Prince and buy him a drink. "His name is Prince," Rupert would say before they had a chance to ask. Prince always got a lot of attention because he was the only collie. Most of the other dogs were brought in for show. A passing fancy. Their owners would park them on a stool and go off to the video games. They didn't sit down beside them and treat them like a member of the family. The novelty seemed to wear off fast too: he hardly ever saw a dog more than two or three times. The only dogs that were brought in regularly were the brutes: mastiffs, Dobermans, pit bulls, some of them in studded collars without license tags. Once he overheard the owners laughing among themselves, about how they could wipe out the bar at a given signal.

Leonard kept it up. He thought he was cute, Billy guessed. One of his favorites was to throw an ice cube down a girl's front. A lot of them didn't take to that; one of them threw her drink in his face. He didn't think that was funny, especially when she wouldn't pay for it. But that never slowed him down; he'd do the same thing the next night, yelling "Watch this," when a chesty woman sat down. Every time Leonard was in their vicinity, Rupert would lean forward over the bar to watch him pour, tsk-tsking aloud or just shaking his head. Billy found himself leaning and watching Leonard short the customers too. Leonard didn't care; he'd wink back at them. He knew they saw him. It was a joke to him.

He knew it was going to happen, the way Rupert was talking, but there was no way to stop it. It was late; Rupert had had his share by then. Leonard went to pour him a last drink, a highball. Rupert tipped the bottom of the bottle with his hand and got three extra shots in his glass. Leonard tried to grab the glass and Prince lunged, tearing his shirt sleeve. Leonard grabbed a broom and before anyone could stop him whacked Prince off his stool. Billy grabbed Prince under his arm and tried to get Rupert out the door. Rupert was shouting, "You'll get yours, you scut. You never poured full measure in your miserable life."

They stood on the corner catching their breath. Even old Prince was panting, his big tongue out. "He should never have hit Prince," Rupert said, starting to cross the street. Billy followed.

He didn't think Rupert was going to come in the next night. It was after twelve. But after he'd given up watching the front door open, Prince leapt up on the stool next to him and Rupert eased himself up on the stool on the other side. Leonard kept his distance, and Rupert didn't mention what had happened.

Instead of leaving Rupert at his corner, Billy walked him all the way home. It was nippy and Rupert was wearing his old Post Office cardigan. Billy could remember him delivering the mail in the neighborhood when he was a kid. His father, out of Rupert's hearing, called him the Irish speed-demon because, unlike a lot of mailmen, he moved right along. Now he shambled, glasses so thick and heavy they slipped down his nose.

He'd never had much to say, Billy thought as they stood out in front of his place for a while. A big jet passed over and they both tilted their heads back to watch.

"You know, when I was born there weren't any airplanes. Can you imagine that? People then no more thought of getting off the ground than Prince here, and now whole bus loads of them are up there." Billy waited for him to say more but he didn't. He was watching the next plane circling to land at the airport when Billy said good night.

He drove his father home. It had been three weeks. The day before he'd spent four hours cleaning the place up, besides painting the bathroom and having the rugs shampooed.

"Jesus, they charged me four dollars for a tablespoon of cough medicine. What if I would've had a headache and needed aspirin. Money-hungry bastards," his father said, unlocking the front door. "I hope Medicare covers everything. Ask Kay for me; she'll know."

"I will," he said, setting down the blue plastic basin and water pitcher his father'd got at the hospital.

"Did you water my plants?" his father asked, going over to the window and jabbing his forefinger into a pot.

"I watered them."

"Dry," his father said.

Billy phoned Rupert to say good-bye. He hadn't been down to Danny's the last couple of nights. Someone had said Prince was sick.

"My father's back, Rupert. Drop by; he'd like to see you. How's Prince?"

"He's better. He's got the rheumatism in his hind legs when it gets cold like this. Old age too, I guess."

"Well, you take care of yourself."

"Oh, I'll do that," Rupert said with a chuckle. "I have no choice; no one else will."

He didn't go back to the neighborhood for a while. He phoned his father on Sundays. Spring was the busy time at the lab and he was getting a lot of overtime. He'd read in the paper a couple of times about trouble at Danny's. A wife took a shot at her husband. The place got held up. Gus, who he'd finally seen the last time he was in, got roughed up in the toilet; they took his money and gold railroad watch.

Then one evening after he'd popped a bowl of popcorn and sat down in his chair for the ten o'clock news, a picture of Danny's came on the screen. "Scene of riot," the announcer said. He couldn't believe what was happening. First Leonard comes out the front door on a gurney, blood all over his face. Then out comes Rupert, handcuffed, a policeman on each arm. People milling around, ambulances, cops all over. Out comes Prince. They'd thrown a net over him and were dragging him to an S.P.C.A. truck. He was still game, barking and snapping his teeth.

He was on the phone to his father before the picture faded. "Did you see that; they got Rupert."

"I told him not to go back there," his father said. "He was always getting into it with Leonard. I told him. It didn't do any good."

"Christ sake," Billy said. "Should I go down there and see if he needs bail?"

"No, he's got a brother that's a lawyer. He'll take care of it."

120

"I didn't know that."

"Yeah, he's good too; he got Rupert out of a little trouble before. Years ago."

"I don't remember that."

"You know how the Irish are. You weren't born, I don't think. They all stick together. When we came from home they'd barely talk to us; Kansas might have been on the moon."

"What did he do?"

"Beat hell out of some guy."

"Rupert?"

"He was tough as nails."

"What did the guy do?"

"It was a long time ago. I think it was an old boyfriend of his wife. Tried something, I guess. Don't get me wrong; she was a good woman. I don't remember if the guy recovered or not."

His father phoned him at six the next morning to tell him it was in the papers. Rupert Delaney, retired postal worker, accused by Leonard Gilchrest, owner of Danny's Bar on Second Avenue, of ordering his dog Prince to attack. Gilchrest has been treated and released from Mills Hospital. Police reports state that during the incident other patrons of the bar took advantage of the confusion to loot and wreck the property. When asked about the alleged attack, Delaney stated, "I had nothing to do with what happened. Prince hasn't been getting full measure since Leonard bought the place. I guess he just couldn't take it anymore. I intend to stand by him to the highest court."

He tried phoning Rupert that morning from work, but the line was always busy. Finally after three o'clock Rupert answered.

"Are you all right, Rupert? This is Billy."

"Couldn't be better."

"And Prince?"

"He's in his chair."

"Do you think we should start a defense fund for him?" He laughed to show it was a joke.

"Won't be necessary: the Humane Society is after that bastard. And I heard he's going to drop the charges."

"You've got to take it easy, Rupert."

"I know, I know, but he deserves what he gets."

He went over to his father's the next night after work with a fifth of Lord Calvert. He phoned Rupert from there and invited him over for a drink. His father made a point of saying several times that he'd just have a diet cola because of his diabetes. He put some peanuts on the table and had a place ready for Prince and a clean ashtray. Billy waited until Rupert took a sip before asking, "What the hell happened there?"

In his shy way, not looking at anyone, Rupert started out, "As soon as Prince took on Leonard, all hell broke loose. Those kids started busting up the place. Grabbed all the bottles off the back shelves, then started tipping over the pinball machines and video games for the money. Then they all took off when the cops came." He took a long sip. "They just got me and Prince." Rupert paused again. Billy poured another round, his father watching from his chair as if the farthest thing from his mind was joining them. "You should have seen the look on Leonard's face when Prince got a hold of his ear."

"I'd like to have seen that," his father said, shaking his head.

"Well," Rupert said after the third round, "we better hit the road." He stood up. Prince got to his feet too. He and his father walked them out to the sidewalk. They watched them go down the street and turn the corner.

He was turning to go in when his father said, "Come on, let's take a walk. See what's left of the old place." They were down there in five minutes. Billy was surprised how fast his father walked. There were still small chips of glass on the sidewalk. Plywood covered the front windows; a notice of a six-month revocation of license was stapled to one corner. It started to drizzle and they hurried back.

He got home late, ate dinner, watched television, finished the remains of the Halloween candy he'd bought in case any trick or treaters came, then went to bed. When he heard the ringing he thought it was his alarm clock and reached for the button to stop the sound. When it didn't stop he realized it was the phone. It was after three o'clock. His father was excited, out of breath. "Danny's is on fire. I'm phoning from the gas station across the street." For some reason he said, "I'll be right down."

There must have been half a dozen fire trucks, men running all around, shouting over the crack and pop of the burning wood. He watched from his car. The roof came down. The neon sign disappeared in the smoke. A lot of people from the neighborhood were across the street, watching. He saw his father, Rupert and Prince on the edge of the group. Rupert was looking up at the sky, stroking Prince's head.

It didn't take long for the place to burn down, maybe an hour, an hour and a half. It had been there almost seventy years. The firemen had blocked the street, so Billy didn't go over and talk to them.

Even after his father phoned several times at work asking him to stop by, he made some excuse. He didn't want to know what was going on. And once he decided, he made himself wait a couple of days before going over. When he walked in, his father nearly jumped out of the chair. "Come on," he said, "let's take a walk."

He didn't think he'd ever been inside Rupert's house before. It was pretty much like his father's. Couch and matching chair. Recliner. Family photographs on the TV. Venetian blinds and an old worn faded rug smelling of dust. They all had a fast drink, his father making no pretence this time. When they finished that, Rupert poured another. He sat back in his chair with his glass and a shy smile on his face. "You want to know how I did it?" he asked Billy.

"If you want to tell me."

"I filled a clean plastic dish-soap container full of gas from my lawn-mower can. I took Prince for his walk, later than I usually do, and I had the container with me." His face had become flushed as he talked. He forgot to sip from his glass. "No one was around at that time of night. I squirted the gas into the letter slot. Prince was watching at the corner. Then I threw in a match."

He didn't know what to say. They were both watching him. Waiting. "You going to report me?" Rupert suddenly asked.

"You know better than that, Rupert."

"It doesn't matter. I'd do it over. At first your father tried to talk me out of it."

"That's right. I did."

"In the old days Leonard wouldn't have lasted a second," Rupert said. "Not in this neighborhood."

"You're right there," his father said.

"But don't you think that might have been a little strong, burning it down?"

"No, I don't," Rupert said, raising his voice. "I'm serious. I thought it out. It wasn't just what he did to Prince, or cheating the customers." He stopped and looked around the room. Then in his normal, quiet voice he said, "Anymore, going down to Danny's was like watching old movies on TV. No one remembers that time, and the actors are all dead."

Billy looked down at his drink. Before, he might have agreed with Rupert, but now he wasn't so sure. Maybe you shouldn't get rid of the past. Maybe you couldn't burn it up. He looked over at his father.

"A person might as well stay home when that happens," his father said.

Kay, 1983
Ring Around the Rosie

The problem with losing weight was it never came off evenly: twenty-five pounds off the top half of her, not her rear, and where the fat had melted away in her face there were furrows from her nose to the corners of her mouth. If Rose looked like Ann twenty years ago, who did she look like? Not Garnet. Maybe a blue jay, in this new blue suit; her nose had got more pointed when her face got thinner. She had to stay on the subject here: it was Ann who'd called. For Ann to even mention a problem in passing, it had to be getting out of hand. "I don't know what to do anymore." It was Rose again. Sixteen and careening. Unmanageable, her grandmother would have said. Didn't come home till after two on a school night. And when Ann had asked, "Where were you?" Rose had said, "It's none of your goddamned business."

"What did you do?" She could already guess what Ann had done.

"I must have tried to grab her." There was a silence on the phone. "She got away and ran, locked herself in the bathroom."

As a C.P.A., she understood human frailties. She liked to use that word to cover unusual or unexplained behavior. When clients seemed to want to self-destruct. Destroy their way of life. The people around them. Get so far in debt that they lost their jobs. Spouse. House. Family. She gave advice, too freely, probably, but it worked sometimes. One time out of five, say. That was an exaggeration, but it did work occasionally. Clients would snap out of it as if they had been sleepwalking and stepped on the family cat. Cut their credit cards into slices and send the pieces back to the company. Stop spending money. Stop buying things. Follow some system for getting their creditors off their backs.

Stop shopping. No zombie mall visits. She even made a deal with one client, a professional, a newspaper editor, to phone every time she had the urge to buy something over ten dollars. It worked. She got phone calls at all hours, but the woman stopped buying. So Ann's call about Rose started her thinking.

Even her mother had known about Rose. When she phoned on Thursday at her regular time she started out, "Poor Ann." Kay knew what was coming. "If Ruby hadn't taken off, these things wouldn't have happened."

"Mother."

"It gave Opal ideas. That she could run off with your father."

"Aren't you going back a little far there? Twenty years ago? It's just the way things are; you have to accept them."

"Ann was no angel either, if I remember correctly. Chickens have a way of coming home to roost."

"Mother, Rose is just going through a phase; it'll pass. It's like pimples; you get them as an adolescent and then they go away. Skin changes and your attitude does too. It just takes a few years."

"For someone who's never had any kids, you sound like one of those TV authorities."

"That's why I have so many thoughts on the subject; I've never had to test them. How did you hear?"

"Ann's my niece; I still keep up with the family. Even though I'm hardly part of it anymore."

Kay wasn't going to exclaim "Mother!" again; she waited her out.

"One of the women who works for Ann at the flower shop is a friend of my neighbor's daughter. She sees it all. Last week Rose borrowed, or I should say, *took*, one of the delivery vans. Ann caught her out and there was so much yelling you could have heard it for two blocks."

"She'll outgrow it," Kay said.

Kay didn't hear anything from Ann for another week. She didn't want to phone, didn't want to be nosey and intrude. But in spite of herself she was curious. What had Rose done now? She seemed to know how to get a reaction from her mother. Also she was imaginative, to say the least. Last time she'd taken a sheet of letterhead from her doctor's desk and typed a letter to the school with a long medical explanation for why she couldn't take P.E.—a dangerous heart condition—and signed the M.D.'s name. Of course they phoned the doctor's office, afraid she was terminal. Before that, Rose had found a baby pigeon that had fallen out of its nest and raised it in her locker, feeding it, letting it nest in her books, until they had a surprise locker inspection and the pigeon, startled, flew out into the face of the dean. When they asked her what the pigeon was doing there, Rose told them she was teaching the bird to count and intended to enroll it in school next quarter. Ann spent more time at the school than she did at the shop.

Ann phoned the next afternoon. "I have to ask a favor," she started out.

"I'm yours to command," Kay said, trying to make it as easy as she could. They had played Cinderella and the cruel stepsister when they were girls.

"Don't think I don't remember I always had to do your bidding. You made me clip your toenails once," Ann said.

"I don't remember that," Kay said.

"You never gave me my turn to be cruel stepsister, but I'll forgive you if you do me this favor."

"Anything," Kay said.

"Wait until I tell you. Rose got kicked out last Tuesday, just for a week. It was probably a good thing because staying home she got bored as hell. I couldn't take her down to the shop and start a war there. They're going to let her back in again, last chance. But they mean it this time. She goes to continuation the next time she does anything. They want an adult there tomorrow; that's where you come in. Make it a formal kind of situation where Rose might understand this is it."

Kay wasn't going to ask Ann why she couldn't be there. It was so unusual to be given an assignment, any assignment. "I'll be happy to. Just tell me what you want me to do." If Rose was bored after staying home a week, what about her: she was bored, too, after twenty-odd years of coming to this office, listening to the same questions over and over again, giving the same answers. Being a C.P.A. was like being an answering machine. She was ready for anything, any excuse to stop her from sitting behind her desk. On the way back to the office Monday there had been a striped cat up a sycamore tree that wouldn't come down. People had gathered underneath on the sidewalk watching, offering advice. She'd stood underneath that tree calling out kitty kitty kitty in her grandmother's Kansas twang for ten minutes, and stayed around another twenty-five while other people tried, until someone brought over a sliding aluminum ladder and got the cat.

It was cold for February in California, in the low thirties, and people who'd parked on the street were scraping ice off their windows when she pulled up in front of Ann's house at 7:30 the next morning. Before she could open the door to get out, Rose came down the walk. She had wanted to see Ann for a minute, find out what had happened so that she couldn't take Rose. It wasn't like her to allow someone else to take her place, no matter how bad the situation was.

"Auntie Kay," Rose said, "thank you for coming," and she leaned over and kissed her on the cheek. It startled Kay; since she'd turned thirteen, Rose had avoided her, usually going into her room when she came over, as if she and Ann were planning an alliance against her.

For conversation, she announced, "It's cold this morning." Next she found herself asking, "How's your mother?"

Rose became wary. "Okay," she said.

"I saw RubyAnn's name in the paper, when she broke the junior high record," Kay said.

"I was there; I walked over. I've been home all week. She looked good. She was the shortest jumper at the meet, and she went the highest." Rose laughed. "You know what she told me when we were coming home, when I asked her how she could twist herself around and throw herself over the bar backwards, not knowing how she'd end up? 'I pretend I'm a dragonfly,' she told me. 'The way they move up and down sideways and backwards like they're not sure which way they can go.'"

With one eye Kay glanced over at Rose as she spoke. Red cheeked, thick dark hair, shoulder length, in almost iridescent ringlets, as if it were liquid. Her nose was too wide now, but when her face filled out she'd be striking. Curvy, though she still had baby fat around her middle. And she had an air of always being about to laugh. She'd been wrong to think Rose was going to be like Ann. They might look alike, but Ann was estranged from the world; Rose was just waiting to get her share. Their perspective was so different that it almost changed the way they looked, if you knew them. It was the difference between someone running as fast as she could and someone pacing, stopping to check the next step. Even as a girl Ann had brooded, acted like she found it difficult to look at you.

Her head always hung down, askance, as if she couldn't face the next thing that was going to happen. But it wasn't so: Ann could face anything. A mother abandoning her when she was eight. A father who drank, who did the best he could to raise them. She was a widow with two kids by the time she was thirty, with no marketable skills. But she never complained, never admitted there was anything different about her luck.

Kay couldn't help it: when she got to the school, her pulse quickened. She hadn't been back here since she graduated. She felt animated, stirred up as if she were going to take a last test for another A. She felt her wrist with the fingers of her other hand. A steady 72. A couple of thousand kids were trying to get inside the building before the eight o'clock bell rang. Going through the doorway was like passing through the small part of a funnel.

It was like a herd in the hallway; the pace kept quickening. She followed Rose, who almost sauntered through the masses of kids, through a door marked Attendance Office, and through another door. They finally sat down after Rose checked in with a secretary. The second bell sounded and with it a last rush of yells, slammed doors. Then it was absolutely quiet. Kay could hear the big clock over her head begin to tick.

She started having second thoughts right off. What was she doing here, anyway? She would do anything for Ann, that's what. She was Ann's first cousin; their mothers were sisters. Rose was her second cousin. Who called her Auntie. She should tell them that she was a friend of the family; that would be more accurate.

"Ms. Cortner, may I speak to you now in my office?" a counselor asked.

She got to her feet. Rose knew the routine, stayed seated, winked at her and patted her arm. The counselor was young, probably just out of his twenties, casually dressed in open-necked shirt and cords. He wouldn't be mistaken for a high school student but he could be in college, easily. Assured, he said, "Ken," and nodded at the same time.

"Kay," she answered.

He went around behind his desk and sat down, opened a folder. "You're . . ." He paused.

"Rose's aunt. Her mother couldn't come today." She wanted to explain more fully her being there, but stopped herself. He started writing something in the folder.

"That happens," he said as if she'd given him a long explanation. Kay began to have the feeling that she'd just caught the very edge of her new skirt in a machine and was gently, almost imperceptibly, getting pulled in a direction she didn't want to go. She did what she did when she faced an auditor or the I.R.S.: she stopped talking, gave her skirt a tug downward as if to free it, and waited to find out what the rules were going to be. The counselor was playing her, taking his time. Now he was ready. He looked directly at her.

"We all want what's best for Rose. But to be truthful, she's been a problem for us. In my opinion, she should have been put in Continuation a long time ago, where there's less of an audience for her acting out. But as you know, we've decided to give her another chance. The last chance, I might add. Her grades are terrible and her behavior is worse. To put it bluntly, she's a bad influence on the other kids. I never told her mother this," he said, lowering his voice as if to a fellow conspirator, "but she's sexually active, too; she's out of control. Rose thinks this is just a game here, where she can do as she likes. Twenty-three cuts in P.E. in a month, out of twenty classes. That was *after* she was caught with the phony doctor's excuse." He was enjoying himself, sure he had her attention. "She's one of the biggest liars I've ever met."

She listened, composed, while he went on as if he were reading off a long list of Rose's physical statistics: weight, height, color of eyes. When he paused for breath, Kay cut in. "What is your position, exactly?" she asked.

"I'm a counselor, Rose's advisor; what else?"

"Is that Rose's file? May I see it?"

"We're not authorized to show it; you have to make an appointment. You have to be a parent or legal guardian." He closed the file and planted both elbows on the cover.

"Are the things you told me in that file?" she asked. "The liar part and the sexually active part?"

He looked pained. "Of course not. I told you that in confidence."

"What are her test scores like? The California state proficiency tests?"

He opened the file. "Not bad: eighty-seventh percentile in reading, the last one; a little lower in math. You're not questioning my evaluation of the situation, are you?" he asked, smiling, rocking to the back legs of his chair.

"I question your attitude, if you're Rose's advisor. I've found that what you expect of a person is usually how they will respond to you."

130

"You're blaming me for Rose's behavior?"

"No, but you're the last person I'd have advising anyone."

He brought the legs of his chair down hard, catching himself with his hand against the flat of the desk. "Would you like to see the head counselor or the vice principal, Ms. Cortner?"

"Why don't you invite them both in, Mr. Little? I think you and I have gone as far as we can on this subject."

He jumped up and left the room. She wasn't angry or even excited. "Calm," she said aloud. "I am the calmest, most rational person in this building, if not in the entire state of California."

A woman came in, younger looking than Ken, if that were possible. Kay stood up. "I'm Melanie Roberts, head counselor. Ken, here, said you'd like to see me." They all remained standing.

"It's apparent that he and I have come to an impasse," Kay said. "I find his attitude toward Rose one that pretty much cuts out any chance of her ever succeeding."

"All Rose's problems are well documented," Melanie said. "I can bring her teachers in, if you like."

"Is it well documented that she's sexually active?"

"We don't verify things like that."

"If you don't, why say them, then? Why should unfounded accusations be used to tear down a kid in front of a parent? What right do you have to categorize kids in that way?" Kay knew she was repeating herself. "What right does he have to use innuendo against Rose? What business is it of his in the first place?"

"We care about our students," Melanie said, and tried to go on. Kay ignored her, all the time knowing she was railing against a system that was probably beyond remedy. But she was enjoying herself too, as much as she could allow. "Rose needs a new counselor," she said. "Someone who'll grasp the concept that she's sixteen. Someone who will be more concerned about her good points than ones that are neither their business . . ."

"Now wait a minute," Ken tried to interrupt.

"You wait a minute; it's my turn; let me finish. Where was I? Nor pertinent to the fact that she's not doing well in her school work. Why isn't she? Does she need extra help? Why does she cut P.E. all the time? Did you ask her, Mr. Little?"

"I have 150 other students to counsel, you know."

"Ms. Roberts, get Rose another counselor. He or she couldn't be any worse."

"I object to that," Ken said. "I'm not going to stand here and listen to this." He walked out.

"What do you do for a living?" Melanie asked, watching Ken go out the door.

"I have my own business. Accountant. Tax consultant."

"C.P.A.?"

Kay nodded.

"None of us are perfect, Kay; not Ken or me."

"Neither is Rose," Kay said.

"That's a good point. It's going to be complicated, but I'll take Rose, be her advisor. Tell Rose my door is always open and I'm ready to listen."

"I'd appreciate that," Kay said.

"It was nice talking to you, Kay." They both smiled at each other.

When Rose saw Kay come out she got up and followed her to where they'd parked. "What happened?" she asked. Kay had to admire her for lasting that long before asking.

"Nothing; you go back Monday."

"Why did Mrs. Roberts go in there?"

"She's your new counselor."

"She is?"

"That's right." Kay felt tired, as if she'd been doing aerobics for the last half hour instead of just talking. "Rose, I have one question I'd like to ask you."

"Go ahead."

"How can anyone get twenty-three cuts in a class that's only held twenty times?"

They both started laughing at the same time. "They count you off for tardy, they count you for not dressing down, they count you for not showering, they count you for leaving early. Sometimes I do all four."

"Why?"

Rose thought for a minute. "Everyone does it; I know that's no good. But it's such a waste of time. Volleyball. I'm not good at games. Which means when I play I'm miserable, and so is everyone else, over my mistakes. And I don't like taking off my clothes. Half the kids fake it going to the showers. I told them it's my time of month for a shower excuse so many times one teacher said I belonged in a record book for the longest period in biological history. I just don't feel like dressing down and hopping around for an hour, so I get in trouble. I didn't come to school to be a jock."

"What do you come for?"

"I knew you were going to ask that. To have a good time. To eat my lunch and look at the boys." Kay caught Rose's smile and had to laugh. "You know what my grades are like. The worst is, I know I could get decent grades, please my mother, the teachers, counselors, myself, probably, but I can't, I just can't. I start out thinking I'm going to do it this quarter, I'm going to show them all. But I don't. I just don't. I don't read the assignments. I don't even take the books home anymore and try."

"Why don't you quit, get a job, if you don't like it?" Rose stared at her, looking shocked at the thought. "Why make yourself miserable and everyone else? I don't know what the legal age is, but they'd probably be glad to get rid of you. Or take that test to get out, the equivalency exam."

"I can't get a job. How would I support myself?"

"Work in the flower shop. You've done that for years."

"Are you kidding? All the time, with Mom?"

"I'd hire you," Kay said. She waited, but Rose didn't say anything. "One thing I learned before I had any time to fool around with is don't waste it. That's what you're doing, wasting time. Yours and theirs." She let Rose off in front of the house.

"You want to come in, Auntie?"

"No, no, I can't."

"I'll make your lunch."

"I've got to get back."

"Thanks for coming with me. I've never seen Mr. Little so mad."

"Rose, that's beside the point. You start considering your options. I'll phone you Saturday or Sunday, see if you've come up with anything."

That night Ann phoned. "Kay, how'd it go?"

"Okay. Didn't Rose tell you?"

"Are you kidding? We don't even say pass the salt around here."

"She goes back Monday."

"Good."

"Rose said you went to the doctor. What's wrong?"

"Tests."

"What kind?"

"What are you, the I.R.S. or the F.B.I.?"

"I'm just asking."

"I took a lot of tests. He's supposed to let me know as soon as he finds out anything."

Kay let it go. When she'd found out she was pregnant, she'd let Ann know about her appointment for the abortion. "I'll go with you," Ann had said; "those nuts are picketing the place again." She'd hoped she'd come. But Ann wouldn't allow any interest in her affairs unless she initiated the information, and that rarely happened. It had taken weeks before she'd understood why Ann was acting so irritated, even for her. She'd caught on finally, worked the conversation around to loans. But it was like pulling teeth. Rose reminded her of Ann with a sense of humor.

Rose improved. Kay made a point to phone when she knew Ann wasn't there. "This is your probation officer," she started out.

Rose played along. "Five whole days without a cut. I'm not going back to prison, officer, I'm already there. Do you realize that you interrupted me while I was doing my homework?"

"Quit it, Rose, you wouldn't know how."

"Really, a book report. The librarian at school gave me a book, *Precious Bane*; did you ever read it?"

"Are you kidding? I read Sylvia Porter at your age; now it's the new revised I.R.S. tax code."

"It's good; I recommend it. It's awfully sad: it was hard times, and they didn't treat each other very well then. I don't know if I could stand having a cleft palate."

Kay interrupted. "What's RubyAnn up to?"

"What else, exercising or something."

"Well, get back to work; I was just checking up on you. Don't tell your mother I phoned," she said to be funny.

"You don't have to worry about that. Can you imagine what Mr. Little thinks now?" Rose said.

"Don't worry about him," Kay said. "You have enough on your own plate. This is not a game," she added before she hung up. She decided later she shouldn't have said that to Rose. She didn't want to sound like a mother. But on the other hand, Rose had had the nerve to say once, "I want to be like you, Auntie," after she was caught out in a lie.

On her lunch hour Kay went to the bookstore at the mall by her townhouse and ordered the book Rose had mentioned. She was surprised it wasn't there with the paperback romances. When the clerk looked it up on microfiche, he told her it'd been published in the twenties. She'd got back to her office and was hanging up her coat when the phone rang. It was her mother. "They just took Ann to the hospital in an ambulance. Rose went with her." Kay was back out the door before she remembered she hadn't asked which hospital.

She kept driving, hoping it was the one they'd taken RubyAnn to when she'd broken her wrist high-jumping in the back yard. At the reception desk they told her what floor, and she hurried faster, imagining the worst, Ann breathing her last. But as she hurried down the corridor she heard Ann laugh. She stopped at the open door to catch her breath. They were all there: Billy, of course, still wearing his lab coat, and he had picked up Uncle Frank, who was sitting in the only chair, next to the bed. Rose stood on the other side by the window, she and her mother so much alike the clear glass could have been a mirror, except that Ann had one eye almost swollen shut.

"Aunt Kay." Rose saw her first, came up and gave her a hug. "Mom fell against the sink," she said before Kay could ask what had happened.

"I was looking at myself in the mirror," Ann said. "I must have been too startled; I fainted."

Uncle Frank got up and kissed her, familiar whiffs of Chesterfields and bourbon. "I better hit the road," he said. Then Billy kissed her. It was an occasion; a family get-together. But no one left; they stood around telling hospital stories, taking turns. Uncle Frank as a house painter had the advantage, having spent most of his life working on top of twenty-eight-foot ladders. Billy's were from being a medic in the army. Rose did a girlfriend's story; she didn't have one of her own. And she joined in by asking, "Ann, how long are you going to be in here?"

"Don't know; he's going to take X-rays tomorrow morning. I feel fine now, just tired."

"RubyAnn and Rose can stay with me tonight."

"I've already promised they can stay at the house."

"We'll be fine," Rose said, trying not to bubble over.

"Well, that's settled," Billy said for the second time. "I better take Dad home and get back to work."

Kay was the last to say good-bye. "Well, you'll get a rest anyway. Do you want me to do anything?"

"I've already phoned the shop. It'll take care of itself. Keep an eye on the girls for me."

"I will." For some reason, Kay hated to go. Ann was half asleep, her eyes sliding closed. "I've got to go," she said, but she kept on talking. Finally she left; Rose was waiting out in the hall. She would have liked to find Ann's doctor, but Rose wanted to go.

Kay went through the house with them. "Make sure the door into the garage is locked," she said. "Leave the porch light on."

"Aunt Kay," RubyAnn said. "We've stayed alone before."

"Just do it," Kay said. That was the wrong thing to say, wrong tone, she knew it before it reached the girls, who were standing by her on the porch. Instead of lightening up the situation with I'm a fuss budget, humor me, she added, "Do what you're told for a change." Both the girls watched her leave with sullen looks. What made her speak those words, what gene? Her grandmother?

Her mother phoned when she was eating her dinner cup of strawberry yogurt. She was going to stay thin if she dropped from malnutrition. "Doesn't sound good," her mother said. "You don't just pass out for no reason. Pregnant, a fever maybe."

"Mother, she was sitting up in bed entertaining us all."

Her mother changed the subject.

After Ann spent a second day in the hospital, Kay found out the name of her doctor and phoned him. "She's had some kind of seizure," he said, "but we can't find out what caused it yet."

"What did the X-rays show?"

"Nothing; we're taking more today. I'd been treating her because she was complaining of dizziness; that was before she was admitted. So whatever is occurring, it must be progressing. She should stay in the hospital, by the way."

"I'm not arguing against that opinion."

"She is."

Kay snorted. "I bet she is."

"I've never seen anyone so quick to fly off the handle."

It was a phrase her grandmother used. She was thinking of Grandmother more now, she'd noticed, the older she got. "Where are you from?" she asked.

"South Dakota, originally. Why?"

"Just asking. Let me know as soon as you find out anything," Kay said.

The third night, having stayed until visitors were asked to leave, over the intercom at nine, she went home tired. Took off her dress and put on her quilted robe. Sat on the couch trying to read the paper long enough so she wouldn't go to bed before ten. RubyAnn phoned. "Rose has taken Mom's car again. I don't want to stay here by myself."

"I'll be right over," Kay said.

They watched TV until RubyAnn started yawning. "Go to bed. I'm going to watch the end of this movie," Kay told her.

"You're not going to leave me here."

"I'm going to wait for Rose. I'll be here." If Rose looked exactly like Ann, Kay thought, RubyAnn was a good mixture of both Carl and Ann, long legged, with Carl's blue eyes and fair complexion, Ann's dark hair and cleft chin.

She slept on the couch in her clothes, an afghan over her legs, a pillow against the armrest, her head turned to the clock on the TV. It was 2:50 when she heard the key in the lock, then the bang as the door swung the length of the night chain. She turned on the light. "Welcome home, Rose," she said, trying not to sound smug.

Rose ignored her, only saying something like "I'm sixteen" or "I have a license" as she walked past.

"But you're not supposed to be out at this hour. And you're not supposed to use that car," she said, loud enough for RubyAnn to wake up and come out in her pajamas.

"You told," Rose accused her. Then she went down the hall into her bedroom and shut the door. RubyAnn went back to bed and Kay went back to the couch but couldn't sleep.

"I'm ready to get out of here," Ann said when Kay came by at lunch time. "It's Wednesday; I've been in here three whole days. I've caught up on my sleep."

She did look good. She didn't look sick. "You just want to go back to work because you don't want anyone to know that the shop can run by itself."

"You're right, it can, and the girls can take care of themselves too. Rose phoned me before she left for school this morning. She made pancakes for her and Rube. They've always got along so good. I could stay here a month and not have to worry; the girls would be all right."

To change the direction of the conversation, Kay said, "Why did you name her Ruby? Besides the obvious reason, I mean."

"We named Rose after Carl's mother; her name was Rosebud, but we left the last part off. Then when we had RubyAnn it was kind of automatic, Carl's idea, we name her Ruby after my mother and Ann after me. In a way it was a good idea. I got used to the name without thinking of my mother. When Nana Rosebud died she left her complete button collection for our Rose. Eleven thousand." They both smiled. "Her namesake. Rosebud."

"It's not any worse than my mother's name. Garnet. Or Opal's, or your mother's. I think people who were poor and worked with their backs had different dreams for their children. Jewels or sweet-smelling flowers."

"I don't have any dreams," Ann said.

"I dream of cream puffs," Kay said. "Hamburgers and french fries." It was warm in the room. Ann had thrown the covers on the bed back; her bare legs showed beneath her nightgown. She was laughing about the cream puffs, and the top magazine of the stack Kay'd brought slipped off the edge of the bed. Kay reached down to pick it up. When she straightened up, Ann made a noise, then arched her back, her whole body shaking. White foam showed at the corners of her mouth.

For a moment, Kay couldn't move. Then she reached out to stop the rest of the magazines from falling off the bed before jumping up to press the emergency button. Then she grabbed Ann, who was thrashing around, by the shoulders and tried to hold her on the bed.

A nurse came in, then another. Someone else with a machine on a cart. Then

138

a doctor. Kay had stepped away from the bed by then and was forced back as more and more people came in until finally she was standing in the hallway, unable to see Ann.

When Kay got home there was a message on her answering machine from the head counselor, Mrs. Roberts. Please phone. When she did, a secretary said, "Mrs. Roberts isn't here right now, but she left a note. You're to come and pick up Rose."

"Why?" Kay asked.

"I think she's been expelled."

Rose was sitting where she had sat before while they waited to see Mr. Little. She gave a nervous giggle when she saw Kay and stood up. "What happened?" Kay asked.

"They caught me drinking a can of beer in the parking lot at lunch time. They're making a big deal out of it."

One of the secretaries came over to them. "Mrs. Roberts phoned in; she's been held up at a meeting at the county office, but she asked me to give you this." She handed Kay a note written on yellow paper. "Dear Ms. Cortner," it said. "Rose was written up with nine other students found drinking in a van in the east lot by Security. Forty-eight twelve-ounce cans of beer were confiscated, and one 750 milliliter bottle of brandy. All seven boys and two girls are suspended until further notice."

"What did she say?" Rose said, leaning over to see the note, her breath full of beer.

"Come on, Rose," Kay said, starting to walk out. Mr. Little came past them, straight-faced. They got into the car without another word.

Kay wondered what made one person react one way and another so differently. She was calm. She had to understand what was expected of her, exactly. Like the instructions for filing the most complex I.R.S. forms: you read them over and over until you passed the ordinary meaning and started understanding what would change when you added your information; then you came up with what you had to do. She hadn't been over this enough, she decided, to understand about what was happening to Ann. She wasn't sure yet.

"Why are we going this way, Aunt Kay?" She didn't answer. "Why are we going this way? I have to go to the bathroom."

It was hard to pay attention. "We'll be there in a minute. I'm taking you to my place."

"I want to go home."

"You're going to stay with me for a while."

"You're not my mother."

Kay was gripping the wheel so hard her wrists ached. She couldn't stop herself, heard her voice loud, shouting, angry. "Your mother's in intensive care. They're going to try to operate on her tonight. She has a brain tumor."

"Go to bed," Kay said, and Rose, who'd stayed over before, ambled into the other bedroom and shut the door. Kay sat down at her desk near the phone, listening to the sounds of Rose sitting down on the bed, kicking off her shoes, then the headboard rocking against the nightstand as she stretched out. She had phoned Billy, who would phone Uncle Frank, and her mother, who would pick up RubyAnn at school and take her home. The doctor was going to phone her if they could operate that night. She was thinking about what Ann had said, after the seizure. First she kept asking, "What happened? What happened?" Then, "Mommy," Ann said. "Mom. Mom." She'd been too startled to say anything. Then the shot they'd given her started taking hold and Ann closed her eyes. Even when she was picking up Rose, she kept going over that awful feeling, the dread she felt when Ann called for her mother.

The phone rang. She looked at the clock: past five; it was Billy. "Kay, it's as big as a lemon," he said. "I saw it in the X-rays. Right behind her forehead. You know what she said when I told her? 'It started when I fell down the back stairs and landed on my head. That's what I think.' She was laughing. She's kind of rambling with the medication. But she can talk. They're going to operate at seven-thirty. Kay, are you still there?"

"I'm here."

"Say something, then."

"Did she say how she fell, when she hit her head?"

"No, I don't think she did."

"I pushed her; we were both trying to get down the stairs first. She got ahead of me and I couldn't stand it."

"Kay, that isn't why she got a tumor."

"I know, but that's what happened."

"Anyway, there's no way of telling if it's malignant or not. But it's growing, pressing against her brain, and that's why she's had the seizures: they have to take it out to relieve the pressure. Are you coming down?"

"I'll be there. I have to do a few things first."

"Dad's here too. I'll see you."

Kay put down the phone and got out her old address book, started looking down the pages under R. The phone rang again. She picked up the receiver and said, "Mother?"

"How did you know it was me?"

"I just knew."

"I have RubyAnn here with me now; we stopped over and got some of her things, picked up the papers and left a light on. We're almost ready to eat."

"You sound like you've covered everything."

"Do you think this is the first time I've helped out Ruby's and Frank's kids? I don't know how many times we had Billy and Ann stay with us."

"I didn't think you kept score."

"I don't, but I'm always ready for emergencies."

"I don't think it'd be good to take RubyAnn or Rose to the hospital and wait. The operation could take four or five hours."

"I agree; I'm going to stay here with RubyAnn, then."

"I'm going down in a little bit. I have something to do first."

She found the unlisted number and only hesitated an instant before pressing the stainless steel buttons. She'd just talked to her a couple of minutes that time the three of them had gone down after Billy had found her. That was almost five years ago. No one had gone back, but Billy phoned on Mother's Day every year, in spite of the circumstances: Ruby abandoning Billy and Ann and then being completely uninterested when they found her. It depressed her when Billy talked about the calls. It was so awful to pursue someone who was indifferent to you. He must have caught on, because he hadn't mentioned it in the last few years.

"Ruby Kent." Kay recognized the voice.

"I don't know if you remember me: I'm Kay, Garnet's daughter."

"I do, I do, the C.P.A. How are you?"

"I'm fine. How have you been?"

"Busy: we've added another hundred forty units to the hotel part of the convention center. You either grow or you die; the bigger ones will choke you to death. You know that, too. Christopher's in law school, engaged to be married. Next June. Wonderful girl, daughter of an executive at one of the studios."

"Ruby," Kay got in, "Ann's sick, really sick."

"I'm sorry to hear that."

"Your daughter, Ruby."

"I know that."

"She's going to be operated on tonight. She has a tumor, a brain tumor."

"How's Billy?"

"He's fine."

"He phones me, you know; we talk."

"I understand that."

"It's always good to hear from him. It's inconvenient sometimes, when we're in conference or something like that . . ."

"Ann's going into surgery at seven-thirty. When I was there she had another seizure; she was calling for you. There's a flight leaving L.A. in about forty minutes. You could be on it. Be in time to see her before the operation. I'd pick you up at the airport."

"I'm so busy, this is the busy . . ."

"It's your daughter, Ruby."

"You don't have to tell me; do you think I could forget, with Billy pestering me?"

"Does your son know he has an older half sister and half brother, Ruby?" She was trying to say it casually, but it came out with too much volume.

"Don't threaten me, damn it. When I left that life, I left it for good. It's over. Do you understand that? It's over, for me. I can't come up there now, I just can't. It's impossible. Please understand that," she said in a normal tone.

Kay couldn't help it, stop herself: it was more important even than having Ruby come up to the hospital. She heard herself ask, "How could you leave your kids like that? I can understand a husband. But your children. Just walk out and never come back?" She could hear Ruby breathing.

"At that time it was the easiest thing in the world. Easier than leaving Kansas, where I'd lived my whole life. When I came out, I was seventeen and carrying Ann. I had her, then Billy, all before I was twenty. I used to think about them a lot. But you forget by stages when you don't see someone. You can imagine the changes, but really Ann and Billy are still eight and six for me. I'm not callous. But I've concluded it's best not to think about the past. You probably don't understand that."

"No, I don't."

"You couldn't, because you can't imagine how poor we were. The Depression. We were a town joke, the Stecker jewels. Ruby, Opal and Garnet. I left Kansas when I married their father. If I loved Frank, I don't remember it. When I decided the children were what were keeping me, I had to leave them. It was the only way I could escape. I couldn't wait another sixteen years. If I stayed I'd have always been Ruby Stecker. I brought Kansas with me with the kids and Frank. I didn't see that right off. When I did, I left. She's selfish; that's what you're thinking."

"No, I was looking at the clock. Phone her, Ruby; here's the number." She read it off. "Do you have it?"

"I have it, but I can't promise anything."

"You can't promise?" Kay was talking as loud as she could. "You're not selfish, Ruby, you're disgusting, did you hear me? You're despicable and disgusting. You stupid self-centered piece of trash." Just as she was in the motion of slamming down the phone, she saw Rose standing in the open doorway. She didn't try to arrest her arm. The mouthpiece missed the receiver and careened off the desktop. Rose came over and picked it up, untangled the cord, and handed it back to Kay. "That was your grandmother, your mother's mother, Ruby. She lives in L.A. Are you hungry?" Kay was still out of breath from yelling, knew she was red faced, but pretended everything was normal because the words she was speaking were. Rose was just watching her. "We have plenty of food. I haven't eaten in so long . . ."

"I can cook something," Rose said.

"Look in the freezer compartment. Defrost something in the microwave. I keep buying stuff even though I'm not eating anything but yogurt and for a special treat a can of water-packed tuna on Friday night with a bowl of butterless popcorn."

Rose laughed.

"I shouldn't have talked to your grandmother like that. She can't help the way she is."

"I feel like that too, sometimes. Things just happen," Rose said. "There's nothing I can do about it."

"Come on, Rose, you know better. Sooner or later you have to be responsible. Not just for what you do now, but your past. Own up to the mistakes too." Rose was looking at her blankly, one hand on the freezer door handle. "We all have to learn that. Some people learn it later than others." She was going over Rose's head. Maybe some never do, she thought. Like Ruby. That kind of indifference was incomprehensible to her. The phone rang. "Cook something, surprise me, Rose."

She picked up the receiver knowing it had to be Ruby with some pat excuse, answer or accusation.

"You'll never guess who called," Ann said.

"I probably won't, but let me try. That land-rich flower grower over on the coast who wanted to marry you. He's changed his mind."

"No, be serious. Mother phoned; she wanted to talk to me. She was crying and all; it was hard to understand her. But it was nice speaking to her, and she wished me luck. It makes it all easier, having the loose ends taken care of."

"Is Billy still there?" she asked.

"He's outside at the nurses' station, passing out samples of mayonnaise, I think. Telling the surgical nurses he's my brother and to take care of me like I was ten. I'm older than he is. How are the girls?"

"Fine, RubyAnn's at my mother's and Rose is here. Cooking up a storm in the kitchen. I'm coming down as soon as I get organized here."

"You don't have to. I'm almost calm."

"I better. Some of those doctors might need some advice on their IRAs."

"Suit yourself. I've already ordered what I want for breakfast. It was really thoughtful of my mother to phone like that."

"You mean after all these years."

"Better late than never. I'm relaxed now. I don't have a worry in the world."

"Yes you do; you haven't shaved your legs in weeks."

"How do you know?"

"I saw them in the hospital."

"Do you think they'll notice?"

"It's the first thing they're going to see in the operating room."

"Quit it, Kay, you're just saying that." They both started giggling.

Kay, 1983
Waking Up

She was in her car, driving, she realized halfway to the new place, and she didn't remember getting behind the wheel. A faded California poppy swayed among dead weeds in someone's side yard at the turn off El Camino. If heaven was a place, it ought to be fields and fields of flowers, tidy tips, blue lupine, orange California poppies. Wildflowers. If they had any authority, any power, Ann would wake up. Was this going to be the day? The operation three weeks ago had been a success; the doctors couldn't explain why she hadn't regained consciousness. Yesterday they'd moved her from Mills to a convalescent hospital.

Ann had never been interested in flowers: why she'd picked a flower shop to buy was a mystery. The business had gone bankrupt once and been abandoned another time, but that hadn't stopped Ann. She wanted it. Wanted the building. The refrigerator units were old, ruined, had to be replaced; she'd pointed that out to Ann. The ceiling was stained where the roof leaked; the front plate-glass window had a big crack. But Ann walked around the empty, dusty rooms as if the place were already filled with flowers.

The flower shop changed Ann. It wasn't just the time she gave it, making sure the flowers she sold were the freshest, driving over to the growers on the coast herself, sometimes doing the cutting, always haggling over the prices. But she also felt obligated to donate huge bouquets of flowers she made up herself to convalescent homes, the Veterans' Hospital, anyplace that asked. Flowers made Ann a different person, or maybe brought out a part of her that was dormant most of the time. Like that day when they were driving over to the coast on a flower run. Ann had slowed down—the road was curvy—and rolled down the window and emptied a plastic bag into the wind. She'd turned her head back to see what Ann had done. Nothing had changed; the same winter-damp ground ran downhill on one side; the same matted dead grass lined the bank on the other to where it met the dark brush that covered the slopes of the coast range. It always stayed the same. She wasn't going to ask, but Ann would never tell her if she didn't. "What did you just do?"

"What?"

"That stuff you threw out the window?"

"Seeds." After a minute, Ann went on, "Poppy seeds. California poppies. In the spring they'll bloom. I threw out baby blue eyes last Tuesday."

"Any particular reason?"

"No, not really."

Ann didn't always throw seeds out the window on their trips. Mostly just in the winter. She'd phone: "You need an outing; you look peaked. I'll pick you up at ten." It always sounded better than what was on her calendar. Over the years she'd kept track of the wildflowers. There must have been some there originally, but now, each early spring, there were banks and banks of orange, yellow and blue. Looking at the fields of growers' flowers from the highway never gave her the same feeling: those colors were unnatural, too consistent, as if the ground were covered with neon lights that blinked off and on.

She'd told Ann once, maybe it was last spring, how much she liked watching for the wildflowers. "I like it too," Ann had said, and then had surprised her by going on: "When I bought the shop, I wasn't sure of the whole idea with flowers. I didn't know anything about them, but that wasn't what bothered me. It was having to cut them, sell them, when they only lasted at the outside a week, ten days. Seemed like a waste. Impractical, you'd say. Spreading those seeds that come back year after year was more permanent. Anyhow, it made selling the cut flowers easier for me."

She ought to stop at the flower shop, see how things were. Put in an appearance. Why? Ann's business would run itself; her assistant manager was sharp and loyal. Before she had a chance to deflect it, she started thinking about her grandmother again. She resisted any part of that thought that suggested it was up to her to do something. She didn't have to concentrate very hard for her grandmother to come back. But now it was always from her point of view as a little girl. She wasn't driving; she was sitting in the front seat, her short legs sticking straight out, nine years old in the blue Chrysler. They were traveling north to the hospital to visit Uncle Wally.

She wasn't going to think about that. Ann was going to get well. It was only a matter of time. She knew that. The tumor wasn't malignant. Ann's head under the bandages was scarred and bristly, but she was fine. She looked like she was asleep. At ease, now, with a faint, very faint smile on her face, like the first time she threw the seeds out the window. Instead of stopping at the flower shop, Kay went on to the hospital.

She tried to be a spectator, make a distance between herself and what was happening. She watched the others for signs. Billy came from work and stayed until they drove him off, way after the time. Came back early in the morning before he drove to NatureFresh. Started out, "Now where were we?" Talked for hours to his sister, about when they were kids, about his ex-wives. Read from magazines. He held her hand, her face turned up to the ceiling, tubes running into her arm, a small machine over the bed that blinked. She breathed easy, content to be with her brother.

Rose could sit there for hours too. It was startling to walk into the room and see the two faces so alike. She read to her mother from her schoolbooks. Continuation school wasn't demanding, and she did what homework there was. They were spending the afternoon class making plaster casts, ten inches high, of famous men in history. They spend one whole class each day, five hours a week, making change, working a cash register in preparation for jobs in fast food places. "Aren't you bored doing that?" she'd asked Rose. "You know how to count." "I don't mind," Rose had replied. She seemed subdued by the experience, seeing her mother lying still on a bed, day after day. But she visited every day, kissed Ann on the forehead hello and good-bye.

Uncle Frank sat in the chair by the bed fidgeting, wanting to smoke, to light up a Chesterfield, unable to think of anything to say if he were alone with his daughter, though if someone else was there he'd talk a blue streak.

Her mother came too, regularly, announced, "It's your Aunt Garnet," and sat down and took out her knitting. Occasionally she'd say something: "Ground round can't go up any higher, or I won't buy it," or "Ann, you won't believe how patchy your hair's coming in. You had the curliest hair when you were born." She'd watch from the doorway, touched, as her mother squinted at her knitting,

147

moving the needles as surely as if they were part of her fingers. She never gave time or age a thought now, since the divorce. The gray hair and pink or turquoise pantsuits became her now, just like the wash-faded cotton house dresses she wore when she was a girl in the old photos from Kansas. Kay could almost stop thinking about Ann when her mother was there. Watching Garnet once, she suddenly felt time had got broken or knocked askew, that the two of them were sisters, not mother and daughter. She didn't understand the thought. She went up and kissed her mother on top of her head, through her wiry hair. Startled, her mother dropped a stitch. "What's got into you? I could have ruined this, and then where would I be?" They weren't a hugging or kissing family usually. Kay kissed her again on the same place. Her mother, pleased, reached back and swatted her on the leg.

Garnet got agitated if someone wasn't there by three o'clock to relieve her—there were no set times, but everyone made a point never to leave Ann alone—because RubyAnn was staying at her house now, and she came home from school at half past. "There's time, Mother; it's ten till three," she'd tell her. "You have to be there when they come home," Garnet said, "or it's no good." Then she'd add, for the twentieth time, "You recall how often Ann and Billy stayed with us. RubyAnn is just like Billy; you have to be there."

But RubyAnn wouldn't come to the hospital anymore. Not even Garnet could talk her into that. "She's like she's dead. I'm not going anymore." There had been that one yelling match and it was over. No one tried after that.

The Kansas family came. Her father and Opal, when they knew her mother wouldn't be there. Drove up the six hours and stayed one, trying not to look at their watches. She saw her father at least a couple of times every year. He stayed with her when he came through on his semi-annual route through the northern part of the state, still selling the same line of car polish he always had. Still spent months on the road. Fit, suntanned, trim. Opal. She remembered Grandmother saying about Opal, "I've seen chickens that had more brains." Opal was the same; talkative, almost clucking with false enthusiasm to be back with the family.

People from the Kansas Day Picnic, which was held every other year now, came by. Neighbors of Ann's, women she'd worked with. A couple of flower growers from the coast stopped every Saturday, their delivery day. Sometimes the room was filled with visitors, others standing outside in the hall, talking to each other, going over the past, while Ann lay there sleeping away.

Religious people stopped by the room: they left cards with saints' pictures, homegrown flowers. Once they put them around Ann's pillow. It amused Kay at first: Ann a shrine, as if those nuts were looking for someone to venerate. When she came in one day and saw someone had drawn a small cross on Ann's forehead with a felt tip pen, though, she asked the nurses not to let anyone in the room but family. But not long after that she walked in and there were five of them on their knees, resting their heads on the bed, speaking in tongues to Ann. "She's just unconscious," she said to them, remaining calm. "She's going to wake up soon. And I want you to leave here now." They got up. A woman her mother's age explained at the door, "She's more than halfway there; she can't come back. But she can take a message." "Get out of here," Kay told her, louder than she meant to.

Kay got regular phone calls from Ruby, mostly at home, but sometimes at the hospital, person to person. "You're not busy, are you?" Ruby would start out, and whatever Kay was doing, she'd stop to listen, still, in spite of herself, interested in what Ruby had to say. "How is Ann?" The sound of the voice, the question, would infuriate her: it sounded manufactured, observing a death-watch decorum, the voice modulated to a whisper, as if she didn't want to wake Ann up. Then Ruby would go into why she had never come up, why she couldn't in the future, either.

Finally, alone with Ann, late at night, after visiting hours were over and the hospital was quiet, Kay would sit in the semidarkness thinking of her grandmother. Uncle Wally. "It's not up to me," she said aloud once. The sound of her voice startled her. Made her look around to see if anyone else was listening. She had to stop thinking these thoughts. Stop now.

But driving home she wondered who it *was* up to. Who was going to take the responsibility for making a choice? Stop it, she told herself. Stop it now.

She stopped off at home one afternoon because her shoes were soaked; it had been raining again. The place was too quiet, vacant. Rose didn't get back till later. She sat in the kitchen drying her feet with the dish towel. Rose wouldn't make a snide comment if she saw her, just say, "I'll get you a towel from the bathroom." She had developed bad habits, living alone. There were advantages, having Rose here, but she could be a real pain, too. On the other hand, she didn't mind cooking, cleaned up her mess, and was extremely neat, almost fastidious. In her person, in her room, in the whole house. Everything had its place now, from the *TV Guide* to Kay's shoes, which she usually just kicked off anywhere and then went looking for later, when she needed them. Rose picked them up and lined them up neatly in the closet rack.

It was hard to get used to having someone at home; the sound of another voice always caught her unawares. Before, she'd had to phone someone, Ann, her mother, a friend, to make small talk. But Rose could prattle on like a chirping bird. And it was amazing how much she knew about things. The name of every music group in the country—that was to be expected—but she understood what the government was doing or not doing, too. She knew the names of all the cabinet members, the leaders in the state and federal legislatures. Who could keep up with all that? They were always changing—fired, resigned, going to jail. Kay had given up on the government years ago, didn't even vote anymore. Rose read more newspapers and magazines in a week than Kay did in a month; Rose checked out magazines from the high school library that Kay had never even heard of before, and bought a couple of newspapers at random from the newsstand each day besides reading the *Examiner* and the *San Mateo Times*, which were delivered to the house. Ann hadn't read like that: mysteries, maybe, but not everything that was printed on paper. "How come you like the news so much?" Kay asked Rose once.

"In the seventh grade we had this teacher, Mr. Grant. He made us bring a clipping of a current event every morning, and we'd read it in front of the class and answer questions. It could be about anything. I just got used to it, reading the papers every day, magazines. Our high school librarian is always giving me articles to read. I asked her about one I'd heard about, and she got me a copy from another library. You know that saying 'I only know what I read in the newspapers'?" Rose started giggling. "That's why I read magazines too." She broke into whoops of laughter.

Kay started reading more herself. Rose brought home a form for registering to vote. Just left it on the end table, never mentioned it. After a week or so of seeing it there, Kay finally filled it out and sent it in. When the news came on, Rose would interpret. "Watch this guy now; he'll try to lay a smoke screen, but it's not going to work; he has no credibility left. He's on his way out." Then she'd explain why. It was like having your own anchorperson around.

She was putting the dish towel into the laundry hamper when she heard a noise. She cocked her head, listening for the sound. It came again. She looked at her watch. It was only two o'clock; Rose was still at school. She went down the hall. Her bare feet against the carpet didn't make a sound. Her bedroom door was open; there wasn't anyone in there. She went in and got her black shoes from the closet, shut the door quietly. This was silly, she knew. The security here in the complex was good. She was the last person to leave a door or window open. She turned the knob of the other bedroom door without making a noise, flung the door back. Rose was in bed, smiling, her arms crossed over the covers pulled up to her chin. Next to her was a boy, his elbows pointed at her, his hands locked behind his head. He was grinning. Kay was so surprised she was dumbfounded.

"We got wet," Rose explained, "and we're drying our clothes," and she glanced over at the open door of her bathroom. There were clothes hanging from the shower rod; the portable electric heater glowed orange red under them. "Our class had a demonstration at a computer firm, and we came here from there instead of going back to school. It was almost over, anyway."

Kay heard in her head, plain as day, control yourself. But what kept intruding, looking at the bed, was Ann, comatose, her body starting to form an S under the white hospital bedspread, her mouth slack. How could Rose do this while her mother was . . . what? her mind couldn't find the word. She heard her voice, loud, ask, "What's your name?" to the boy.

At his ease, promptly, with middle-class assurance, he answered politely, "Cliff. Clifford Locke."

"Get the hell out of here, Clifford," she yelled as loud as she could. He looked surprised. Rose threw the covers back—she was in her peach-colored half slip and white tank top—grumbling, "What is this, a prison," went into the bathroom, and got the pair of trousers. Came back, thudding her heels like stones against the floor, saying, "Do you mind, Aunt Kay?" as she handed the pants to Clifford.

She backed out of the room, shutting the door. Marched back to the front room and picked up a magazine. Tried not to listen to the whispering at the opening and closing of the front door. Rose came back and sat down beside her on the couch. "Do you want to eat something before we go down to the hospital?" Kay was so surprised at the question she couldn't answer, just stared back at Rose. "He was just a friend, Aunt Kay, no big deal. It's not like I'm going with him or anything." Rose went on in the same breath, "I boiled some eggs this morning after you left. I'll make us a deviled-egg sandwich before we go. I'll use mustard." Rose was careful, didn't allow her to gain weight, no mayonnaise, ever. It was as if she, Kay, were the sixteen-year-old and needed to be comforted.

She drove relaxed in the heavy traffic: she'd always found a certain kind of satisfaction, for some reason, to be among the long lines of cars five rows wide passing the same number of cars and people going the opposite direction, separated only by two strips of yellow paint. Maybe it was the satisfaction that she could keep her place for hours, if necessary, both herself and her car holding up under the test. The stop and go movement was soothing. Rose kept talking as if nothing had happened of significance, giving her opinion on how the governor in his last evening's news conference had proved beyond doubt he was a registered dimwit, being funny, making Kay laugh. So when she interrupted with "I hope you're being careful, Rose," she surprised even herself. Rose looked puzzled. "Taking precautions. Contraception. Safe sex," she said louder.

"What for?" Rose asked.

Kay forgot to breathe, to take in her next breath. She had to slam on the brakes before she rear-ended the Ford in front of her.

"Oh, I get it," Rose said. "I know what you mean. I better tell you something. I decided a long time ago, when I was eleven or so, in junior high, that I wasn't going to seriously consider sex until I was a lot older, maybe twenty. I didn't know enough then and I don't now. The whole business is too physical, too personal to take a chance on random choice. Exchanging the big L word isn't reason enough in my book. And besides, it always makes me think of traipsing around in P.E. on the way to the shower, trying to cover yourself with just two hands, only a thousand times worse."

That explanation seemed to satisfy Rose, because she went on talking about the governor. Had Kay missed something? Was she listening carefully enough? But it didn't seem to be a communication problem, or even a time problem, a lapse between generations. It was a point of view problem, a set of instructions she hadn't read yet that Rose understood. She had to take her time, listen, figure out where she could obtain a copy of the directions.

Garnet gave Rose a ride home so Kay could stay. It was getting harder to sit in the quiet room. She'd muse, listening to the discussion in her head, trying to get all the voices to speak at length. She wasn't her grandmother. Her Uncle Wally had begged to die. Ann wasn't even conscious. She lay there with her mouth in a parody of a smile. Happy now? But in the end, it was going to be up to her. How many years was it going to take? To be sure, to convince herself that Ann had really died on the operating table and now she should be buried? But comatose patients came back, woke up in three or four years, sometimes. Longer, even. Was she going to judge? Her grandmother had. Wally's severed spine was enough. It was her obligation to do something. But what?

She'd been almost eighteen, a little older than Rose, when her grandmother died. The family had known it was coming, after the two operations. The last one they hadn't done anything, cut her open, saw there was nothing they could do. She sat in her straight-backed chair, an afghan over her knees, after the surgery. She refused to get in bed during the day, no matter what. Kay stayed with her on weekends and vacations, stopped by every afternoon after school.

"Just wait until I get stronger," she'd say. "Gain my strength back. We'll go to the movies." She liked sitting in the theater. TV screens weren't big enough for her. "You can't believe what people say if they're only three inches high."

She knew she was dying. "I don't have any regrets, I did what I wanted to do most of my life. Never made an enemy, not to this day," and she'd knock wood on the arm of her chair. Kay knew it was a saying, and they both knew it wasn't true in her grandmother's case: Kay's own mother couldn't stand her, hadn't talked to her in four years. "I would have done some things differently, of course. Everyone says that. But I wouldn't change anything I did." Another time she announced, "I'm seventy-three years old, and what I miss most about before is the horses. It was a pleasure to harness a good horse up to a wagon and know he was going to do his best for you. And you in return would respect him by not overloading, not going too far. You took care of him and he took care of you. Just like a member of the family."

"What about the Chrysler?"

Her grandmother had thought a minute. "You can't talk to something made of steel, glass and rubber and hope for any understanding. Am I boring you, Kay?"

"You couldn't if you tried."

"Where was I?"

She hadn't really believed her grandmother could die. She knew there were cemeteries, filled, but not with people like her grandmother. They had to be there. To comment on things, to remember what went before. What it was like in Kansas in 1893. Seeing Theodore Roosevelt when he came to her grammar school in a coach drawn by six yellow Belgian horses.

The family assumed Grandmother wanted to be taken back to Kansas when she died to be buried next to her husband. But no one would broach the subject as she lay dying. It was too close to asking about her will, which no one wanted to mention. Her bank accounts, bonds and properties were legend in the family. Finally Kay asked, for her father.

"There's no sense in going back there in a box. There's no one back there anymore. And I've lived out here thirty-odd years, so I might as well stay here. I'd like to think I'm a transplanted Kansas cottonwood, but the tree turned into a California redwood without me even knowing. And besides, no one would come and visit me back there."

She remembered her sitting in her chair in so much distress she couldn't breathe by herself, using the plastic mask attached to a green oxygen tank for air. When she found it hard to talk at length, Kay got her one of those magic slates: you could write and then erase by flipping up the cellophane cover. She was amused. Wrote: Kay, this is a good trick, to make words disappear just like people. Kay couldn't answer anything. She'd given in, decided her grandmother *was* going to die, after a year of watching and waiting. Not because she was old or couldn't breathe enough anymore. But because she'd given up her place in the family. She didn't want to know anymore about her son Lester running off with Opal. She didn't care if her daughter-in-law Garnet was miserable. Or that her granddaughter Kay was waiting for her to do something about it.

Kay invited her mother and RubyAnn for dinner. Rose cooked. It was important to try to keep Ann's family intact, for the sisters to be together. Rose could always go over and see RubyAnn, of course, but she hadn't so far.

What had she expected? RubyAnn and Rose barely talked. Sat there eating like two rabbits. Rose tried. "How's the jumping?"

"Okay," RubyAnn said.

Garnet added, "She's done her best height so far, in the backyard last Tuesday. She's got legs like a grasshopper when it comes to jumping."

RubyAnn kept getting up to refill Garnet's coffee cup. Already she was picking up Garnet's Kansas twang, duplicating the way she held her fork and leaned in and over the plate as if someone might try to grab it away. Kay's own table manners came from her grandmother; at her house she'd practiced sitting up straight and bringing the food forkful by forkful to her mouth to be chewed twenty-eight times. She'd practiced on her own when she realized she talked like her mother. She must have been ten, in the fifth or sixth grade. She'd trained herself not to have that twang by listening to herself; when she caught herself slipping, she'd bite down hard on her lip. She could imitate them all at will, but she didn't want to sound like her mother, or her grandmother, for that matter.

After dinner they watched the news. Was Rose taking on any of her characteristics, Kay wondered, like RubyAnn was her mother's. She didn't notice any. What traits did she have to pass on, anyway? Former overweight glutton, good at taking care of other people's money, and her own. Efficient. This one plus Rose did not consider worthy of imitation. She approached all problems, tasks, hurdles, hoops, life in general in a higgly-piggly manner and with loud raucous laughter. She was laughing now, in fact. "My theory is," she was saying, "that given the chance, every politician will succumb to the most efficient and direct way of corrupting themselves."

"So what would you do to change things?"

"That's easy. First, require everyone to vote. Give them a hundred dollars off on taxes."

"I'd vote then," Kay said.

"Have a national election-day holiday in the middle of the week—no one has to work that day. Second, make lists of public-service volunteers, and for some elective positions, draw names from the list by lottery for the nominations."

"We better get you home," Garnet said to RubyAnn. "It's past eight."

Once they'd left, after RubyAnn pecked Kay good-bye on the cheek but passed up Rose without even a see you, Rose went on with her theory as they loaded the dishwasher. "Third, I'd move the capital of the country to a more central place. Or better yet, have a rotating capital, going from state to state year by year." Rinsing the knives, Kay realized suddenly that no one had mentioned Ann the whole evening. She hadn't even thought of her. Not until now, when she looked at the clock and realized Billy was at the hospital. It was like her heart was a siren and went off: it made her body hurt like she was slowly coming apart from the sound. She wanted to let out a wail as loud as she could. She stopped in midstride, reaching down to put a handful of silverware in the basket.

"When they get all through with the fifty, start over again. That was . . . what's wrong, Aunt Kay?" Rose noticed everything.

She had to answer. Let it all out. "We never talked about Ann tonight. Your mother. Not one word. How she was doing. Or something she did in the past. Nothing."

"It's not that we forgot her," Rose said. "A person can't just worry all the time about something you can't change."

"Like the stupid government, Rose?"

"No, the government you might not fix, but you can tinker with it, alter things here and there. That might make a difference for the next generation. But there's nothing we can do in her case."

Kay yelled back, "Mother. Why don't you say *mother*. My mother. You always avoid that word. My mother," she yelled.

Rose turned off the faucet, dried her hands, and walked off.

"What now?" she thought when she picked up the phone and heard a secretary say "Rutherford B. Hayes Continuation School, please hold." Click.

Another voice. "This is Jim Erickson, Principal. I understand you're Rose's guardian."

Kay wanted most to ask what's she done now? "That's right," she managed to say.

"We'd like to put Rose on the list to see the district psychologist."

"Is there any particular reason?"

"She was recommended by a counselor. Apparently there's a family situation she's having difficulty coping with. Just someone to talk to. Problems seem so big at that age."

"Have you asked Rose?"

"No, we haven't; we usually get permission from the parents first and then the school sets up an appointment."

"Ask her, and I'll think about it. By the way, why do you spend so much time making those plaster of paris casts?"

"I wasn't aware it was an excessive amount of time. The students seem to enjoy the experience. It's part of our art/geography/history/clothing unit."

"I understand the art part, and maybe history, but the geography and clothing? I don't see the connection."

"When they replicate, say, Alexander the Great, a personal hero of mine, they learn what color to paint his clothes. We're big on accuracy. We use encyclopedias, videotapes, and so forth."

"I see," Kay said.

"And the geography, well, if they have extra time, they look up where he lived and so forth."

"How interesting for sixteen- and seventeen-year-olds," Kay said.

"I thought so when we organized the unit. Hands-on history, we call it."

When Rose came in to her office that afternoon, Kay asked, "How's Genghis Khan?"

"We're making the Three Stooges now on the sly. Some of the kids are doing the twelve apostles," Rose said, pouring herself a glass of water from the cooler.

"Did you talk to the principal? He said he'd ask you first."

"I don't want to see a psychologist. My home life is almost bearable." Rose was trying not to crack up. "You're normal, aren't you, Aunt Kay?"

"Sometimes. It's up to you."

Driving to the hospital, Kay asked, "You want to go to a private school? Business school? You don't have to go there."

"I've been thinking about that," Rose said. "I put in for the equivalency test. The end of the month, I think." She paused. Kay waited. "Maybe I'll get a job. I should probably start getting better organized. With the situation like it is."

"You mean your mother?"

"That and RubyAnn. I'd like her not to think what I'm doing is the best way to go. Copy me. If she—my mother—doesn't wake up, I should be ready. I can't live off you the rest of my life."

"I'm keeping strict accounts at 9 percent interest." Rose gave her a poke in the ribs.

The swing shift had changed at the hospital, the visitors were all inside the rooms, and the halls were quiet. Billy was sitting by the bed reading Ann a story from one of his magazines. She lay curled up on her side. Whoever'd combed her short bushy hair had put a bright blue ribbon around it with a bow on top. Billy motioned to his throat to Rose and handed her the magazine. She started reading. He went out in the hall for a drink. There was no physical resemblance at all, but Rose was like Billy, it dawned on her. Determined, a kind of endurance that never ran down. He would be here for another twenty years, or however long Ann lasted, hoping. Never giving up on her or himself. Reading book after book, going through whole libraries, if that's what it took. He would never understand having to put an end to it. She followed him out into the hallway.

"I get dry," he said, taking another drink from the fountain. "I think she's listening. I know she can hear me. It's like when we were kids and we used to hide at night under the blankets with the flashlight to read. Till you two wanted to go to sleep. But I never wanted you to stop till the chapter was finished and always talked you into reading on, even after Ann was asleep. And the next day Ann would say I remember, I wasn't asleep; I can tell you the story. And one time she did."

When they were ready to leave, Rose touched Ann's forehead with her fingertips. Then her cheeks, along her eyebrows, her lips, nose, then around her jaw, outlining her face. Billy didn't resume reading until they were out of the room.

In the car, Rose asked, "Do you think she'll wake up?"

"I don't know," Kay said.

"What'll happen then, if she stays that way?"

"Sooner or later her body will atrophy. Stiffen. Curl up like an old carrot." Why was she being so brutal? "Then things will start breaking down until she dies. It could take years."

"Who's paying for this now, and what happens later?" Rose asked the question as if Kay were showing her how to operate a new machine at the office.

"She's fully covered for six months, which means about 85 percent. But she's in a group plan too, and I'm still trying to get them to say what they'll do."

"Then what, after that runs out?"

"Then you and RubyAnn will have to decide things. Sell the house and the shop. To keep her going longer, with good care. The state helps when everything's gone." Rose didn't ask anything else, but Kay couldn't stop. "You two kids will get your father's social security until you're eighteen; that won't change. RubyAnn can finish high school. Your mother has some investments in your names. There's probably enough to send you through college or buy a car or take a trip, whatever you choose."

"My mother's going to wake up," Rose said, looking straight ahead. "She's too hardheaded not to. I'll bet you by my birthday."

They were both sitting in the front room, she at her grandmother's old desk, first Saturday morning of the new month, writing checks out for household bills, Rose stretched out on the couch, reading a magazine. Talking back and forth. Kay heard her voice ask, "Do you remember your father?" She startled both of them with the question. She was embarrassed: "You don't have to answer. It just came into my head; I'd never thought of it before."

"I don't mind," Rose said. She rested the magazine flat against her stomach, thinking. "I was six, almost seven, when he died. RubyAnn was two. I know what he looked like. But what I remember most was that day. Mom and I were sitting on a gray blanket spread out on the sand. The tide was going out. It was cold. RubyAnn was in the back seat of the car; it was parked right behind us on the beach. My father was putting on his black rubber wet suit; it had two yellow stripes down the sides. He had to really tug to get the bottom part on; it was too tight. Mom was telling him he was gaining weight and should get a size bigger.

"When he was ready, he strapped his mask up on top of his head and said I'm going to bring home the bacon or something like that, Midwest talk. Then he bent down and pushed my wool stocking cap further down over my head to keep my ears warm. Picked up the clamming fork that was leaning against the bumper of the car and started walking toward the surf. My mother called after him, 'Get enough and I'll make clam chowder.' He turned and raised the fork in the air that he'd heard.

"I must have taken a nap then because I don't remember anything until Uncle Billy was there. And the helicopter was going up and down the beach. There were a lot of people. Mom was crying." Rose had sat up as she talked, and now she stood up. "It's time," she said, making a joke of their sparse lunches. She broke up the lettuce while Kay put out the bowls and the diet dressing. They were going to have a treat because it was Saturday, add beets, grated carrots, string beans, and then a big spoonful of low-fat cottage cheese to the lettuce.

While they were eating, Rose went on: "I knew what dead meant then. I understood he wasn't coming back. The Easter before, I'd got a bunny, an angora rabbit. He died, and when he died we had a funeral in the backyard. Me, Mom and RubyAnn. Put flowers all over him in a shoe box. Buried him. Put his name in pencil on a cross we made out of sticks. I must have forgotten what Mom told me when he died. Because about three months later I convinced myself Oscar was alive and hungry and I had to feed him. So I dug him up to give him some food."

Kay kept her eyes on her bowl.

"RubyAnn doesn't remember Dad. We talked about him later. Dad this or Dad that. But not that much. Mother always answered when we asked about him, but never mentioned him on her own. Never. I feel guilty sometimes that I don't think about him anymore. Sometimes something will remind me, but not very often." Kay had finished her salad, and Rose hurried to catch up so they could go to the hospital.

Rose received her equivalency test score on May second. She came down to the office after school and put the slip of paper in front of Kay, who read it after she got done on the phone. She didn't get a chance to comment until Rose came by with an armload of folders to file. "What now?" she asked. She wondered if that was the right thing to say. She worried too much which way Rose was going to jump at a word, a look, a suggestion. But Rose knew about irony and could laugh at herself some of the time. Children were treated a lot like wild animals that were bigger than their trainers, she decided. Elephants or polar bears. But Rose was not a child.

"I don't know," Rose said. "I"m going to have to think about it."

"Whatever you decide, take your time. I'm sure it'll be interesting," Kay said, stopping herself from adding, "Think, for a change." Later, when it wasn't so busy, she phoned a longtime client, who gave her a number to call. She got an answer from the private number at the capitol building on the first try.

"We start the interns out at the beginning of the school year."

"Oh," Kay said. "What kind of requirements?"

"Usually they're kids on the fast track. Good grades. Ambitious. Think politics is where the action is. Like the power as well as the glamour."

"How do you apply? I have a niece . . ."

"May I call you Kay?"

"Certainly."

"When Gwen gave you this number, Kay, she expected me to tell you straight. She'd be angry if she found out different. It could save you some time."

"Go ahead," Kay said.

"These nine positions for gofers are for kids with some juice. It's a prestigious job; something they get to put on their resumes, intern. Their parents usually are big contributors and so forth, or have some other in. Not always, but most of the time. And I'll tell you something else. These people here are not who I'd want my daughter or son to associate with, to tell you the truth. The only kids I've ever seen benefit from the experience were the ones who like to watch things, step back and look. That's not very clear, but not like TV. Like state government as a spectacle."

"That's Rose," Kay said. "She thinks it's Gilbert and Sullivan. An operetta. She thinks they ought to be made to sing when they hold hearings and when they're in session."

"How old is she?"

"Almost seventeen. She's passed the high school equivalency test."

"There's an opening, an intern that got pregnant, left abruptly. We weren't going to fill the slot. How soon could Rose start? Just to finish this month, another three weeks. Can she use a computer?"

"She's good."

"Tomorrow morning. Ten sharp, be at my office. The guard at the door will show her where to go. Tell her to wear comfortable clothes, not to dress up. Tell her it's going to be just like going to the circus."

When Kay mentioned the offer on the way home from work, Rose started laughing.

"What's so funny?" Kay hadn't known what to expect, but not so much hilarity that Rose couldn't speak.

"I've been out of school for five hours and you find me work." And she started laughing away. Kay couldn't see what was so funny.

She loaned Rose her car for the commute to Sacramento. Stood on the curb in her slippers waiting for her to put the key in the ignition. "Don't worry," Rose kept saying, "if I don't like it, I'll come right back."

"You'll do fine," Kay said for the third time. When Rose finally drove off, she watched until she got to the corner and made the turn out of sight. She felt really tired.

She kept Ann informed, sitting by the hospital bed in the semidarkness. About Rose's job, how she'd come home with an appetite; how she'd cooked a Kansas meal, pot roast, mashed potatoes, white gravy, carrots, peas, and chocolate cake and ice cream for dessert, Friday night to celebrate. Rose hadn't volunteered much about the job beyond "I don't know yet. But I never felt like taking a nap, like at high school. And I don't think politics are irrelevant to our lives. I had an argument with some of them over that." And RubyAnn broke the league high jump record by a foot. She had started to grow, Garnet reported, penciling the record on the doorjamb like she had for the three of them, one and a half inches in two months. Kay spent nearly two hours talking, giving up all the news she'd accumulated. It felt good, like a transfusion of nourishing vitamins and minerals going from herself to Ann. Not that it was really unusual, she decided after she'd finished, to talk so much. Ann normally let her do all the talking anyway.

Ann looked exactly like she was asleep. Her eyes closed, her knees drawn up a little more. For the first time she could remember, Ann looked at peace. Happy, almost. As if she had no worries. She couldn't end it, put her in the ground to be covered up by yards and yards of dirt. Would her hair turn gray when she was asleep like this, in five years, in ten years? Would she allow that much time to pass, telling herself another week, another year? In God's hands, she thought. Hands. Fingers. She couldn't imagine a God's hands. Only her grandmother's hands.

No one in the family had ever gone to church. It was because of her grandmother, who'd had an uncle who was a minister "and a hypocrite," she'd always added. "You can't advise people on good and bad and escape that fate." And her mother had always said, "They're not hypocrites; it's plain unvarnished greed.

Like any other business." Billy was the only one who'd gone, off and on. His wives were churchgoers. Ann, never. She herself thought religion had lost so much ground in their time because of TV. If religion could survive mass communication, God had to be a comic, a tease. If Jesus came back today, he'd have to come as Curley in the Three Stooges. Her grandmother had said once, when someone offered to pray for her to ease her pain, "If I want comfort, I'll get me a softer pillow for my rocker."

Billy came in. "Any day now," he said. "I've got a feeling. One of the day shift nurses said she heard a groan yesterday. Can't be long. Some just take more time to recover than others."

Kay couldn't shift away from what she was thinking for a minute; she didn't say anything back. "Are you awake?" Billy asked.

"Come to dinner next Sunday," Kay said.

"Can't; have to work."

"The Sunday after that. The girls like to see you."

"I saw RubyAnn break the record. She's like a kangaroo, that kid."

She realized that Billy was always around—at the girls' birthdays, school functions. He took them to the museum, aquarium, zoo. Camping. Uncle Billy. Or was he just being Billy? Neither had kids to raise. But she'd never think of going to a track meet. Was *he* her grandmother, with that feeling for family? Treating it like some exotic flower, worthy of constant attention? She did all the maneuvering of everyone, and Billy did the watching. Knowing the answer, she asked, "Do you still go to church?"

He didn't look surprised, just shook his head. "I go to Breakfast Lions, that's enough. I went before because they did—Norma and Jennifer, I mean. I went to Masons once because Dad was one back in Kansas."

"Do you think it would hurt if we prayed? Let those religious people back in here?"

"You mean the ones that pass out those will forms to leave a little something to their church, the ones that say, what do you have to lose, if you're dying?"

She laughed too. "Sunday after next," she said. "We'll be expecting you." She paused at the door. Billy had already taken up the thick book he'd been reading lately to Ann. She wanted to tell him about what she'd been thinking, how sometimes she felt she had to stop Ann from turning into a machine-breathing corpse, to let her die naturally. How she couldn't stop thinking about it sometimes. He was waiting for her to go before he started in. The book was open. "I'll see you," she said.

She was finding it hard to concentrate, even to sit at her desk any length of time. She'd get up and wander, sometimes into the other offices, sometimes all the way out to the sidewalk. One of her first investments: a turn-of-the-century Victorian three-story she'd bought for nothing and turned into her place of business. She looked up into the summer sun: the paint was still good. It must have been five or six years since the last coat. She went back inside and got her purse.

She drove fast so as not to change her mind, thinking it was too late now to take Rose over to the coast to see Ann's flowers, to tell her how she'd tossed the seeds out the window. Now she was working; there was no time. Most of the wildflowers would be gone now anyway. She parked in front of her mother's house, the place she'd grown up in. She didn't like thinking about the house, much less coming back.

Her mother tried not to look surprised when she opened the door. Welcomed her, backing up to leave the doorway clear for her to pass. Offered her tea and cookies. A visitor would call it cheerful: sunlight coming through the old venetian blinds, illuminating bars of shag rug and overstuffed sofa and chair. Dusted. Her high school graduation picture still on the TV, mortarboard with the tassel in front. Propped up next to it was a new Polaroid photo: she had to get up and look closer to see who was in it. RubyAnn in her sweats, looking noncommittal. Her mother was talking from the kitchen, clinking cups against saucers, opening and closing drawers louder than necessary, she thought, suddenly irritated.

Her mother had got the house when she divorced her father, and now it was worth a bundle in California real estate. The lot was apartment-house size, two hundred by four hundred. Kay had insisted at the time that she get rid of it. "Why do you want this place?" It wasn't only so she wouldn't have to come back. "I'll buy you a smaller place, be easier to maintain."

Her mother'd refused. "It's the first house I ever lived in that I owned." She'd worked until she retired a couple of years ago, in their old grammar school cafeteria as a cook. Not once in the last twenty years had she ever failed to mention within at least the first five minutes of conversation that Lester her husband had run off with Opal her sister as if that was the most important thing that had ever happened in her whole life.

Her mother came in with a tray. She had acquired some genteel ways—from her mother-in-law, Kay realized: her grandmother would have brought in the same kind of tray, but she wouldn't have left the canned milk in its can. Her mother's family had been so poor in Kansas that when her mother died she and her two sisters had dug the grave in the county cemetery to save money. "Where was your father?" she'd asked as a kid.

"He was off."

"Where?"

"That time he'd gone to Missouri, I think it was, to meet a man who'd found a way to roll cigars with a machine, a thousand a day. He wanted to see it with his own eyes, just to shake the man's hand, if it was true. He was that kind of a person. He was hard on himself as well; he walked the whole of the four counties. We were too poor to have a horse, much less a car. Left us in a shack; we did what we could. Hired out to clean up. When she got sick, we just watched, wiped away the fever sweat. Your Grandmother Cortner came when she heard and drove her into town, but it was too late. She never said it after that, but before, every time we came to borrow something she always made fun of us: 'Well now, come in, come in; if it isn't the Stecker jewels, Ruby, Opal and Garnet. What can I do for you today?' She stopped even thinking it when I married your father."

Over the years her mother's stories had become more specific, the facts sharper, as if with time certain incidents were revealed in their final meaning. Kay had always turned the subject to something else. She'd always liked hearing the Kansas stories from her grandmother, even from the few old clients she had left who'd come about the same time, after the war, from Kansas to California. But not her mother's. She found it hard to stay in the same room with her mother. She became aggravated. Irritable. Upset. Something.

Her mother sipped her tea, unusually quiet, as if she were thinking something over.

"Mother," she started out. She wanted her to know it was a formal question. "What would you want if you were Ann, lying in the hospital?"

She didn't hesitate. "Just what we're doing, taking care of her kids. Getting on with things."

"I mean with Ann. Just leave her to dry up, wither away in a bed for twenty years until some organ fails?"

"If it was me, I'd want to die, not be a burden on anyone. But I can't speak for Ann. It's not easy," she said, talking slow in her Kansas voice, "to watch anything die. Whether it takes ten minutes or ten years. But there are worse things." Kay knew better than to ask what, but that didn't stop her mother. "Have someone stop caring about you. I was fourteen when my mother died. But it was worse when your father left me."

This was too hard, Kay decided. She wasn't going to get an answer, or the right answer, or any answer, from her mother. She finished her tea so she could leave. Suddenly the front door opened and RubyAnn yelled out, "Auntie, I'm home, I'm home, I'm home," and broad-jumped from the threshold to the middle of the room.

"I can see that," her mother said.

RubyAnn came in talking a mile a minute. "They let us out early because they had a meeting and might strike next month if they don't get what they want." Stopped when she saw Kay. Went over and sat next to her mother. Reached for the cookies.

"How are you?" Kay asked.

"I'm fine," RubyAnn said. That was all.

It wasn't until she got out on the sidewalk that Kay realized she wasn't any more or less agitated when she came out than when she went in. One of them was getting older. Or mellower. She was going to have to be more observant about herself. But she knew now what to do. Or what not to do. Grandmother had made a choice, for right or wrong, and lived with the consequences. I can't speak for Ann, her mother had said. That was a choice too.

She had to go get him, but Uncle Frank came too. He kept forgetting, got back out of the car three times to check if the burner on the stove was off, to get his Chesterfields—he allowed himself three a day now, to leave a note on the door in case Rupert and Prince came by. Finally they got off the street and on their way. Would she ever be that patient for her mother, she wondered.

Rose had stayed home to get the dinner ready. She took her grandfather's hat and made sure he got the chair with the ashtray nearby. A big glass of ice water, all that anyone would be drinking, with Frank at the dinner table.

Billy came next, a little flustered—he'd had to leave Ann about halfway through the chapter—still carrying the volume, as if he might need it there too. When he put it down, Kay had a peek. Hubert Bancroft, *History of California*, Vol. XIX. She opened it at the bookmark. There was a half page of footnotes, a list of mission possessions for the year 1809: 1200 mules, 1600 chickens, 3181 sheep, 179,000 steers. No wonder Ann was still in a coma. She laughed out loud.

The sound made Uncle Frank jump. Rose came out of the kitchen to see. Billy came back from the bathroom. "Don't lose my place!" She knew Billy read every word, too. They wouldn't think it was funny, she decided. But Rose would. RubyAnn and her mother came in, took off their matching pea-soup green cardigans, and started cutting the french bread.

It wasn't supposed to be a festive occasion, but everyone was smiling when they sat down to supper. My family, Kay thought, lifting the mashed potatoes to her mother, when the phone rang. "It's always something," Uncle Frank said as Kay got up.

"Hello," she said.

"I take a little longer than expected to recover, and you all abandon me," Ann said. "Boy, do I feel groggy. If you're still as slim as before, you're probably trying to fit into my clothes too."

"Ann," Kay managed.

Her mother heard. "She's awake?" she asked. Kay could only nod.

"I knew it," Billy said; "as soon as I leave, she pulls this." He was up and on his feet with the rest following him out, leaving the front door open. Kay looked across the dinner table: the roast was still steaming, condensation was dribbling down the outside of the water glasses.

"So what's new?" Ann asked.

"Not much," Kay said. "Same old thing."

Billy, 1983
Yosemite

If she wants to stay with me, I'm going to keep her," Garnet said.

"Mother, you can't," Kay said. "RubyAnn belongs with Ann. You don't just keep someone because they want to stay with you. And it's what Ann wants, not what you want."

Why was it, Billy thought, that Kay could deal so well with everyone except her own mother. They just naturally took opposite points of view. Even Ann at her worst could at least hear the other person out. No, that wasn't true. Not with their father. It must be the way they perceived the other person, in some continuing argument. Both Kay and his Aunt Garnet were hardheaded. Maybe Garnet was only opinionated. What was the difference? And what was he, then? Ann had told him once, in a restaurant, loud, so everyone could hear, that he had so many tread marks on him from people running over him he could be the tire industry's poster boy. It had struck him as funny and he'd laughed, which infuriated her even more.

"Mother," Kay was saying. Was it the same tone that Garnet had used on Kay when she was a girl? Did you get to be your own mother's mother when they got old? He was never going to find out. His own mother couldn't be bothered with Ann or him. It made things easier once he understood that. But not better. Who was his mother? His older sister Ann? She'd never have agreed to that. Garnet? He'd stayed with Garnet, for months, sometimes. No, she was always Aunty. This was like that book he used to read the girls, with the little bird asking everyone, "Are you my mother?" It was too late to matter, if not to know. Kay? The thought made him pause. Think back. He couldn't remember his real mother, not at home. No matter how hard he tried, or insisted he could re-member. And the woman he'd met that time in L.A. didn't want to be his mother. Didn't have time. Didn't want to admit she'd had another life. Another family. A daughter and a son. Was it genetic? Blood? No, it had to be acts that one person did for another. Kindnesses. Without thought of reward. Without reservation. There was no doubt that his father was his father. Ann's father. Common knowledge shared between them. Certain characteristics. Subtle im-itations, on their part.

Kay used to take him everywhere. Only four years older, she'd walk the nine blocks from her house to include him. Take him by the hand, Ann following along, skipping, playing hopscotch on the sidewalk squares. Wherever Uncle Lester and Aunt Garnet went, they always took Ann and him. Even then, he knew it was Kay who insisted. He couldn't tie his shoe laces in second grade, not well enough to last the whole day at school. The other kids made fun of him. His laces were always loose, whipping around his feet, like strands of spa-ghetti. Kay would walk over in the morning, the opposite direction from her junior high, and double tie his shoe laces. This was after she'd spent hours showing him how. "See, this is easy," she'd say. "You're just lazy," Ann would yell. But Kay would repeat, "It's easy, Billy, you'll catch on." And he did. One day he reached down and tied the double knot and it stayed, just like it had so far today. He glanced down to be sure.

Kay wasn't twelve now. She looked her age. After all those years of dieting she was thin, but her face had sagged around the mouth without the extra pounds, and her forehead had permanent straight lines like a music staff. She didn't look like her mother, but she looked comfortable with herself. Assured. "What do you think?" she asked him.

He wasn't ready, hadn't really given any thought to the situation. RubyAnn didn't want to stay with her mother because Ann was acting strange and it scared her. She wanted to go back and live with Garnet. Who wanted her. He said the first thing that came to mind, something he'd been wanting to do for a couple of years. "I'd like to take RubyAnn to Yosemite." He went on with the idea. "Talk to her. Explain to her that Ann is going to get better." He paused. "And that she can help her mother."

"I haven't been there in years," Garnet said. Kay rolled her eyes.

He never hesitated. "Of course, I'll have to ask RubyAnn first if she wants to go, but come with us, Garnet. The tourists will be gone now, or at least there won't be so many."

"When do you think you'll go?"

"I'll phone, see what kind of reservations I can get. Are you up to camping?"

"I can do anything," Garnet said. They both laughed. Her enthusiasm was catching. Kay was watching, not with amusement. Dismay? As if he'd sidetracked her, made it impossible for her to finish grappling with the problem she'd started after. Put it off; he was an expert at that.

He stopped by Kay's office to let RubyAnn know about the trip. She'd worked for Kay last summer, and now she put in three days a week after school. It had been her idea; she'd gone down on her own and asked the manager—Kay wasn't there—for an application. "Aren't you a little young?" the manager had asked. "We need someone to run the copy machines." RubyAnn had just turned fourteen and looked more like ten or twelve. But she could run the copy machines. Kay hired her when she saw the application.

He looked into the copy room from the hallway. She was wearing a skirt here, he noticed. He hadn't seen her in one since she was a little girl. Dresses Ann made for her, then. Usually jeans or sweats now. But the skirt didn't make her seem more feminine. It was askew, the back zipper over to one side, and hiked up high around her waist. And the blouse was too small in the shoulders because she'd lifted weights the last eight or nine months, and now her upper arms were rounder than her skinny legs. She had dressed up for work. Who was she imitating? Not Ann or Garnet. Kay? Intent on unwrapping a ream of paper to reload a tray, RubyAnn didn't notice him in the doorway. He'd already talked to her on the phone, and he was sure that Garnet had mentioned it to her. She had been noncommittal. "I don't want to go camping," was the first thing she said.

"They have cabins, tents and hotels. We can go any route you want."

"Let me think about it," she'd said.

He crossed from the copy room to Kay's open door. "Madam, is there any chance of employment for me here? I need to make a lot of money, fast." His jokes were never that funny, but Kay always laughed. "How's the number factory?"

"Couldn't be better," Kay said. "I was thinking about you. Whether you should be incorporated, now that your barbecue sauce is catching on a little more. You're making enough now that it's getting hard to put it places where the I.R.S. can't take big chunks out of it."

"Do what you like," he said. "Money doesn't mean anything to me. Now that I have some." She laughed at that, too. "I thought I'd stop and give one of your employees a ride home, since I'm going that way."

She motioned him closer to her desk. In a low voice she said, "She's so unlike Rose that it's startling. In a month, Rose was trying to run the place. She stays with that one set of machines and runs that. Never even looks around. I know, I know, they're different people, but I expected . . . I don't know what I expected."

When RubyAnn finally saw him standing two feet from her, she waved over the noise of the copier with a shy lift of the hand. Rose would have yelled Uncle Billy and given him a big hug. It was only natural to make comparisons; how else could you understand differences. When the machine came to a stop on its own, he said, "This Friday. I have the reservations confirmed."

She was so serious. Didn't she ever laugh? "Aunty too?" she asked.

"She's coming. She mentioned she was going to bring her clothesline rope in case you and she wanted to go mountain climbing." RubyAnn peered at him as if somewhere on his face or chest was written the meaning of what he said, or more information, so she could answer. "Well," he said, "you look like you're working hard."

"I like it here," she said. "I have time to think." He didn't know if he should ask about what, so he waited. She didn't say anymore.

"Do you still have time to jump, now?"

"In the morning," she said. "Before school. Then, instead of P.E., I have track practice. Three hours are enough. I do my weight program at night. My weights are in my room at Aunty's."

"Sounds like you're doing fine, then," he said. He always felt awkward with her, as if he was never able to get on the same channel. The closest he got was two or three pictures on the same TV screen, but he was never sure which one she was watching.

He tried not to overdo everything. Let them see for themselves. He didn't stop or pull over for the views like he did when he was alone or if he was with someone who hadn't been before. Didn't comment either, just drove, until he came to the place.

In this part of the valley the road ran in through the trees along the river that followed the round bumplike boulders that kept the water to its work. On the other side of the road piles of broken sharp-sided rock were waiting their turn, having fallen to make the smooth cliffs smoother, cliffs that still could pulse and move to shed their skin. No matter how many times he'd been here, this part always surprised him. Always made him stop to store up what he was seeing to take with him until the next time. No one's imagination could have designed this; no one could fit this into a theory or belief to diminish it.

"Uncle Billy, we've seen this now," RubyAnn said.

"I was just thinking," he said, starting the car up.

Garnet sat in the front with him; RubyAnn was in the back, her head resting on the front seat between theirs, quiet, listening to Garnet. "I remember this. Do you see that? A waterfall used to come down there. It must be the drought. Black oaks are turning. We went up the same time of year as this. During the war they put soldiers up here that had problems."

"What kind of problems?" RubyAnn asked.

"Bad ones; they couldn't forget things. The government thought this would be a good place for that."

"Was it?"

"The person we came to visit didn't think so. He said it was too quiet. He didn't like it. There were no tourists then. I don't think we passed another car, going or coming."

"Who was it?" RubyAnn asked. "Do I know him?"

"No, someone from home; he went back to Kansas."

"Should my mother be in a place like this?"

"Why do you say that?" He kept his voice neutral.

"Just because."

"There's nothing wrong with your mother."

"You wouldn't say that if you saw her sometimes."

He waited a minute; was going to point out that Ann had had major surgery and had been in a coma for months, had been home for only two weeks. But RubyAnn knew that already.

"There's the falls," Garnet said. "I'm surprised how well I remember everything."

He couldn't leave it, was going to ask even before he had the question in his own mind. "What did she do?"

RubyAnn must have known he'd ask, because with perfect timing she said, "She came in my room the week before last. Turned on the light. When I woke up, she was at the foot of my bed looking at me. I said something to her like Hi Mom. I hadn't looked at the clock yet. She started asking me questions then. Who are you? What are you doing here? I thought she was kidding me, trying to get me up. Then I saw it was only a little after three. She scared me. I said Mom, it's me, RubyAnn. She said, I'm having another dream, turned off the light and went out of the room."

"You never told me that," Garnet said.

"I thought I was the one having the dream. But the next night she woke me up when she did it to Rose."

"What did Rose do?"

"Told her to stop wandering around. Go back to bed. Had to get up and take her back into her own bedroom."

"She's just confused."

"That's what Rose said the next morning. I'm not going to live with her if Rosie leaves."

"Then who's going to be there with her?" he asked. He felt he had to take the conversation to the end. "Who's going to help her get well?"

"I don't know," RubyAnn said.

"I recall this," Garnet said, "this meadow. Must be fed by springs all year. The grass is always green all summer, like Kansas."

The trouble with the parks in California was they'd turned into wonders of the modern world. The places that had to be seen by everyone else. He said that out loud as they waited in a long line of cars to get into the parking area.

"Oh, I don't know," Garnet said. "It's not only the parks, it's all of California. When we went back home from here after the war, it was like we'd returned from paradise. What's it like, everyone asked. The jobs were out here. That's why we came back and stayed. A person had a chance to make something of himself. I don't blame any of these people for coming. Just saying California always made me feel hopeful."

"What do you think of this place?" he asked RubyAnn.

"Nice," she said. Then added, "It's beautiful. It looks like when I'm jumping, going backwards over the bar. The sky looks like it's falling and I'm coming down on top of it. It looks like that here, with those cliffs." She patted his shoulder.

They checked into the hotel. The place was busy; he waited in another long line at the desk. He wondered if this had been a good idea. This wasn't going to solve anything. More than likely, put things off for the weekend. It had been habit that made him want to take to the mountains when something came up like this. But he wasn't RubyAnn. And a different location didn't mean anything to most people. He'd taken Jennifer up here and she'd stayed in their room the whole time, watching her programs on TV. She hadn't wanted to be his wife. But he hadn't understood anything either, trying to force the issue. You don't come up with a solution just because you need one.

Garnet and RubyAnn went up to their room. He waited for them downstairs. He wasn't going to go over what had been said or what points he should try to make. He leaned back in the soft chair, made himself look around, watch the other guests. He couldn't look without trying to guess: newlyweds over there? How could he tell? Did women wear dresses like that any other time? Too formal for this place, but not for after a wedding.

"Uncle Billy, what are you thinking? Daydreaming?"

He gave a start; he hadn't seen them come up. "Speculating. On if those two waiting for the elevator are newlyweds."

"Hard to know anymore," Garnet said. "We used to say you could tell by the stars in their eyes. But now that couples live together before they marry, why go on a honeymoon? What is there to find out about each other?"

As Garnet was talking, RubyAnn took a few fast steps and followed the couple into the elevator. He looked at Garnet. "She wouldn't ask them, would she?"

She shrugged. "I don't know."

That's not part of the game, he thought. You just guess: knowing for sure isn't important. RubyAnn came down the stairs instead of the elevator. Walking straight, her shoulders back, perfect posture, as if she were taking the first step

175

of a run at the bar. She was never going to be pretty, he decided. She looked like two crossed popsicle sticks in brown cords and a green sweater. Her permed hair stuck out like a giant bird nest, made her look silly. A born wallflower, but completely unaware of it. Confident. A Kay.

"Can we walk down by that river we passed?" she asked, coming up.

"I don't see why not," Garnet said. They went out, passing the lobby coffee shop, stopping to watch as a waitress went by them with five strawberry sodas on a tray.

"We've got to come back here," he said. "We've got to see if they're as good as they look."

"You don't think they might run out before we get back?" Garnet said. The two of them laughed. RubyAnn looked puzzled, as if she were thinking wouldn't they have a whole freezer full of ice cream?

He wanted to ask well, what happened with the honeymoon couple, but missed his chance when they got outside and saw the cliffs. The place was like a kaleidoscope; you could give yourself a shake and see something no one had ever seen before. It was overwhelming. The only intrusion came from the Steller's jays, squawking and hopping around on the mat of yellow leaves like blue wind-up toys. No one spoke.

They walked along, not looking where they were going, not even watching their feet, because Garnet stumbled twice and he took her arm. He noticed she was stoop-shouldered now, as if she were carrying a heavy shopping bag. They passed what looked like Indian mortar holes in a big creek rock, but they could have been natural. RubyAnn just pointed. The river was low; it hadn't started raining yet. There was a pleasant odor of wood smoke from the camping area. RubyAnn went ahead, came back, then went down closer to the water, jumping from one boulder to another. Picked up a walking stick and threw that in a pool and picked up a feather. Held that out. He didn't know; shook his head; he couldn't tell. Brought back next a small pointed stone. "Arrowhead?" she asked.

Garnet took a look. "No," she said. "Not likely."

"Why not?" he asked. How could she be so sure about everything? She handed it back to RubyAnn.

"Because it's not worked. That kind of stone isn't the kind that can be chipped right."

"How do you know?" RubyAnn asked.

"When I was younger than you we used to find them all over the farm. After plowing, after a good rain. We used to gather them up in our aprons and take them back to the place. Then break them up on my father's anvil."

"What for?" RubyAnn asked.

"I'm getting to that."

He paid closer attention. He had never heard this one before. And over the years he'd listened to a lot of them: her stories were all circles: a beginning, an end, and a middle that came back to you again and again.

"We sold eggs. The chickens had to have some gravel in their crops or they couldn't grind up their food, and you didn't find rock in that part of the county. They'd pick up the pieces of arrowhead with their beaks just like they were pecking after a piece of corn."

They walked along. A wind that he could only see, not feel, stirred the very tops of the trees, but it made him think it was going to get cold that night. He could feel it in the toes that were missing on his right foot. They not only itched when he walked any distance, they hurt when he thought there was going to be a frost.

"Rose gave me a book," RubyAnn said, "and I read it twice." She was walking backwards in front of them. "It was about a woman and her brother in England who worked so hard—they had a farm, worse than yours, Aunty, in Kansas— and it was all for nothing. All because the brother didn't know when he had enough. The first time I didn't understand anything, but the second time I did. You can read it, Aunty; I'll bring it over."

"Remind me," Garnet said.

They made a loop and were back at the hotel. It was hard to go inside. He looked around the valley once more, almost a full circle. He had stopped taking photographs, sold his expensive cameras. It had been a relief not to have to fiddle with meters and lenses. To rely just on his memory. Garnet and RubyAnn were poised to go up the steps. He looked at his watch. "This isn't going to ruin our dinner?" he asked.

"Not mine," RubyAnn said.

"I'll only have one," Garnet said.

His hot fudge sundae was better than it looked, if that was possible. The chocolate sauce was still warm and malleable. Garnet was served hers last but finished first, not even pausing for a breath. RubyAnn couldn't finish, slid hers over for Garnet. He barely made it himself. "What do you guess?" he asked them. "Were they honeymooners or not? The two in the elevator."

"Not. They were complaining about the price of their room," RubyAnn said.

"That doesn't mean anything," Garnet said. "Everyone has to be practical sooner or later."

They started out on another walk out to the meadow. There were still long lines of cars and buses coming in on the roads, gangs of people waiting to get into the shops. It felt like some event, a parade maybe, had just ended, and the spectators were still milling around.

They stopped where a group of people were looking up at the face of the cliffs. He'd forgotten his binoculars in the car, but they could see the two small patches of orange moving straight up the face. "I wouldn't do that for all the tea in China," Garnet said.

"I tried it," he said. "but I wasn't very good. I didn't have the concentration. I kept daydreaming about what I was going to do when I got down. But I never went that high, either."

"Coming down is what I'd like," RubyAnn said. "I'd like to parachute off of the top."

"I don't think that's allowed anymore," he said. "Too dangerous." He led the way, passing up the road along the river to the meadow for another one he wasn't sure of. It turned out to be the long way around. They passed a park ranger leading a group of foreign tourists on a nature walk. He was in full uniform, wearing a gun, as if he were in costume, looking for just the right background for them to take his photograph. Passed the snack bar, supermarket, souvenir shop, restaurant, camping-gear store. Nozzles attached by tentacles to a big vacuum cleaner ready to suck up tourist cash.

The meadow was some kind of grass he wasn't familiar with, long but laid over, wiry, deep green. Damp soil underneath, with narrow gullylike streams running zigzag everywhere. They wandered along the paths. "I was wrong," Garnet said. "This isn't like Kansas. It's more like the rough on a golf course. He hadn't realized she'd played golf. It reminded him more of the hospital grounds in the army. During basic training, twenty-six members of his company had contracted spinal meningitis. He'd lain in bed for weeks looking out a window at an unkept field, waiting to see if he was going to die. There were never any flowers, but it must have been watered, because it was always green, though it never seemed to grow. Never saw a bird either, he realized. Seventeen of the recruits had died. He was the last to be declared out of danger. After that they'd sent him to school to be a medic. He'd always thought that was funny.

They went on. The sun suddenly disappeared behind the rim, but there was still enough light in the sky for the walk back to the hotel. You could just see the moon above Half Dome. It must be because he was with Garnet that he kept thinking back, further, the way she did. Normally the past was like his own personal paperback history book that he carried around but never had to open because he already knew what was inside. He heard himself say, "When I was little I used to think the sun became the moon at night. And the stars were the part of the moon that was missing."

"What did you think when there was a full moon?" RubyAnn asked.

"I can't remember." Suddenly it was darker and there was no moon or stars. It began to drizzle. He took Garnet's arm and they all walked fast. "And I said it wasn't going to rain. I looked in two newspapers," he said.

"You can't expect it not to, up this high, in October," Garnet said.

They had reservations for eight o'clock in the dining room. In the planning stages of the trip, they'd decided they'd all dress for dinner. He'd brought his black suit that he'd got married in last time. But he was surprised when he met them in the lobby. Garnet had on a powder blue formal, all fluffy, like a prom dress, and her hair was done up in a different way. He thought she had been joking when she said, "I'm wearing a formal." RubyAnn had some kind of evening dress on too that went to the floor, the color of a red tulip. He was so surprised he didn't know what to say. "You bought that for here, Garnet?" he blurted out.

"Thirty-five years ago, for Eastern Star. I must have worn this a hundred times."

"You look nice," he said. "You both look nice. That's an interesting dress," he said to RubyAnn.

"It's Rosie's; she let me use it."

He took their arms. As they were seated, he noticed the couple from the elevator, sitting at a big table with friends. He nudged RubyAnn, who whispered to Garnet. They both gave a quick glance that way. He looked around too. Three or four hundred people inside here, he guessed. The room was enormous, one whole wall glass onto the dark outdoors, all the way up to the high-beamed ceiling. "The sky's the limit," he said when they got their menus. He ordered a bottle of wine after Garnet said she'd have some with him. "Do you want some?" he asked RubyAnn.

She looked at Garnet. "Go ahead, it's made with California grapes; a little can't hurt you," Garnet said. She made jokes all through the first course. "I'm having to force myself, you know. I wonder what the common people are having for supper." RubyAnn held out her glass again for more wine. He gave her just a little. She was already giggling. "It's sour, but it makes my tongue feel good," she said.

Garnet had ordered scallops *en brochette flambés* for the second, and they all oohed when the waiter touched a match to the skewer and blue flames flared up. "When we get back, Aunty," RubyAnn said to Garnet, "I'll bring the rest of my clothes over after school. It's a good thing I left most of my stuff at your place."

He didn't say anything, kept chewing. "She's not going to get any better, Uncle Billy," RubyAnn said, touching his arm. "I accept that."

"But you were sure she wasn't going to wake up from the coma, too."

"That was different."

"She needs you," he said. "You're giving up on her. Not giving her the chance she needs. Like you did when she was in the hospital."

"What good would I do? She doesn't need me home. She's got Rose. She worries me all the time."

"You're her daughter," he said.

"Well, I don't understand what difference that makes. You're her brother; what does that mean? It's like saying I'm fourteen years old for a reason. I don't want to be a keeper for anyone," she said too loud.

"That," Garnet said, "was a good meal." She moved her linen napkin across her mouth. "If this place wasn't so elegant, I'd wipe my plate with a piece of bread."

"No one's looking," he said.

"I can't," she said. "I was barely able to finish. But I might have saved a little room for dessert. I've noticed that cart they've been wheeling around. I haven't seen layer cakes like that for years. Used to be a German bakery when we first moved to the Peninsula, you could gain ten pounds just looking."

"What would you do, Aunty?" RubyAnn asked.

"About dessert?"

He was the only one who laughed.

"About my mother. It's not fair."

"All I know," Garnet said, "is you can't force people to face their responsibilities. They have to decide if they have one or not. No one else can do it for them." She paused. He realized she was trying to stop there. But then she went on. "I took care of my sisters when I was younger than you. And I worked for people, helped them cook and wash and clean. One family put a cot behind the stove for me to sleep on. They didn't invite me to eat at the table. I waited on them at dinner, but I got to eat later in the kitchen after I cleaned up. They gave me more than enough. A big heaping plate of food, kept hot in the oven. Every night as long as they had me, I had to decide whether to go home, be cold, and share that plate of supper with my sisters, or stay where I was. Nothing is fair. You do what you have to, when something happens that you can't help. You make the best of it. That's all you can hope for."

RubyAnn wasn't looking at anyone, just moving a single tine of her fork back and forth through the sauce on her plate. "And who at table nine is going to have dessert?" their waiter said.

"I know of one," Garnet said.

They stayed up late, stretched out in the overstuffed chairs in the great hall, listening to the pianist, comfortable, at ease. A fire roared in a fireplace big enough to drive a car through, cracking, popping sparks. It was really raining now, the drops hitting the big glass windows with so much force from the wind it sounded like waves were striking the building.

"How's the jumping?" he asked RubyAnn. Garnet was having coffee and he'd had a brandy.

"Better competition in high school," she said. "Some can jump higher."

"But they're older," Garnet pointed out.

"It doesn't matter," she said. "I don't know why I said that. I don't jump against them. I try and better myself. Go up, see if I can do another half inch.

Inch by inch. I sound like I'm a worm," she said, smiling. "Don't get me wrong; it's nice winning. I like it when they make a big folderol over me. Did I say that right?" She turned to Garnet, giggling. "But it's basically when I see them move the pole up another notch and I have to get myself over that's the challenge."

No one was hungry for breakfast the next morning. He tried to get RubyAnn to go horseback riding or rent a bike. "Let's go walk along the river we were at yesterday," she said. "I liked that."

The rain had cleared the air and the tree leaves glistened wet. The sky was all pure blue, and again the only sound came from the jays. They started out the way they'd gone the day before and stopped at a crosswalk with other morning strollers. He heard a ring-a-ringing coming from somewhere. He didn't understand at first what the sound was. Birds? Ring-ring-ring. Hundreds of rings. He looked down the road. He didn't grasp what he was seeing.

"It's them," RubyAnn said, "it's them!" It was the young couple from the hotel, on bicycles. She had on a long white wedding dress and he was wearing tails. Pedalling their bikes, ringing their bike bells. She had a bouquet of flowers and was smiling as she went by, her veil flaring out behind. Dozens of people on bikes came after them, bridesmaids and ushers, a big bunch of family, then guests, all dressed up. All were smiling, laughing, ringing their bike bells, those tinny-sounding handlebar bike bells, ring-ring-ring.

The people waiting at the crosswalk were clapping, yelling out "Hurray" and "You'll be sorry" and "Sucker." Garnet was laughing and clapping, yelling "Good luck, good luck" after them. He was clapping too. It felt like he was getting married, he was so hopeful, all of a sudden, at the sound of that ring-a-ring under the dome of the sky.

"Did you see that?" RubyAnn kept saying, clapping, "Did you see that? When I get married, I'm going to have my wedding here."

"Then I better practice," Garnet said. "See if I can still ride a bike."

It was late when they got back. He turned up Garnet's street, heard RubyAnn waking up in the back seat when he braked the car. Garnet got out, stiff, carrying her big purse and overnight bag. "I must have snoozed," she said, sounding groggy. "What a time we had. Thank you, Billy."

"We'll go again," he said. He realized the back door hadn't opened. "One of these days."

"You can count on me," she said, hesitating by the car.

"I'll stop after school tomorrow, Aunty," RubyAnn called out from the back seat. "Before I go home."

"Okay then," Garnet said, starting up the walk.

He waited until she opened the front door and went inside. The porch light went off, and he put the car in drive.

Kay, 1984
Pretty Frank

Nothing went back to the way it had been. There was that time, a couple of days after Ann had come home from the hospital, when Rose came back from work and caught her on all fours on the way to the kitchen. "Mother, Mother," she'd said, taking hold of her flannel nightgown to stop her, "wait, I'll get the wheelchair."

"Let go, I'm just going to see if there's any more ice cream."

"Let me get it for you; go back to bed," Rose told her. When Kay heard that story she went right out and bought a walker and took it over that afternoon. In a couple of days, Ann was thumping through the house as if it were a cell and she wanted to check and recheck the dimensions. Something was different, though. The only time she lost control was over things that were nothing. They were sitting in the front room once; Rose was there. Ann looked down and noticed that a button was loose, dangling on her striped shirt. They had been talking about recipes for pound cake. "Just look," she said when she saw the loose button, loud enough to make Rose jump, sitting beside her. Gave it a yank. "What are we going to do about this?" She held the button in the palm of her hand. "I can't stand it anymore. I won't have it."

"I'll sew it back on," Rose said. "Tonight."

"What about now?" Ann yelled. "Everything of mine always gets lost," and she started wailing.

"Do you think Ann's all right?" Kay asked her mother when she phoned that night.

Her mother seemed surprised at the question. "She was knocked out for months. You can't expect her to be her old self right away. It's only been six weeks. She's fine to me."

After the first couple of days back at work, Ann would only stay at the flower shop an hour or two at a time. Didn't say why. But Kay thought it was too fast for her now: customers coming in to order, phones ringing, the back room full of flowers, employees putting together the arrangements, delivery vans coming and going. Too much movement: it must be unsettling for her. "Let's go for a drive," she'd say, and then Ann would look out through the windshield at whatever they passed as if she were seeing it the first time, bemused equally by the tall buildings downtown in the city or the glaring blue of the ocean. "Absolutely no brain damage," the doctor said when Kay phoned him. "The tumor wasn't malignant. She should be just fine."

"Did they have any extra parts left over when they sewed you back up?" Billy would tease Ann and she'd reach out and grab him by his ears like they were kids again. He took her to the movies: she couldn't get enough of them, sitting in the dark, eating popcorn; three in a day, once. Ann was fine with Billy. Why did she seem so stiff with her?

In February Kay took her on a ride over to the coast to see the wildflowers. Rose and RubyAnn came along. Kay told them how their mother had thrown out the seeds. "You did all this, Mom?" RubyAnn said. The California poppies had moved up the hill on the bank side where the road cut through, finding good holds in the hard brown shale. They looked like enormous butterflies flapping their orange wings among the blue lupine and spills of buttercups. The girls oohed and ahhed. Ann was smiling, she noticed, until she turned her head her way; then she frowned. Ann couldn't know her thoughts in the hospital: Kay was petrified for a moment, remembering what she'd considered. No one knew about Grandmother and Wally.

When she got around to it, she phoned Ann's mother. Ruby sounded excited. "She's all better? Isn't that a miracle? I was so worried. Really concerned. I lost weight over it. I'm a whole size smaller. Did I mention that I'm going to be a grandmother? Christopher's wife is expecting." Kay was silent until Ruby caught on. "Of course, there's Ann's two. How are they?"

Kay gave her a short version. Rose had been hired by their assemblywoman as a liaison in the local district office. Full time. Loved the work. Rejected the idea of going to college. Said she was the only one who'd omitted that step and therefore she thought differently from the rest. "Says it's her strength; people point her out," Kay laughed.

"She should get an education," Ruby said.

"Your namesake is in high school now, jumping over five feet."

"Jumping?"

"High-jumping in track, over a bar. You never saw anyone so dedicated. My mother said she's just like you. Determined."

"Garnet said that?"

"Said you were the same way back home. In Kansas." Kay was enjoying herself, but she knew she should stop now. She was always ready to make too much up, put too much together. She should leave Ruby alone. But she couldn't, until she'd said all she'd ever wondered about, considered. "The way you went after Uncle Frank."

"I did what?"

"You know."

"I don't know where you got that piece of information. If your mother is telling tales out of school . . ."

"I guess I always assumed that. My mother always talks about how poor you were. Didn't have anything . . ."

"I could have married anybody I chose," Ruby cut in. "A lot of boys wanted to marry me. I had my pick."

"Why Frank, then, only to leave him when you got to California?"

"I'll tell you why; I was two months pregnant with his baby, that's why. He came back in his Navy uniform and sweet-talked me. I thought he knew what he was doing. I was wrong then and I was wrong later when I married him. It wasn't like now. You got married to whoever you were going with, if you missed your period." She was calm-voiced, conversational.

Kay tried to phone back a few times, but Ruby was never available. She'd asked Ann once, "Do you want to speak to your mother?"

"I don't care," she'd said.

Uncle Frank phoned one evening, surprising Kay. She asked him about Ann.

"I don't notice any change, not that much. She's back working, isn't she?"

"Half day," Kay said. "She gets tired easy." Had Uncle Frank ever noticed anything? Ann and her father: it was all new ground after the operation. You could see her try, make an effort to be kinder to him, even as disorganized, unsettled, as her mind was. But she couldn't keep her usual impatience or dislike from seeping through. Now you're sure that's *all* you need, she'd say sarcastically.

"What I phoned about, Kay, is could you take me to the doctor? I've got an appointment for next Thursday."

"What's wrong?"

"Nothing, I got some pain in my hip. Where I fell that time and got the fracture. You have to make an appointment a month ahead of time. What if I was dying or something?"

"I need to break out of the office anyway. Is it the same place I took you to last time?"

When the phone rang again at just past one a.m. the next morning, Kay kept thinking it was part of her dream, that the ringing was the sound her car was making as she drove down the coast road past the colors Ann had planted like rainbows arching over the round hills. But it was Uncle Frank. "It hurts too much, Kay. I can't stand it. It's bad."

"I'll be right over," Kay said. After she got in the car and started driving, she began thinking of her own father. How he and Uncle Frank would tell Kansas stories back and forth, one after another. They had been best friends. Went to grammar school and high school together, joined the Navy together. But her father hadn't bothered to stop at Frank's, when he'd come up to see Ann when she was in the coma. Frank hadn't known he was in town. He always asked after her father, before getting down to what he needed.

She drove off the freeway and down the off-ramp, amazed at how uncrowded the road was. The Mercedes ran soundlessly through the avenues. The front door was open, the screen door unlatched; Uncle Frank was sitting in his chair. He didn't respond when she said, "I'm going to call an ambulance, Uncle Frank."

The emergency room doctor said, "Kidney stone," and gave him an injection. "Your father?" the doctor asked later, in the waiting room. She was Kay's age but had let her ash blonde hair go gray. Her name tag said Dr. Anthony.

"Uncle," Kay said.

"His blood sugar is two-ninety."

"He's diabetic."

"And his liver's shot. Do I sound like a mechanic?" she asked. "Describing what's wrong with your car?"

Kay had to laugh. "A little," she said. "He drinks some."

"That's the way we talk in our family about our Aunt Mary. Who must guzzle a quart of vodka a day. Do you want to hear the rest?" She went on without waiting for Kay. "He has emphysema, bad; his lungs look like the inside of a chimney. I know he smokes."

"Chesterfields," Kay said. She remembered the doctor from somewhere.

"Do you want to hear about his heart?"

"Angina. He takes nitroglycerine tablets."

"Not only that, his arteries look the size of bicycle tubes."

Kay couldn't pay attention; she felt as if she were already back in her car. It was old, sixteen years, 190,000 miles on it; she'd driven it brand new off the lot. For the last five years she'd meant to get another one before something happened, went wrong, but she never did. She didn't know if she was just tired or what, but she couldn't get excited about the prognosis, the forecast for Frank. She didn't know if it was because he was old and she knew there were things wrong with him, or if, after Ann woke up in the hospital, she couldn't be surprised anymore. And there had always been something the matter with Frank. If he wasn't falling off a scaffold, he was drinking too much, in some kind of trouble. But now he looked so frail, insignificant, almost. Stretched out on the stainless steel examination table, he seemed like an arrangement of clothing in the shape of a man.

"We're going to have to admit him," the doctor said. "Try to get his blood sugar down. Wait and see if the kidney stones pass. Find out what's left of his liver. He's come to the end, so far as his body's concerned."

"Do what you have to," Kay said, "but he's going to surprise you."

She stayed with him until seven, then drove over to Ann's house. On the way she remembered where she'd seen the doctor before. At that Women's Clinic in the city, when she'd had the abortion. Dr. Anthony. Was it ten years ago? Almost ten years. Sailing to Tasmania with Gene.

Rose had already left for work and RubyAnn was just going out the door for school. Ann was only using her cane when she felt really tired or weak. She told her about her father while they drank unsweetened tea in the kitchen. "This family spends more time in the hospital than your average nurse," she said.

Ann didn't laugh. "What can you expect, all the things he did. He's lucky he's still kicking." She sounded indignant. "I've had enough of hospitals, Kay."

"Well, he wants his slippers and his own pajamas. Shaving kit. I'll go get them and take them over."

"I'll go with you. You're not supposed to do everything for us. Even if you do like to be put upon." She laughed too loud, as if she couldn't hear herself. Kay was about to get mad, but when Ann laughed, she did too.

They drove over to Frank's house, Ann not saying another word. "Shouldn't we call Billy?" Kay asked, standing by the phone.

"No, let him alone. Billy would just run over there. This isn't an emergency. It's been coming a long time."

Kay said it before she had a chance to think. "Your father came nearly every day to see you."

"Who asked him to? And what does that have to do with anything? Do I have to pay him back?"

"I think you're recovered," Kay said. They were standing in the front room at either end of the coffee table, their coats still on.

"Why do you always think you have to be the judge, the one who decides everything for us? Who made you our official referee?"

Ann wasn't angry, Kay realized; her tone was matter-of-fact, like she was discussing a dress she planned on making. On her part, Kay didn't get worked up either; she decided to ask a question that had bothered her for years, since they were girls. "Why don't you ever try to compromise? Try once in a while to get along? Why keep this up? When do you say: with all his blemishes, he's still my father. You're almost forty now. How long does he have left? Why can't you accept him like he is?"

"Because he's so pitiful, that's why. Always whining. I understood even at eight years old why Mother left. Who could put up with a man that never stopped complaining? I was only sorry she didn't take me with her. And that's the truth."

"He's an old man now."

"So? Does that make it better? Does that help me forget the way he used to knock me and Billy around?"

Kay couldn't think of anything else to say. She wished she was back in her dream, driving her old car down the freeway, no traffic, cruising along the white dashes like a shadow. "I'll drop you off at the flower shop and then take the things to the hospital."

"No you don't. I'll have them taken when the van makes its regular delivery there this morning. Just take me to the shop."

Neither said a word the whole way. "And don't phone Billy; I'll do that," Ann said when she got out.

Kay went back home to dress. She'd left in such a rush that morning she'd forgot to put on a slip. What had she expected? Not Ann's reaction, that was for sure. It wasn't the first time. Ann had called her nosey once. But what was she reacting to? She wasn't competing with Ann. Maybe she was nosey. Maybe she couldn't think of anything better to do. She had never tried to be her grand-mother. Putting on her makeup, she remembered the watch. It had taken almost a year for Ann to forget and leave that watch on the windowsill over the sink after they'd done the dishes. She hadn't hesitated a moment, slipped the watch into her pocket, made some excuse, and drove fast to the Broadway Jewelry Store. The clerk had whistled when he saw the name. "Easily over two thousand dollars," he'd said, turning it this way and that. She'd been almost afraid to look at Ann, sitting on the couch writing something for the school paper, when she got back. Who was she, anyway? And what had she done to get that watch? She'd put it back on the windowsill, held out for all these years, waiting for the right moment to ask. Always waiting for exactly the right time. The watch wasn't a good example of anything, she decided. Only of her own duplicity. Like the rings Ann had tried to keep. She'd done the same thing.

When the phone rang, she knew who it was. Uncle Frank. The van wouldn't make the delivery to the hospital till the afternoon.

"What's up?" Billy said. "Rupert phoned, heard an ambulance this morning take off in the neighborhood. And now Dad isn't home. I phoned and there's no answer. He's worried."

"Your father's in the hospital."

"Why didn't you tell me?"

"He's not at the one Ann was in. Community."

"Does Ann know?"

"She knows."

"What's wrong with him?"

"Kidney stones. They're going to keep him until they pass. He's tough; he'll be all right."

"I'm going over," Billy said.

In two days Frank was back at home. After a week or so, Kay went over when she knew her mother was there. He was wearing his old flannel robe; the purple nap had worn off and the cloth looked slick, like leather. His thin legs were as hairless and white as paper. There was no smoking Chesterfield in the empty ashtray, and his face didn't have that loose look around the mouth that meant he'd been nipping at the bourbon. He still held an empty mug from the soup her mother had brought over.

He wants to live as long as he can: the thought caught her by surprise. She'd stayed away, from the hospital and from his house, not because of what Ann had said; just to see, she told herself. Not if they could do without her. Or she could do without them. What other reason? She didn't need all this aggravation, that's why.

"Where have you been?" Frank asked. "The hospital almost wouldn't let me leave until Billy signed a form saying he'd be responsible. They screwed up the paperwork. I kept telling them you'd come, tell them how. Billy tried phoning, at least a dozen times. Left messages." He stopped, waiting for an answer.

"I've been busy," she said.

He went on. "Can they charge me $130 for a blood test?"

"They do that," Garnet said. "When I had that cataract operation, it was eleven dollars for a dab of salve. Couldn't believe it; still can't." Her mother had an old, two-pound Whitman's chocolates box on her lap. Two more were stacked up on the floor beside her, with corners and wide-bordered edges of old yellowed photos sticking out. They went on exchanging hospital stories. Doctor stories. Then back to Kansas stories. She sat next to her mother and took the box off her lap. The old Kansas photos. It took a minute to focus, still thinking what Uncle Frank had said. Is that all they wanted her for, to do the paperwork? Straighten things out? If they did, she allowed it, encouraged their dependence on her. Except for her mother. She took care of her own business, appointments and affairs. Kay hadn't even known she'd taken some tire company to small claims court until it was over and she'd got her four hundred dollars back, or about her eye operation until it was over.

She had to look close at the first photo: she didn't recognize Frank right off, but she remembered the stories about his car, the 1925 Whippet. He was standing in front, one foot up, heel hooked on the bumper. He'd been the only son, the only child after his older sister and parents died in the scarlet-fever epidemic. His aunt and uncle in town raised him. They owned the largest furniture store in the three adjoining counties. Photos of the store, the employees lined up in front on the sidewalk. Awning. High-curbed streets. The building was three stories. Her mother began another. "Remember Mrs. Clare?"

"That old woman," Frank said, shaking his head, attentive, waiting as if he didn't know the rest, had never seen for himself or heard this before.

"I was out at their place. I don't recall doing what. Using that summer kitchen they had off the yard, in the shed. Putting up fruit, it was."

"She was a character," Frank said.

"Time for supper, I guess, she reached out and grabbed a passing chicken. Held it by the legs, talking to me. Telling me to get the water hot enough to scald the mason jars. I added more wood to the firebox. 'Bring it to a good boil, now,' she told me. She was standing right next to the chopping block. I could see the hatchet in the shed. I didn't know what she was doing, when she lowered that pullet so that the head was resting on the ground, the one red eye going around and around. She was still giving me directions: 'Fill each jar with twenty-four peach halves, two ladles of syrup, one peach pit on the bottom.' She put her big man's boot she was wearing on the eye, not hard. But when she pulled up on the legs she kept the boot bearing down. Wings flapping, white feathers flying, blood squirting all over the bottom of her dress when the head tore off. Half buried in the soft dirt of the yard. All the time still giving me directions: 'Wipe off the outside good, nothing sticky.' There was a wire made into a hook on the clothesline. She tied the legs together and hung the poor thing to drain."

"I saw her do that too," Frank said. "Me and Lester went out there. After the fire, it was. She used to knock off a dozen then to feed the hay crew. I used to avoid watching if I could help it, to tell the truth. She didn't know any different."

"Well I can tell you I didn't eat any chicken while I was there," her mother said.

In spite of herself, Kay listened, rapt. She didn't know this side of the family as well as her father's. Because of her grandmother, of course. And her mother never talked about hers much until the last ten years or so. Were they telling these stories now for her benefit?

Neither her mother nor Frank were talking. "How did you get the furniture up to the top floor?" she asked.

"Freight elevators. They had them then," he added. He was going to go on, but there was a knock on the front door and Ann came in.

"It's old home week," Garnet said.

"Did you get the medicine?" Frank asked. "If I don't take it on time, they said I'd get sick all over again."

"Here." She handed him a white paper bag. "The receipt's inside."

Neither she nor Ann said anything to each other, but Ann sat down on the couch on the other side of Garnet.

"I'm going to take this medicine," Uncle Frank said, "and lie down then. The stuff makes me dizzy. I'll be back," he said.

They sat there a minute before Garnet said, "I better get a move on."

"I have to go too," Kay said, startled at how quickly it came out. But no one moved. There was an old photo in a studio holder that opened with a flap. Nervously, Kay lifted one side of the dark gray cardboard. The photo was of a young man. They had used color somehow, and the cheeks were too pink and the lips unnaturally red. His dark hair was slicked back exposing his wide forehead and sharp nose.

"Who is it?" Ann asked.

"It's your father," Garnet said. "We used to call him pretty Frank." Ann took the picture and held it by her chin, then drew it away, arm's length. Kay didn't have any doubts: there was that resemblance.

"There wasn't a girl in the county that didn't want to snare him. But his aunt was too smart for them. Kept him working at that store, all hours. And sent him to Missouri to relatives for vacation."

"Then how did my mother marry him?" Ann asked.

"When he came back from the Navy. The whole first string football team enlisted when the war started. Here," Garnet took the box off Kay's lap and sifted through the mound of photos, "I was just looking at them. Here's this one."

Again the same person, in a Navy uniform. "Here's another." In a blue suit and a vest. "He was something. I had a crush on him too. He was your father's best friend, you knew that," Garnet said to Kay. "In Kansas they palled around together. My first date was with Frank. That's how I started going with your father."

"I never knew that," Kay said.

"It was like one big family back then. Everyone knew everyone else in high school. Only about seventy in the whole school. After I married Lester, Frank took out Ruby. He was a catch."

"That's hard to believe," Ann said.

"Because he's old now," Garnet said. "You wouldn't say that if you'd seen him then. He was not only handsome, he had a good disposition, too."

"Why did you take up with Uncle Lester then?" Ann asked.

"One," Garnet said, "Frank never asked me out again. And two, for some reason, Frank reminded me too much of my own father. And number three, I fell in love with Lester's pompadour." Both Kay and Ann started laughing, rocking the couch and spilling the top photos out of the box. "It's funny, I know, but he had the waviest hair then, way up high in the front. It made you want to touch it." Garnet started laughing too.

"Pretty Frank," Ann said, making a face.

"They said things like that then," Garnet said. "The town treated him different," she went on. "He was an orphan, of course. And his aunt and uncle had money, compared to the rest of us. But that wasn't the reason. When the store burned down without a penny of insurance and the bank took the family farm, all by the time he was twenty-one, nothing changed in the way people thought of him. He was still Frank, that drove around with Lester in that white coupe. Never a hair out of place, in high school. He was like his uncle, I think, just plain kind to the bone. Never talked about anybody or made fun of you. Took me home to meet his aunt and uncle on our date. I didn't know what to expect. They treated me nice, sat in the parlor talking, Mr. Bennett asking me what I was going to do after school. Mrs. Bennett knew I was one of the Stecker girls. Not a pot to piss in."

"Aunt Garnet," Ann said in mock surprise. "What language."

"It was true. Words aren't enough to cover the subject or give any idea what it was like. It took away our will; we lived on the county. Our shame was we took a fifty-pound sack of rice and beans they gave us for the month. We had no place where we could put our eyes not to look at other people."

"Mother, where did you go on the date?"

"To the movies in the next town. Danced at some grange hall. Took me home; my father was sitting on the porch stairs, and we sat with him and talked for an hour. That's when I realized there was something similar between the two of them. When either of them laughed, it was the same way, same sound. That's where he started talking to Ruby for the first time. She came out and joined us, sat on the glider with me and we went back and forth, back and forth. She was younger, four or five years. I wasn't going to go, because when you're like we were, people take advantage of you. Think you're just something they can use up and then discard. Not Frank. He never took advantage of anyone."

"I wasn't born premature, was I, Aunt Garnet?" Kay noticed her mother looked like she was listening for something more. But Ann was finished and waiting for some kind of answer. "When I was working for the airline after I graduated, they needed to see my parent's marriage license," she added. "Kay isn't the only one in this family that can count."

"I'd probably say you should ask your mother about that."

"Why don't you tell me," Ann said. "You're the one that mentioned my father never took advantage of anyone. And you know I can't ask my mother."

"The fire that burned about a third of the town happened after the war, about a month after Frank came back from the navy. Him, Lester, and Lester's brother Wally, all in white uniforms. They were all pretty then. Of course, Lester and I were already married; when he came home from the Mediterranean in 1943, we got married then. He shipped to the Pacific then and I followed him out to San Diego and waited there. When it was over, we went back home. I had Kay by then. It didn't take long to know that we couldn't stay in Kansas. We had all changed too much or something. Anyway, Ruby started going with Frank. It was kind of a surprise; she'd been more or less engaged to a big farmer in the next town. She hadn't been going out with Frank more than a couple of weeks when she said to me, 'I'm going to change my name to Bennett tonight.' I didn't understand what she was talking about until after the fire. All of a sudden, Frank was unemployed. And she was morning sick. I still didn't catch on until after she took about a quart of castor oil. She was sick as a dog. But it didn't take. When she wanted me to go see Mrs. Clare with her, then I understood. That old woman used to use a length of baling wire dipped in bleach to abort with. I wouldn't do it. And they got married. Came to California right after us."

Kay glanced over at Ann. She looked the same, noncommittal.

"You can't consider the right or wrong of that without first being in Ruby's shoes." Her mother pushed her glasses back up her nose. "You can't judge some-one without some kind of understanding of what you would have done. I used to hate my father worse than I could tell. When he came back from Missouri that time and I told him Mama had died, he said, 'Well, at least she waited until you were old enough to take care of your sisters.' That's the way he was. I stopped feeling that way, finally; it took a long time; I was in my thirties, I guess. One day the hate was just gone, used up. So you can see that Ruby had a hard time, too. But Frank didn't do anything alone, as far as I was concerned. And now I really have to go." She lunged to get herself to the edge of the cushion, rocking Kay and Ann toward the middle.

After Garnet left, they sat back down with plenty of space between them, the Whitman chocolate box on the middle cushion. "You know those things I said," Ann started out. "I'd been thinking that off and on, even before my operation. I always thought those things, but I don't know if I believed them. But I had to say them."

"You don't have to explain anything," Kay said.

"But I want to explain. It's not easy for me. That's all." They were facing each other now. Ann made her mouth smile then. "Another thing, you gave one of those rings we found at the auction to Rose, didn't you? I feel so ashamed when I think about them. I saw her wearing it to work this morning."

"It was a birthday present."

"You want me to thank you, don't you, about Rose."

"Come on, Ann."

"I never seem to be able to arrange my feelings, or the words you're supposed to use about them; I'm always behind or ahead, describing something that hasn't happened yet or has already passed. I never used to think about anything, and now I think too much. I still can't fit things together right." She looked around the room.

Kay was about to say her mother's line, I better get a move on, when Ann started again. "You know I could dream when I was in the coma? Whatever I wanted."

"What did you dream?" Kay asked.

"They didn't have a subject; no one I knew was there. But they were pleasant. Simple. Always wonderful. I didn't want to come back. I wanted to keep dreaming and dreaming my life away."

"Kay," Uncle Frank called out. "Kay, got a minute?"

She didn't move. "You go," she said, not looking at Ann. "He's your father."

"He's calling you. I'm going over for flowers tomorrow. Come with me. It's supposed to be nice and foggy, the way you like it. Early," she said, opening the front door and stepping out.

"I think I can," Kay said after her. Ann nodded her head as she shut the door.

Ann, 1987
Geography of the Heart

Is that you, Ann?" her father said, looking surprised to see her. He unhooked the screen door. She stepped inside under his arm as he held the door open, carrying the bouquet of flowers away from her sweater. On an impulse she'd picked out at random some mums, carnations and a few tea roses. She held them out to him. "For me?" he said, genuinely pleased, she thought. She couldn't find a vase, so she put them in a quart jar.

She'd come on the spur of the moment to deliver the flowers. She was surprised when she noticed the time; it was almost five o'clock. "Have you had supper?" he asked. "I made some soup." They sat in the kitchen. He waited on her, forgetting the crackers, getting up again for the butter.

"This is good," she said.

"The whole trick is to let soup bones—you don't get them free anymore—simmer for a couple of days before you start putting anything else in. They make the best soup stock in the world." As her father talked, she realized he must not get much of a chance, anymore, but in spite of herself she started feeling fed up. The sound of his voice was getting to her. Now he was going on and on about what someone had said to him in the social security office. Before, she would have wanted to lean forward and yell at him, quit whining.

"Let's go sit in the front room," she said. "It's more comfortable." She cleared the table and followed him in. The boxes of photos that Garnet and Kay had been looking at when she came in last week were still on the sideboard. She went over and opened the folder of the one Garnet had called pretty Frank. There was no resemblance now. "Can I have this?" she asked, for something to say.

"Sure, go ahead," he said. Just then the doorbell rang. "Rupert," he said. He got up and opened it. It was Rupert.

"Long time no see," Rupert said, coming in with his old dog. They all sat down again and Rupert said, "My wife liked flowers. Tulips. Red and yellow."

"Ann brought them," her father said, and there was a long silence. She had the feeling she was intruding now. They were both looking at the blank TV screen like they could see the news. There was a kind of awkwardness, but both were sitting politely, waiting for her to say something. "Well, I better get a move on," she said, standing up. Did her father look relieved?

When she got home she turned on the radio in the kitchen to some talk show, and most of the lights in the front part of the house. She never listened to what they said; it was the voices that made her—what? Less likely to feel lonely? She'd never been lonely in her life. But she missed the sounds of the girls. Even the yelling? Kay had asked.

She put her father's picture on the mantel. She wasn't sure why she'd asked for it now. Next to the photo of Rose, just her face, smiling. She had never been as pretty as Rose. RubyAnn looked serious. It was hard to believe the girls were gone. And weren't coming back. Not to live, anyway. It was almost harder to adjust to them leaving than it had been having them as babies. Rose was like finding a doll she'd really liked. RubyAnn was colicky: she'd have given her back if she could, some nights, walking the floor, trying to get her to go to sleep so Carl could get some rest and be able to get up at five and go to work. The thought startled her. She let Carl's face appear with his name. He was always so serious looking, like RubyAnn. Like he was thinking about the next thing he had to do on the engine he was building, or tying a fly he'd been considering for his next fishing trip. She was surprised at herself: thinking up Carl, and it didn't even bother her.

She got up and tried to remember where there'd be a photo. She wouldn't have thrown them away, but she would have hidden them some place where she wouldn't run across them. She was always putting things away where she wouldn't find them to remind her. Or getting rid of things. She'd given every piece of the contents of that storage crate to some veterans' group that came around with a truck, so she wouldn't be reminded about the rings.

She thought of the kitchen first, in her junk drawer, but dismissed that. She went into her bedroom, got down on her hands and knees, and started going through the bottom drawers of her dresser. Came up with a whole drugstore envelope of photos of him taken on a fishing trip. In one of them he was holding up a string of fish between his two outstretched arms. She took that one back and put it next to her father's.

There couldn't be two people more different. Carl was like—what? He was smart, but her father wasn't dumb. But Carl had learned to use his head to get the most of himself. He'd wandered through high school, he liked to say, and joined the Air Force because he looked good in blue. They sent him to auto-mechanics school. "I could do a better tune-up when I was ten than what they taught us with all that diagnostic equipment in that Air Force school. My father and older brothers used to go out and pull an engine while they were waiting for dinner, just to switch to one with more horse power. But the school, they had every tool, piece of equipment, mock-ups of cars, all under one roof. That made me start to wonder. I used to think *cooling system* when a car heated up, forget about everything else. But for some reason there, I started to think how interesting the whole internal-combustion engine in a car was, not just how it worked, but the shapes of the parts. How could they be modified? Think what a crankshaft looks like, for instance." He talked like that on their first date. She'd listened half amused, half fascinated. No, that wasn't the word. Surprised.

She had wanted to get out of the house. She was working full time, had got a job with an in-house magazine for the airline because her high-school news-paper adviser's wife was one of the editors. She wrote short biographical cap-tions under employees' pictures: Captain Smiley, with thirty-four years of flying for Central, 44,000 hours in the sky, lives with his wife and two poodles Mimi and Mitzi in Millbrae. The magazine was mostly photos. An article every month by the president, definitely antiunion, about how wonderful it was to work with the other employees. She did the recipe page and the last page, which was mostly the best jokes she could find about flying. She liked her job. So she jumped at the chance to move into an apartment in the city with Jane, who had a degree and worked in the magazine's advertising department.

The first six months were like one of those articles in the ladies' magazines where everything was going according to some scheme that was altogether dif-ferent from the way people had lived on her street. She never got tired of dress-ing up every day. She stopped sewing and bought clothes. Ran up enough bills at Macy's and the Emporium that the salesclerks knew her by name. Took a vacation, flew to Hawaii with Jane. Lounged on the beach in January and came home with a better tan than she'd had in July. Got her first raise and bought her first car, a red '62 VW with a sun roof.

And she didn't go out with just anyone who asked. She was selective. She knew enough about that from her high school days, and what Jane told her about married men. She looked them up in the personnel file if there was any doubt. Whenever the EXIT sign went on, she did just that. She was not only picky, but safe. She had a diaphragm, and Kay had told her about the new pills, which were 99.9 percent safe. She took them for a month, feeling a little silly— there was no occasion to make them necessary. She put them away. But after they went to dinner with Smitty, she fished the pill compact out from behind her underwear in her dresser drawer.

Jane's brother Smitty stayed over at their place when he came to the Bay Area. He'd graduated from college the year before and got drafted into the Army. As a civil engineer, he went around the country safety-rating military roads on bases. He took them both out to dinner at the officers' club at the Presidio. Made them laugh the whole evening. He could imitate anyone. Especially the officer he worked with, who he nicknamed Colonel Lump. " 'Where exactly am I, Lieutenant?'

" 'In the officers' club, sir.'

" 'Well, if I'm in the officers' club, I must be an officer. That follows, doesn't it?'

" 'No, sir, you're one of the waiters.' "

"You didn't say that," Jane said.

"Yes I did. Let me finish. 'If I'm one of the waiters, you better pay for the drinks, Lieutenant.' That actually happened," he insisted, as she and Jane were breaking up.

She loved him. It was easier to think that now than admit it then. But once she got it out, she never stopped repeating the phrase. At least a million times. To him almost as often as to herself.

He was jealous, which made it seem more romantic, more daring. More exciting. They were eating at a restaurant, and he kept insisting a diner at another table was staring at her. He went over and told the man to knock it off or he'd punch him in the nose. And he told her not to go to lunch with her supervisor because he had only one thing on his mind. "You're right," she said.

They went everywhere, to parties, racing around the city, jumping on the MUNI or a streetcar, or sometimes she'd drive her VW. They went to an opening night exhibition at the de Young—she got all kinds of invitations and tickets from the magazine—with a crowd of other people. She wore her new suede raincoat and boots from the White House, caught her reflection in a glass case, knew she looked good. "Want me to take your coat?" he said. "It's warm in here."

"I don't think that would be a good idea," she said. They had wandered away from the others into a dark wing of eighteenth-century furniture.

"Why not?" he said. She opened the top half of the raincoat to show him. All she had on was her Frederick's of Hollywood underwear. She loved the look on his face.

He was away half the time. But she learned to wait. She took a lot of work home. Went to the movies with Jane. Phoned Kay. Never ever went home. Forgot to go to Billy's graduation, even. There was too much to do in the city. And Smitty phoned. He said he trusted her. But if he phoned at his regular time and she wasn't in, he'd start yelling and she'd have to soothe him.

One time they were coming back down 101 from Bodega Bay, the headlights bouncing off sheets of rain coming down like melted glass, the wind gusting the car along, the night as dark as the blacktop. When they got to the bridge approach she could look across and see the Golden Gate outlined by red beacons. What was strange was there were no car headlights or taillights, neither coming or going, as if they were the only people out in the storm heading into the city. They were alone, Smitty was dozing next to her, rocking side to side as the car was buffeted by the wind. She slowed the car in the middle of the bridge, pulled over to the side. She didn't know why she stopped. She didn't know what she was going to do yet, listening to the rain, the sound of her own breath. "Come on," she yelled, jumping out. Getting soaked in the first two steps away from the car. He followed her. "What are we doing?" he kept yelling. She pushed herself up on the railing, got her underclothes off and threw them over her shoulder. She couldn't see down to the bay. "Come here," she yelled. She held on with her legs and one hand for balance against the wind; with the other she pulled him in close and unzipped him. "Love," she kept saying, "love," as her back banged back and forth against the metal railing.

Things got complicated. He accused her of going out on him when he was away. He'd phone her from New Jersey or Puerto Rico, wherever he was, talk easy but end up yelling, "You whore, what are you doing to me." She'd hang up on him. When he'd come back they'd make up, long, sweet weekends. The first time he hit her it was him who started crying, not her. "Forgive me, forgive me. I'm sorry, I'm sorry." He'd punched her in the stomach; she lay on the kitchen floor trying to get her breath, trying to comprehend what had happened, as he ran out of the apartment, sobbing.

It was a long reconciliation. It would never happen again, she knew. Not only because he kept saying that, but because she believed it. He changed; there were no more accusations, no more flare-ups. He did everything she asked him to, for four months.

Then, over nothing—her supervisor had given everyone on the staff a pin with the airline logo, and she was wearing it on her blue cashmere sweater— he started up again. The questions first. Then the accusations. She started yelling back. He ripped the sweater off her shoulder. As she struggled, tried to push him away, he started slapping her. She fell across a chair and felt a terrible pain in her arm. She knew something must have broken.

She had to take her time, get a jacket, call a taxi, cradling her arm. He followed her around the room, saying, "It's my fault; I'm sorry." If she'd had a pistol, she would have shot him right between the eyes. He followed her cab to the hospital and made a scene there, until an orderly made him go outside. "She belongs to me," he yelled on his way out the door. "I take care of her. She does what I say."

Her arm was broken, and they put a cast from her wrist to her elbow. While it was setting up, she phoned Kay. She couldn't face going home to the apartment alone. Kay was there in twenty-five minutes. "You're not going back there, Ann," she told her. She could have hugged Kay for that.

"But I've got to get my things."

"We'll take care of that," Kay said.

All three of them went, Billy too. He didn't know what had happened, just that she was moving and needed help. He'd borrowed a pickup and got cardboard boxes. She didn't have that much: her bed, dresser, clothes, a rocking chair.

Her arm still hurt. She hadn't heard from Smitty since that night. She'd been staying at Kay's, almost a week. She had told Jane at work that she was moving, and Jane already had someone else lined up to share the rent. They had the box springs loaded in the truck and Kay and Billy were trying to get the floppy mattress through the bedroom door when Smitty came in. "You bitch," he said. "Is this your new one?" He pointed at Billy.

"Do you think that's necessary?" Billy said.

"You're goddamned right I do," he said and took a swing at Billy, who ducked and backed away.

"You don't want to do this," Billy said. "It never solves anything. Besides, I've belonged to the Y's judo club since sixth grade."

"No shit," Smitty said, starting to laugh.

"Leave him alone," she yelled. All at once she was furious. "Haven't you done enough?"

"You big bully," Kay was yelling.

Billy was trying to explain, "I'm Ann's brother," when Smitty charged him, slamming him up against the wall, knocking over a lamp. "I'm still going to kick your ass," he shouted. A picture fell down from its hook. Billy grabbed Smitty, Kay reached for an umbrella, and she shut her eyes. It was suddenly quiet. She opened them. Billy had some kind of hold on Smitty's hand and Smitty was on his knees on the floor, a trickle of blood running out of one nostril. Kay was watching, still holding the umbrella with both hands.

"Relax," Billy told him. "I'm not going to hurt you. I want you to get on your feet now and get out of here."

They finally got the pickup loaded and were about to pull away from the curb when Smitty came hurrying down the sidewalk. Her heart sank. Was he going to make another scene, here on the street, or beg her in front of them?

"You," he yelled up at Billy, who had insisted on riding in the back so nothing would fall out. They had hurried, didn't even take time to tie the load down. "I'm going to look you up, wherever you live."

In that calm voice of his, Billy answered, "I've just moved to 2077 El Camino Real, apartment fourteen."

Laughing so hard she could barely get the truck in gear, Kay yelled out the window, "You big blowhard."

She met Carl at the Kansas Day Picnic about five months later. She still worked for the airline and was still living with Kay. She'd got back to normal, had almost stopped thinking about that whole business, now. Went out a few times, but never with the same person twice.

She was helping Kay grill the hamburgers, making patties with a press, when Carl came over eating the last of one. "May I be the first, ladies, to say these hamburgers are exceptional, and I'd be happy to take another off your hands?"

It was Kay who spoke up first. "You can if you'll open that case of meat." He stayed and helped the rest of the picnic. He mentioned he was a mechanic. "You don't say," Kay said. "What makes a car backfire and shake so bad the ashtray falls out? I lost a filling, riding with Ann in her VW."

"Could be anything," he said. "Timing. Bring it around to the adult school on Tuesday at seven. We'll take a look."

She went because Kay kept reminding her. Sat in the classroom in an immense auto shop with two other women and about thirty men. Listened to him spend the first half hour talking about spark plugs. She kept looking at the handout with the diagram of a spark plug as he spoke, trying to follow, trying to understand. It was his enthusiasm, she thought, that made you listen. And he was so serious; about a spark plug, for heaven's sake.

After the lecture, he had her drive her VW into the shop. "Take off that hose," he said, handing her a screwdriver, putting his fingers on the clamp. She just looked at him. "Try," he said. "It's not hard." She got the clamp off.

"If the internal-combustion engine is a cumulation of its components, finding out what's wrong has to be a process of evaluation and then elimination of the functioning parts. I just thought that up. What do you think?"

She didn't know what to say. "I don't know anything about cars."

"You will," he said. "Now take these two screws off the distributor cap."

The car still backfired when she went back to the class the next week, but it had stopped shaking. He showed her how to make another adjustment in the timing. Then put his car up on the rack when she said she'd never looked underneath. He touched the parts, naming them like old friends: drive shaft, universal joint, differential, transmission. "I took one of those apart when I was sixteen on a bet that I could put it back again," he said, patting the transmission. "It had about a thousand parts. I lost."

By the end of the semester she had learned a little, enough to know what parts weren't doing what they were supposed to, like the battery or the starter, but she was never sure if she'd be able to get anything to come off with a box wrench or a screwdriver. Her car still backfired.

"No one's perfect," he said. The last night of the class he was still making adjustments on it. "I'm going to have to confess," he said to the class members gathered around the VW. "I don't know what's wrong with this dumb car." Everyone laughed. "But let's look on the bright side of things. It runs." She signed up for the second semester.

He phoned her one Friday. "I'm a better fisherman than I am a mechanic," he said. "But there's no money in that line of work. Would you like me to give you a demonstration?"

She hesitated. What was she getting herself into? Nothing, she decided. "Only if there's no dying fish involved," she said. "I can't stand to see them gasping and flopping around when they come out of the water." She had cleaned and cooked the fish Billy had brought home as a boy, but they had to be dead first.

He took her to Golden Gate Park early Saturday morning. There was a special pool with blue plastic rings floating at different distances for fly-fishermen to practice casting into. He explained everything to her as if this were just another kind of mechanical system. "It's all in the wrist," he kept repeating. She tried, concentrating, wanting to do well. But the line never cooperated. Or maybe it was the rod. She never even came close. It was so effortless when he did it. The fly popped into the ring as if it were alive. She tried again. "Release at two o'clock," he said. "Now." She knew what he meant, but it never worked out that way. It was only when her arm got so sore that she forgot to think about it that the fly dropped about a foot from the ring. "Good for you," he clapped.

Later they drove back on Highway One along the coast. He'd point at different beaches: "I caught a twenty-two-pound striper there. When they were running, six years ago. Can you see out there, past where that ship is? The Farallon Islands are right there; that's where the salmon pass to come back into the bay. If I could, I'd live out on those islands." They drove past the flower farms all the way down to Half Moon Bay. Parked and walked around the pier, looked at the fishing boats tied to buoys. People knew him, said hello. They looked into a small bait shop and fish market.

"My best customer," a big woman wearing two sweaters said. "Fresh oysters on the half shell. Got 'em this morning. Come on, Carl."

"Do you want to try?" he said. She'd never eaten an oyster in her life. "Watch me," he said, squeezing lemon on an oyster. It quivered, alive. He lifted the shell to his mouth and let it slither down his throat. She couldn't look. She was already thinking up reasons why she couldn't try when he handed her a shell, squirted lemon down its length. She got the oyster to her mouth and let it slide in, chewing, gulping, the old woman cackling. Closed her eyes, closed her eyes. Carl surprised her, gave her a big hug, lifted her off the ground and spun her around. "You're the only one who ever tried," he said. She thought she was going to be sick.

She invited him to their apartment. Sometimes he'd drop in on his own. Sit with Kay and her, watching TV. Once he told them both he was going to take them to the most peaceful place in the state. They ended up walking through the aquarium Sunday morning. "Where else would he take us?" she said to Kay, who got the giggles when he said, "This had nothing to do with fishing." It *was* peaceful. Dark. Quiet.

He lived in an apartment with two other mechanics who worked in the same garage. But he never invited her there. Besides the hug at the coast, he'd never tried anything. She didn't know what she expected, anymore. In high school the boys had been all hands. I could have joined the wrestling team and fit right in, she'd told Kay. Now she wasn't sure about anything. Not after . . . she didn't even want to think his name.

Carl wanted her to meet his parents. Have dinner. Where was this going? Nowhere in a hurry, she thought. Which was good; she was in no rush. He asked her in front of Kay, who was sitting on the couch. She tried to show some enthusiasm; it might be interesting to meet them, after all. "I'd like that," she said.

They were older than she expected; his mother'd had Carl when she was forty. And they were kind. Tried not to brag about their son, who had several patents for tools he'd designed, taught night school, managed the family garage, which turned out to be part of a big truck stop with a restaurant and a store on the highway. She knew the one they were talking about. You could see the dozens of trucks lined up like boxcars at the off ramp.

His parents had been themselves, they hadn't put on for her, she decided later, drying the dishes. Rosebud and Norman Bergstrom. She'd told them her mother's name was Ruby and her aunts were Opal and Garnet. Carl's parents had come out in the early thirties from Wellington. "Everyone called me Okie," Norman said. "I didn't mind, but if I had the energy, busting flat truck tires, I'd say, 'I'm Kansan and proud of it.'" His parents were normal. Gentle with each other. Affectionate. "Go ahead, you tell it, Norm; I told it last time." Nice. Carl too. She startled herself, all of a sudden, thinking: if they were normal, what was she? Her family?

Carl had the Kansas look, tall and lanky, fair rounded face. Didn't have the twang or the down-home toothpick-in-the-mouth mannerisms. He got paid for teaching the Tuesday night adult school class but confided once that he'd do it for nothing. "People shouldn't be afraid of their cars," he said. Watching him once, showing someone how to get his alternator off, she had a terrible thought that he was like Billy, with that endless patience that could wear down any obstacle: with Billy it never allowed him to call it quits, stop and try something different.

She decided that wasn't right, though, because Carl was able to make the jump to a new direction. He didn't just wait for things to happen to him or try to perfect something by doing it over and over. He took a physics course at the junior college because he needed to know electrical theory if he was going to get anywhere. Carl knew, in fact, what he wanted. "I'd like to design a car engine that could get three hundred miles per gallon. Or more," he added. "I think it's possible. There's steam, solar, electric, but I'll still bet the direction to go is the internal combustion engine."

Billy let everyone else decide for him. When his girlfriend Norma took French, so did he, because she wanted him to. He pitched for the varsity baseball team because the coach talked him into it, instead of going out for the diving team, which was what he wanted to do. He even followed their father's advice, who'd already made a mess of his own life: don't enlist like I did; let them come for you. He planned to go to college because Kay told him he should. Carl wasn't like that at all.

What puzzled her most about Carl was he didn't seem in any rush to go beyond the kiss and hug stage. She had taken him into her bedroom to show him the galleys for the next month's magazine: they were on the desk, where she kept a lot of the work she brought home. They sat on her bed while he read the article she'd written. She leaned back on the pillows, watching the back of his head. Who was she testing, she wondered. Him or herself? Having sex didn't prove anything. Fucking didn't have anything to do with loving. Could loving have something to do with fucking? She sat back up.

He kept reading, once in a while making a comment. "This is good. I like this part about the new benefit package. You actually make it sound interesting." When he was through reading, he stood up and grabbed her hand. "Come on, let's go get some pizza. I'm hungry."

Was she disappointed or relieved? She wasn't sure.

She wasn't taking the pill anymore. Couldn't remember where she'd put her diaphragm. No sex: it was too risky. Then sometimes she thought that was just plain crazy. She didn't understand half the time what she was doing. She kept changing her mind, after she thought she was sure. Who was in charge, anyway? Ann Bennett; that's who was supposed to be. One day when she and Kay were driving down the freeway she asked, "Do you believe in instant love?" She changed that when Kay didn't reply. "Love at first sight?"

"You mean spontaneous sex?"

"No, it's not the same thing. Can you love someone without knowing them very well?"

"I'm no authority, as you know," Kay said, grinning. "We don't turn here; stay on Bayshore. Where was I? I would say you have to know someone. The good and the bad. Not just because they're handsome. Or beautiful. I guess there could be an initial attraction from looks. Like male birds have brighter feathers to attract female birds, or sing louder; I don't know which. But on second thought, it should be more than that. I don't know. You should respect the other person. I guess that's too vague. *Like* the other person. I think love has to be cumulative; it builds up like rings on the bathtub."

"That's an awful comparison. Don't forget who scrubbed the tub last time, too."

"Wait, I'm getting close. Decide what your life would be like with that person when you're fifty. Are we talking about anyone I know, here?" Kay was grinning again.

"We're just talking in general terms, that's all."

They gave her a promotion at the magazine, a raise to almost double what she had been making. The president of the company had liked her articles. Sent her a personal note for her file; keep up the good work. She had her own cubicle now and could use the secretary pool.

"At nineteen," Kay said, "that's not bad." Of course, Kay had her own business and apartment at twenty-two, and made probably at least ten times as much money. But Kay had a degree, was a C.P.A. Besides signing up for Carl's class the second year, she registered for an advertising course at the community college.

Carl was the kind of person who liked to invite other people along. Kay, of course. Billy too: boat shows, basketball games, the car museum up near Reno. He even took her father on Veterans' Day when the Navy offered tours of several ships for visitors. They went through a minesweeper similar to the one her father had served on in World War II. They took his own parents along. His older brother's kids. To the zoo. Parades.

Maybe she felt too comfortable with him, as if she knew what he was going to do all the time. She decided she worried too much about things. She was going to let this just take its course. Whatever that meant. But at times she couldn't help herself. She wasn't exactly trying to provoke him, but she intended to be herself. He was going to see her without any pretense. She rolled her eyes when he was telling Kay he'd liked talking to her father. "Why do you do that when I mention him?" he snapped at her.

"Because you don't know him. And you like everybody."

"You're wrong. I dislike a lot of people."

"Who? Name one."

"The presidents of General Motors, Chrysler and Ford."

"Someone in real life," Kay said from the sofa.

"A couple of uncles of mine who beat the crap out of me when I tried to stop them from shooting my dog with a twenty-two. I was fifteen, but if they came back today I'd strangle them with my bare hands."

"Why did they shoot your dog?"

"Said it was too dumb to live. They thought they were funny, showing off in front of the other mechanics. Samson used to growl at people, but he never bit anyone. And he chased cars. They used to be partners with my father. They ended up going back to Kansas."

When Carl went up to the Trinity River for a week of steelhead fishing with his brothers and father, she missed him. It surprised her. It was like she had too much time on her hands all of a sudden. She seemed to be constantly thinking of him. Kay watched her wandering around the apartment, but didn't comment.

She went with Kay over to Aunty Garnet's just for something to do. She usually avoided that because the talk was all going to be about Uncle Lester. Her own home might have been filled with bad memories, but at least no one talked about them all the time. Aunty kept bringing it up, going over and over every detail. She realized that her father hardly ever mentioned her mother, and when he did, it wasn't because he was knocking her. But Garnet was different. Uncle Lester was a no-good bastard. And her own sister, that she'd raised. Screwing in her own bed. She'd caught them. And Opal had the nerve to say, what do you expect? In that room. And she'd point to the bedroom door, as if they were still in there. It made it hard to chew and swallow during dinner, with Garnet working herself up more and more. Kay never said much. But once she yelled, "It's not my fault, Mother."

"No one said it was," Garnet yelled back.

"Then why is it always *your father* this and *your father* that? Why not just Lester?"

"All right," she snapped. "Lester is a no-good son of a bitch."

When Carl came back she was so happy to see him her eyes started dripping all over his chest when he hugged her hello. It surprised both of them. His arms were around her, hands locked at the small of her back. He must have been practicing, because he got it all out in one breath. "The fish were biting good. And I've had time to think. Will you marry me?"

He insisted he wanted to ask her father. That caught her by surprise. "Does he think he's back in Kansas fifty years ago?" she said to Kay, dumping their wet clothes into a dryer.

"I don't know." Kay was trying to read a report.

"He knows we never got along."

"I don't think that's the point."

"Well, what is the point?" She was getting upset, something that didn't occur that much anymore. "You're acting like Carl now. Everything has to be according to some rule. Some etiquette or pattern. My father didn't do anything for me." She realized she was yelling.

Kay put down the report. "Why don't you tell him that. Explain why you don't like the idea."

"I told him already that we don't get along." They had been alone in the laundromat that evening, doing their week's wash. Other people came in to use the dryers and hesitated to come any closer. They both stopped yelling when they realized that, and hurried to fold their clean clothes and get out of there.

She went with Carl when he went over to the house. He'd go without her, he said. She dreaded the whole business. Her father was glad to see him. "You should hear that Studebaker. Runs like a top now. No more pinging."

"All it needed was a higher octane gas, Frank."

"Carl, you want a cup of coffee?" her father asked, starting to get up.

"Sure." Carl sat down, completely relaxed, at home.

"I'll get it," she said. She wanted to get out of the room.

"How's the job out at the refinery?" Carl was asking.

"Finished the storage tanks before the rains come. All we have left is the inside stuff." She heard the front door open.

"Carl," Billy yelled when he saw who was there. "Let's go fishing." All three thought that was hilarious. She'd forgotten Billy might stop by. They might as well get out of there; Carl wouldn't say anything in front of Billy. She was taking her time, putting the canned milk into a blue cream pitcher like Kay did, putting everything on an old tin beer tray she'd found, thinking they'd drink the coffee and then go, as she carried the tray into the front room.

"What I stopped by for, I wanted to ask you something, Frank." Carl hesitated, then went on. "I'd like to marry your daughter. Ann. I wanted to make sure it was all right with you." There was a silence. She felt her face get red. She didn't know where to look. She couldn't keep from watching her father's face. He broke up laughing. So did Billy. Then Carl.

"What's so goddamned funny?" she said.

"It's just . . ." her father started out several times, and then got control of himself. "Me and Billy have been speculating on this subject. But neither of us thought you'd bother to ask me. That was a genuine surprise."

"What it was," Billy said, "was, I thought you'd go off by yourselves to Reno. But Dad said you'd want a big wedding. That was all."

She held the tray out in front of each of them so they could take a cup, milk and sugar. Her father surprised her by patting her hand. "What do you want?" he asked. He wasn't using his snide grin or anything. He was sober. Just coming home from work. Still wearing his whites. He didn't drink on the job.

"I want to marry him, Dad." She made herself lean forward and kiss him on the forehead. Billy clapped.

"Well," he said, "you have my permission. And I'll pay for the wedding, which is traditional." Then he added, "Or I'll pay for the gas to Reno, which isn't." The three of them started laughing their heads off again, as if it were the funniest thing in the world.

Kay, 1991
Last Laugh

Uncle Frank was trying, but the candles wouldn't go out. The third time, she leaned forward, her arm around his shoulders, and added her breath. Then Billy was up, pulling the smoking candles out, cutting the cake, making sure everyone gut a sugar rose, sliding the pieces onto the paper plates.

Ann looked miserable, Kay thought. This was the first one she'd been to in years. She'd barely got started reminding her last week when Ann'd cut in, "I'll be there." Her face looked stiff and unnatural, probably from trying to smile all the time, and she'd moved her lips but no sound had come out when they sang Happy Birthday. On the way over to the coast a couple of weeks ago she'd said out of the blue, "Too bad I never learned to accept the way things are. The things I'm not able to change. My father. When it was me that was unhappy, not him. Someone told me once, 'Regrets are for those who have no imagination.' I should have remembered that."

Frank sat across from her, pleased with himself. He'd mostly stopped fidgeting now, after not smoking for a couple of years. Took his insulin, and might or might not have quit drinking. It was hard to say; he was always chewing gum now. She'd asked her mother, who talked to Uncle Frank nearly every day, but Garnet wouldn't speculate. "We talk about sales and who's died, now. We don't discuss each other's bad habits."

She didn't stay long at the party. When she got home, there was Rose's voice on the machine: "Phone me, oh grand adviser." She kicked off her shoes and made herself a cup of instant before phoning. Rose could talk nonstop an hour just warming up to her subject.

"Almost 100 percent response," Rose started out. She'd taken over the Kansas Association member list. Just twenty-three people had shown up three years ago for the last picnic.

"What's *almost* mean?"

"Eighty-eight replies said they would be interested in attending. All voters, too."

"You asked them which party they belonged to?"

"Of course not, I just asked if they were registered; I'm subtle. There's so much money in that account, we could become a major contributor around here."

"Rose, that money belongs to the Association, and it has its uses."

"What? I didn't notice any withdrawals."

"I paid out for two funerals, year before last."

"Anyway, I feel there was a positive response and we should go ahead with our plan." Rose paused. Kay knew she had to say something and this might be her last chance before Rose was off and running again.

"Rose, I feel obligated to say, as the other member of the executive committee, that we should not make any assaults on the integrity of the Kansas Association. That means we don't bend anything to fit into any other purposes. The Association was started for people who came from Kansas to California for no other reason but to get together and see each other and have a good time."

"If we don't give this thing some structure or backbone, it's finished. I'm not suggesting anything political, I have enough of . . ."

She could only half listen. In six years' time, Rose had become a bulldozer, steamroller, some piece of heavy equipment, and had worked her way past, around or through three or four jobs, until now, with three partners, she had her own consulting firm that managed political campaigns. In the last state election, three of the firm's four candidates had won.

"Did I mention I was back there in Kansas City for a meeting?"

"No, no you didn't. How'd you like it?"

"Not bad. I took time out and went down to where Grandpa was from. Rented a car."

"Your mother and I spent a summer back there years ago, waiting on tables. The place was named the Wagon Wheel."

"The interstate goes through there now. They tore everything down."

"There used to be a street named after your grandfather's family just off the post office."

"It's all crops in there now where the post office was. They moved a lot of the old buildings. I talked to some tractor driver who works for the company who owns it; he said they even moved the cemetery."

"I never knew that."

"Something else: if *you* decide—and I'm emphasizing *you* because I consider you the senior member of the executive board—to have the Kansas Day Picnic, I might be able to get one of the male starlets to make an appearance. Maybe. It just might attract the third generation."

"Write everything down; let me see it all on paper before we go any further."

"No problem, Kay. We have plenty of time. Have you heard from RubyAnn?"

"No, but my mother has. She's doing fine. Loves the school. Her courses."

"What I still don't understand is why she picked a college without a track team. Without a track, even. She was a nationally ranked high school high jumper. She could have got anything she wanted."

"You'll have to ask her; I don't know."

"You can't ask her anything; she just looks at you."

"According to my mother, she's still jumping. Practices every day. Maybe she thought it would interfere with her studies. I don't know."

"And why would you leave California to go to North Dakota to become a marine biologist? There's no ocean there. Never mind. She's just like Mom; she has no system. Anyway, I'll get back to you on the Association doings. I don't want the thing to fold up. The last time I was down, I stopped over at Grandpa's. Did I mention this? What a character. He brought out all those old photographs. We must have gone through five boxes. He insisted on giving me some. It'd be a shame if all that was forgotten."

"It would be," she agreed.

When the phone rang she sat up. She'd fallen asleep in her chair again. She couldn't see the clock or tell the time by what was on the TV screen. "Kay, how are you? This is Billy." His voice was forced, off: he was trying too hard to be cheerful. "How's everything?"

"Fine, Billy, everything is fine."

"I didn't get you up?"

"Believe it or not, I was up and semiconscious. What time is it, anyhow?"

"Almost three. The reason I called is, I got stopped. I was at the Shamrock Club and when I left, they pulled me over."

"I know that place," was all she could think to say. One of the last working-man's bars on this end of El Camino. She took her employees there for a round of drinks every April 15th. Always crowded. Shelves loaded with trophies won by the bar's softball team. The last thing in the world from a piano bar. You could overhear conversations about Local 1406, which represented the employees from the big bakery down the street. Most of the customers wore whites and most discussions were about what had happened on their shift, or some sport. She liked going there because she knew she'd never had to make polite small talk with anyone from any of the professional groups she belonged to. Also because the people in there were right out of the time she grew up in. She'd been sent to pick up Uncle Wally in places like that. Over the bar mirror there was a bumper sticker: NOBODY'S UGLY AT 2:00 A.M. She had never seen Billy there, but it was on his way home too.

"They'll release me," Billy said, "if someone comes down and drives me. I'm at the central jail."

"Where's your car, Billy?"

"I'm not sure."

"Just relax, everything is going to be okay. I'm on my way."

A uniformed officer handed Billy his wallet and his belt and then the barred door snapped open so he could step into the waiting room. The wall clock said 4:07. Ann was quivering with outrage; Kay could feel it through her elbow. Before she could say anything, Ann was yelling, "What's wrong with you?"

"Are you all right, Billy?"

"Isn't Dad enough, without you too?" Ann's voice was getting louder.

Billy leaned over to whisper, "The Motel Six is better," trying to be funny, but then he got fuddled.

"Do you remember where they towed your car? Ann came to drive it home." It was either Ann or her mother, and her mother hated to drive at night.

Billy just shrugged his shoulders. A woman no one had noticed stepped nearer, dangling car keys by a ring. "It's in the back parking lot," she said.

"Who are you?" Ann asked her. Billy looked around the room. He seemed relieved to see there was no one else waiting.

"He was giving me a ride home when they stopped him."

Ann shook her head at Billy. "Don't you ever learn? Don't you?"

Kay took the keys. The woman was wearing white duck pants and a pink ski jacket; must work at the bakery, she thought. "We appreciate your waiting," she told her. "I'll drop you off when I take Billy home."

"Let her take a taxi," Ann said.

Kay ignored that. "Here, drive Billy's car to your house. He can pick it up in the morning." She took Billy by the arm and led him over to the elevators. None of them said a word on the way down or out on the street. Ann went off. They all three got into the front seat of the car. The woman sat in the middle, rigid, her feet planted on the floor. Once they got out of the county complex Kay asked, "Which way?"

"Over to 280. I have a townhouse up off Skyline."

"How do you like it?" she asked.

"Not bad; I lived in a three and two before, so it's a little cramped."

When they'd let her out and were headed back to Billy's place, he said, "I just met her tonight. I wanted to give her a ride. She usually carpools."

"You don't have to explain," she said, and meant it. He fell silent, then began again when they turned off the freeway.

"She didn't vote for Ronald Reagan," he said. "She hopes now that he's out of the White House he'll stay out of the movie houses too." Billy laughed and laughed. "I voted for him," he said. "Just the first time."

"Did you tell her that?"

"Absolutely. Who did you vote for, Kay?"

"I'm not going to say." She was a little embarrassed about the times she hadn't voted.

"I have to get Dad a tree," Billy said. "That's what I thought I saw when the highway patrol pulled me over, that the red light was the reflection from the Christmas decorations along the road. I was wrong." His voice sounded awful. Worse than dejected. When she stopped in front of his place, he got out stiff, like a cripple.

"Look, no one was hurt," she said.

"That's something," he said and added, "I didn't feel drunk." He shut the door and she watched as he went up the walk.

She got piles of mail every day, and she always made herself look through each silly piece. It was a task she set herself before she got down to work. When she got to the long cardboard tube, she took her time undoing one end, pulling out the contents. When she unrolled it, she couldn't believe her eyes. Blown-up photos, eighteen by twenty-four inches, of the old Kansas pictures. Grandmother. Her whole family, Wally up front. Uncle Frank, playing the sax in a band. One she had to look at for a while to realize it had to be her mother and her two sisters astride a pony. There must have been a dozen photos. The enlargement had blurred the faces a little, but you could still tell. A note was clipped to the last photo: *Phone. Rose.* She couldn't leave them alone, kept going back and looking again. Everyone was there. They were all accounted for. Maybe we choose what we need from the past, she thought, but the rest of it just stays there, permanent, waiting, no matter what we do.

She hesitated about phoning Rose. She was never sure what Rose was going to come up with next. It made her feel uncomfortable, like she always had to be ready to put her foot down, say no to something. But that didn't bother Rose. At twenty-four she never let anything stop her, just like when she was sixteen.

She couldn't think about Rose without thinking about herself. Why did she feel everything had passed her by? Like a tree next to the road, rooted in one place. She had missed a chance somewhere, become stationary, an observer, and she'd never noticed. Measuring things by what Grandmother would do, which no longer worked. That wasn't right. It had succeeded. She was Kay Cortner. The sum total of her acts and thoughts, responsible for both. She shouldn't have any regrets. But she could try something different. Look up the road in another direction. At the very least, pretend to see.

She dialed Rose's number. "What about those photos?" Rose started out.

"I never would have thought of that."

"There's more, a lot more; I've got the pictures of the high school graduating classes from 1930 to 1941, the year Grandpa graduated. Everyone likes a little nostalgia these days. I've had another six hundred replies, mostly because of those photos."

"Six hundred! I wouldn't think there's that many people left."

"It's mostly my generation that's answering. In the original questionnaire, I asked for names and addresses of children and grandchildren. Then I sent them a brochure with a half dozen photos. Over two thousand potential voters."

"Rose, you never listen."

"Aunt Kay," she cut in, "there's people who think we *need* apathy, it's built in, like the Greeks needed their slaves: without it the system won't work, like the congress and presidency couldn't function with full participation. But the fourth branch of government should be voters. I just want people to vote, that's all."

"Do you think they'll all come?"

"I don't know; my generation is kind of flighty. Maybe 70 percent."

"That's not bad." She tried to keep the surprise out of her voice. In fact it was very good.

"We'll have it in that park where it always used to be. I've been corresponding with the county historical society back there too; they have old films of parades, homecomings, cattle drives, you name it. I thought we'd set up a pavilion and show the old movies. Everyone's interested in their own past now. Genealogy is a hot topic. There's also a couple of personalities that might be interested in attending. Don't worry; neither is political. A future hall-of-famer baseball player whose grandmother was from Topeka. And this is tentative: a TV actor who will be nameless at this point, but he was raised in Garden City, Kansas."

"It sounds like you've been doing some homework."

"It's relaxing. After dealing with the people I associate with all day long, this is all pleasure. Don't get me wrong. Politicians are all right as long as no one sees you with them. That's a joke," Rose added, laughing. "I better let you go now. I'll keep you informed, don't worry."

"I'm not worried; it's just that I want to keep things as traditional as possible. I don't think that's the right word."

"It'll do," Rose said.

She'd circled the court date on her calendar. She'd only seen Billy once since that night, and that was only for a minute a couple of days before, when he came in to sign his tax forms. She had them all ready. "You okay, Billy?" His face had been flushed, and she'd leaned nearer to him to see if he'd been drinking. As he finished signing, he pulled back. He knew what she was doing.

"I haven't had a drink since that night," he said. She could feel her face turn red, and she sat back in her chair. "I just left the club: didn't I mention I joined a racquet club?" She remembered then. "Working out makes me feel good. Tired but good. I sleep better."

"Do you want me to go with you, Billy?" she asked.

He stopped at the door. "No, that's not necessary. I can do it. Sharon is coming with me."

"Who's Sharon?"

"She was with me the night I was stopped."

"Oh," she said. There was a silence. "Good luck," she said.

"Thanks," Billy said, smiling. "I'll need it."

She didn't want to phone the next day to find out what had happened. She waited. Two days later she got a call from Uncle Frank. "What's up with Billy?" he started out.

"What happened?"

"He comes over here this afternoon and tells me he wants to talk to me. So I say, talk. He hems and haws. Finally he asks me, 'Do you remember when we kids used to pour your Lord Calvert down the sink?' I didn't remember, but I said I did. It looked like that's what he wanted. He tells me, 'That was wrong.' I didn't say anything: he's always remembering things, and he had a woman with him. You know how that is."

"She blonde, with a moon face? Almost pretty when she smiles?"

"That's her, nice enough person. She brought me a whole can of ginger snaps. Diabetic cookies. She didn't know my favorite is peanut butter."

"What happened then?"

"Billy tells me he got a 502, before Christmas. You know I've got a couple myself."

"I remember."

"That was years ago."

"Go on."

"He said a lot of other stuff. He must have went on for a half an hour until Rupert came by to watch the news with me. His TV went on the fritz."

"What'd he say?"

"You know Billy. He always has to say all those things that make everyone uncomfortable. He was sorry."

"About what?"

"The way he'd judged me, gave me a bad time about drinking, something like that. I can understand what he's going through; he thinks he's an alcoholic, because of the ticket. Because of me. He's not drinking. I did the same thing. Stop. Go. I never belonged to AA though. I told myself, why stop; you enjoy the stuff. I just don't drive. My old Studebaker is up on blocks in the garage. There are worse things than drinking."

"What are they, Uncle Frank?"

He laughed. "You're the same too, but I have an answer. I'm ready for you. Lying to yourself is one thing, but to be a liar like one of those politicians you see every hour on TV—even if my own granddaughter is working for them— who run this place against the rest of us, is much worse, in my opinion, anyway. I just hurt myself."

"I never thought of it that way," she said. "I'll see you Thursday."

"They have some good sales on at Lucky; maybe we can stop there too."

"I have the whole morning free."

On an impulse Thursday night she phoned her mother, later than she usually did. "It's all right; I'm still up," Garnet said.

"Today I took Uncle Frank to the store. Why is he so satisfied with himself, the way things turned out?"

"What do you mean?"

"He sits there with that smile on his face. If you were to tell him he had thirty seconds left, he'd break into a grin."

"He wasn't always that way. When Ruby ran off we didn't know what he was going to do next. She is or was my own sister . . ." her voice trailed off, then started up again. "Not that there was anything wrong with Frank, but she shouldn't have married him, just like I shouldn't have married your father."

She tried to change the subject. "What did Grandmother think of him?"

"Who?"

"Uncle Frank."

"I don't know. I don't recall that she ever said. Your poor grandmother. Good thing she's not alive to see how things turned out."

"Why shouldn't you have married Dad?"

"My father traded the three hundred acres he inherited for a team of horses. That's how sharp he was. No one ever lets you forget things like that."

"So how come Dad turned around and married your sister?"

"Maybe he just wanted a change. Opal was younger. I don't know. I've lived twice as long in California as I did in Kansas. It's hard to keep all the reasons straight. But it all started back there."

Grandmother had said that too, that it all started back there. That was at the end, when she spoke in a high cracked voice that it hurt to listen to. Even then, at the end, she dressed each day, down to her sturdy shoes, and sat in her old porch rocker that had come from Kansas. When members of the family suggested she'd be more comfortable in the hospital, she told them, "I'm dying right here in this bed, and that's that," but she did hire a nurse to stay with her at night. When Kay visited, she sat in the spare chair alongside her grandmother's rocker in the bedroom: they sat for hours, sometimes. It wasn't disturbing, being there. It felt comfortable, almost pleasant, sometimes, as if they might decide to go into the kitchen later on and make a batch of cookies. Her grandmother would speak now and then, mention a horse she'd had as a girl, Biscuit. A recipe. Relatives. Storms. And once, on what turned out to be her last day, she said, "Wally. I had to help him leave. I'd do it again if I had to. I don't regret anything in this world. You see how it is, Kay." They both sat still then in the quiet house, and after a while Grandmother said, "You're missing classes." She'd said something in reply, that it didn't matter, something like that, and Grandmother said, "Yes it does. But there's one thing you could do for me before you go. Would you cut my toenails? I don't want to ask the nurse. I haven't been able to for a while, and they're too long; I can feel them."

She got the clippers and the front section of the newspaper, then knelt in front of her grandmother and slid the newspaper under the small white feet. She clipped the nails the way she'd watched her grandmother do it years before, paying close attention to the job, careful not to stare up at the closed eyes in the dying face. Watching the clippings slide from the crease in the newspaper into the wastebasket, she felt such relief, as if she'd got beyond this time, past this place, letting go of her grandmother, ready now to let go.

When she came back from school, her grandmother was in bed, uncon-scious, and by evening she was dead.

"You're not going to believe this," Ann said over the phone.

She had a client sitting next to her at her desk; she was trying to convince him that he couldn't claim his two cats, Gus and Shirley, as deductions. "What?" she said into the receiver.

"Guess. Oh, Kay." She was giggling like she was twelve.

"Tell me."

"Billy got married."

"You're kidding."

"No, to what's her name. Came into the shop to buy her some flowers. They went to Reno over the weekend. On an impulse, he told me. I was so flabber-gasted I couldn't say anything. Three times now. He never learns, never."

"It's his life," Kay said, imagining Billy laughing if he heard this conversation.

"He met her in a bar; how long is it going to last?"

"I've got to go," she said. "I'll get back to you."

After, when she had time to think about it, she decided Billy was amazing. He did what he wanted. If it sounded like a soap opera, who cared. He went ahead and married who he liked. The time he told Charlotte to go to hell, an-other potential bride, she'd thought he was crazy. She had seemed perfect. Not to Billy. She couldn't do that. It took time for her to get her emotions in order before deciding anything. Billy's were always ready.

She phoned that night when she got home to be sure Uncle Frank knew. "He just left," he said, laughing. "Brought me over a fifth to celebrate. He didn't have any but Sharon did. Nice girl. Has a good job at the hospital. She's going to be all right for Billy."

"This is the third, Uncle Frank." She felt she had to say that.

"That's what Ann said too. But who's to say."

"How come you never remarried after Ruby left?" She had always wondered that.

"That whole business took the wind out of me. Something happens to a per-son when you're taken by surprise like that. Ruby disappearing, not knowing what happened to her. It's like you can't get back to where you were. I had the girl friends, you remember. But nothing permanent." She remembered when they were kids, him telling her mother some woman was going to keep house for him: the woman was in the bathroom. "Nothing else, Garnet. You know me from way back." Her mother standing, her hands on her hips; Billy and Ann with their coats on. She'd nodded her head but she took the kids home until the woman moved out. "Let me ask you one now. How come you didn't find anyone, Kay?"

"I don't know." She had to think about it for a minute. It was hard to forget who she was talking to. But she wanted to get it right this time. "I guess I was never willing to take a chance on myself guessing right. Or on waiting for another person to choose me."

"Billy never had that trouble. You should be more like him."

"Maybe you're right," she said, at first to be polite, but all of a sudden it came to her that it *was* Billy she admired. For not giving up. All those disasters, and he was still game, trying for love. She'd always thought it was Grandmother she should be like. But maybe it was Billy.

She could relax now; April fifteenth was past. If she had it all to do over again, she'd become a sheepherder in Montana. Being a C.P.A. was like being a doctor; everyone waited until they were terminal before they came for help. The doorbell rang. She looked up at the clock: it was after eleven. She put on her robe and marked her place in her book. Looking through the peephole, she saw Ann standing outside. She tried not to seem surprised when she opened the door.

"He had the gall to bring that barfly to the house," Ann said, marching in and unbuttoning her raincoat. "Can you believe it. Why does he think I want to meet them all?"

"Probably because you're his sister," she said.

Ann shook her head. "You're so smart," she said, smiling. "That's what I get." She went on conversationally, "She doesn't seem a bad sort. A nutritionist or dietician at the hospital. I give it a year, maybe a year and a half. Long enough for her to get to know him. She had a long talk with Rube about diets. All three are going to run in some race—she runs marathons—before RubyAnn goes back to school next Wednesday."

"You want some coffee and a little warmer upper, as your father would say? I'm going to have some."

"Just coffee. No brandy. Since Billy got caught I'm not taking any chances.

226

He had to pay a big fine, and now he has to pick up trash along the freeway for three Saturdays. Which he'll probably enjoy."

She went into the kitchen and Ann followed. "While we're on the subject of love, Kay, whatever happened to that dentist you were going out with? The orthodontist."

What had happened to Stan? He'd used words like *sharing* and *commitment*. Wanted her to move in with him at his place.

"That time you brought him over, he told me RubyAnn was going to need surgery for her overbite. Surgery and braces for three years."

The offer had startled her, taken her by surprise. She couldn't assimilate it, or separate it from what she'd expected. But she hadn't expected anything. She was satisfied with herself, with the way she was. Change made her nervous. Sudden change was unbearable. That was the part she couldn't jump over. Hesitating made him more urgent; he wanted to marry her. Insisted. All or nothing.

"He was only interested in my teeth," she said. "I didn't trust him."

"Seemed nice enough. I never followed up on the overbite. Billy said he'd never even noticed RubyAnn *had* an overbite."

Unscrewing the lid on the jar of instant coffee, she started laughing.

"What?" Ann said.

It took a few seconds before she could stop enough to answer. "What do you think Billy is doing right now, this minute?" She started laughing again. Ann started laughing too. She could barely talk.

"I know," she said, shaking her forefinger. "They're watching TV. Billy has just said 'I'll make us some popcorn.' He dashes into the kitchen and takes out his special butter-flavored oil and places it over the pilot light on the top of the stove to heat up slightly."

"Then," Kay said, "he gets out his special imported kept-in-the-freezer popcorn. Checks the kernels by holding them up to the light to see how they are."

"Takes out his popper that we used as kids. That old blackened aluminum pot that used to be the bottom half of a pressure cooker. The special lid is out."

"My turn," Kay said. "Special oil in the bottom. Two long droplets. What is Sharon doing? We forgot her."

"Sharon is looking on adoringly. What else?"

"That's exactly what she's doing: no matter how long it lasts, that's what she's doing now."

Ann led the way back into the front room, carrying her cup. "Do you know how old I'm going to be on the seventh?"

"I know," she said, folding her legs under her as she sat down. "It's the same age I was a couple of years ago. It starts with a four and ends with a four."

"It's the craps," Ann said. "I feel the same but I don't look the same. Sometimes I think if I could only stop time passing, go back, I could make it different."

"I don't think about it," she said.

"Do you know what Billy told me tonight? That this was the happiest time of his life. He meant it, too."

Kay put her empty cup down on the coffee table. She was going to say You have to hand it to him, but she didn't open her mouth. She looked over at Ann, who was staring into space. All at once she felt so comfortable, reassured, as if she were happy herself. "You have to hand it to him," she said.

JACKET DESIGN BY ANNE GARNER.
JACKET OIL, *FRUIT TREE IN BLOSSOM*, BY RUSSELL CHATHAM.
COMPOSED IN BERKELEY OLD STYLE AND GOUDY
BY WILSTED & TAYLOR, OAKLAND.
PRINTED BY ARCATA GRAPHICS, FAIRFIELD.

ERNEST FINNEY IS THE AUTHOR OF
BIRDS LANDING AND *WINTERCHILL*.
HIS WORK HAS BEEN INCLUDED IN A NUMBER
OF SHORT FICTION ANTHOLOGIES.
HIS STORY "PEACOCKS" WAS FIRST PRIZE WINNER
IN THE 1989 O. HENRY AWARDS COLLECTION.
HE LIVES IN CALIFORNIA.